A LITERARY SENSATION, ACCLAIME

"Mr. Lerner is among the most interesting young American novelists at present.... In his books, little happens, yet everything happens. Small moments come steeped in vertiginous magic."
—DWIGHT GARNER, *The New York Times*

"Ingenious...This brain-tickling book imbues real experiences with a feeling of artistic possibility, leaving the observable world 'a little changed, a little charged.'"
—SAM SACKS, *The Wall Street Journal*

"Ben Lerner is a great writer and 10:04 a great novel."
—ALEX PRESTON, *The Guardian* (London)

"This masterful, at times dizzying novel reevaluates not just what fiction can do but what it is." —TIFFANY GILBERT, *Time Out New York* (five stars)

"Remarkable...Lerner is doing something different with his metafictional plot: He's showing us, in good faith, how fiction gets written."
—ELAINE BLAIR, *London Review of Books*

"Genius-level...[A] deeply smart and witty novel."
—EMILY DONALDSON, *Toronto Star*

"Lerner is an astonishingly deft writer.... 10:04 is an exciting book, one that thinks seriously about what contemporary literature can do and whom it can reach."
—CATRIONA MENZIES-PIKE, *Australian Book Review*

"[10:04 is] disarmingly clever, unstintingly intelligent, and intensely a product of our contemporary moment."
—JOSH LAMBERT, *Haaretz*

"Reading Ben Lerner gives me the tingle at the base of my spine that happens whenever I encounter a writer of true originality. He is a courageous, immensely intelligent artist who panders to no one and yet is a delight to read. Anyone interested in serious contemporary literature should read Ben Lerner, and 10:04 is the perfect place to start."
—JEFFREY EUGENIDES, author of *The Marriage Plot*

"Frequently brilliant... Lerner writes with a poet's attention to language."
—HARI KUNZRU, *The New York Times Book Review*

"Ben Lerner is a brilliant novelist, and one unafraid to make of the novel something truly new. 10:04 is a work of endless wit, pleasure, relevance, and vitality." —RACHEL KUSHNER, author of *The Flamethrowers*

"What is 10:04 by Ben Lerner? It is a book for people who like great writing—'great,' here, meaning frequently brilliant, electrically hyperconscious, extravagantly verbose, aggressively sesquipedalian throw-the-book-across-the-room-in-despair-that-you-will-never-invent-that-metaphor-because-he-just-did writing."
—DEREK THOMPSON, *The Atlantic*, "Best Book I Read This Year"

"A sneakily visionary novel masquerading as a comic one. The world Ben Lerner describes is recognizably ours. Why then is it so thrilling and unnerving to wander through it?"
—JENNY OFFILL, author of *Dept. of Speculation*

"Lerner's work feels so fluid, so natural that it feels like a magic trick when he moves from meditations about fatherhood to greater considerations of the world at large without batting an eye."
—KEVIN NGUYEN, *Grantland*

"Lerner, with his keen poetic eye, manages to fill 10:04 with deft, breathtaking observations and possibilities."
—CHRISTOPHER BOLLEN, *Interview*

"Ben Lerner is a courageous chronicler of meditative ambulation, of the mind reflecting on its own vibrant thinking processes before they congeal into inert thoughts."
—STEVEN G. KELLMAN, *San Francisco Chronicle*

"10:04 is wonderfully intelligent, full of intricate formal devices, literary references, and various hidden repositories of meaning.... It is also a tentative, tender, and achingly uncertain story of a man becoming a father."
—WILLIAM HEYWARD, *The Australian*

Matt Lerner

BEN LERNER was born in Topeka, Kansas, in 1979. He has been a Fulbright Fellow, a finalist for the National Book Award for Poetry, a Howard Foundation Fellow, and a Guggenheim Fellow. His first novel, *Leaving the Atocha Station,* won the 2012 Believer Book Award, and excerpts from *10:04* have been awarded *The Paris Review*'s Terry Southern Prize. He has published three poetry collections: *The Lichtenberg Figures, Angle of Yaw,* and *Mean Free Path*. Lerner is a professor of English at Brooklyn College.

ALSO BY BEN LERNER

FICTION

Leaving the Atocha Station

POETRY

Mean Free Path

Angle of Yaw

The Lichtenberg Figures

Additional Praise for *10:04*

"A brilliant novel . . . As promising a second effort as *Atocha Station* was a debut."

—Juliet Lapidos, *The New Republic*

"A work that is tender, reassuring, uncanny, on occasion sublime."

—Matthew Adams, *The National*

"*10:04* may be the best contemporary work of meta-fiction that I've ever read."

—Emily Temple, *Flavorwire*

"Like the light from a dead star, *10:04* will illuminate you to yourself for a long time to come."

—Emily M. Keeler, *National Post*

"It's clear Ben Lerner is stupendously, murderously talented. *10:04* is clever, strange, funny, and original."

—Joe Dunthorne, author of *Wild Abandon*

"The boundaries between *10:04* and real life are porous, and it's exciting. But none of it would matter if it weren't for Lerner's excellent prose, which is galloping yet precise, his humorous, complex scene-settings (including one of the best extended party scenes I have ever read), his charming obsessions, and poignant worldview."

—Halimah Marcus, *Electric Literature*

"*10:04,* with its slippery relationship between narrator and author, its beautifully wrought sentences, and its intricate network of leitmotifs, allusions, and recurring phrases . . . demonstrates the pleasures and insights . . . literariness can still afford."

—Daniel Hack, *Public Books*

"In an era of ironic detachment and political apathy, Lerner's *10:04* makes a strong case for art that can move from irony to sincerity." —Alisa Sniderman, *The Last Magazine*

"Lerner's perceptiveness makes his writing not only engaging but funny. . . . Ben Lerner tells a story that moves and provokes." —Maddie Crum, *The Huffington Post*

"Rampant self-deprecation and deft humor . . . separates *10:04* from other novels that focus on writers writing about writing. . . . Lerner has now established himself firmly in the realm of fiction, adding to his triumphs in poetry and criticism. He will prove, if not already, to be an important figure in contemporary American literature."

—Alexander Norcia, *Slant Magazine*

"Deeply intelligent, just as deeply funny, and ultimately quite moving. Plus, it's the only book this year to talk about *Back to the Future* AND Walter Benjamin with equal insight."

—Anthony Domestico, *Commonweal*

Praise for *Leaving the Atocha Station*

"A work so luminously original in style and form as to seem like a premonition, a comet from the future."

—Geoff Dyer, *The Observer*

"Lerner's writing [is] beautiful, funny, and revelatory."

—Deb Olin Unferth, *Bookforum*

"[A] subtle, sinuous, and very funny first novel . . . There are wonderful sentences and jokes on almost every page."

—James Wood, *The New Yorker*

"One of the funniest (and truest) novels . . . by a writer of his generation."
—Lorin Stein, *The New York Review of Books*

"Flip, hip, smart, and very funny . . . Reading it was unlike any other novel-reading experience I've had for a long time."
—Maureen Corrigan, NPR's *Fresh Air*

"Remarkable . . . A bildungsroman and meditation and slacker tale fused by a precise, reflective, and darkly comic voice."
—Gary Sernovitz, *The New York Times Book Review*

"The overall narrative is structured round [these] subtle, delicate moments: performances, as Adam would call them, of intense experience. They're comic in that obviously, Adam is an appalling poseur. But they're also beautiful and touching and precise." —Jenny Turner, *The Guardian* (London)

"*Leaving the Atocha Station* is a marvelous novel, not least because of the magical way that it reverses the postmodernist spell, transmuting a fraudulent figure into a fully dimensional and compelling character."
—Sam Sacks, *The Wall Street Journal*

"An extraordinary novel about the intersections of art and reality in contemporary life." —John Ashbery

"Utterly charming. Lerner's self-hating, lying, overmedicated, brilliant fool of a hero is a memorable character, and his voice speaks with a music distinctly and hilariously all his own." —Paul Auster

"Last night I started Ben Lerner's novel *Leaving the Atocha Station*. By page three it was clear I was either staying up all night or putting the novel away until the weekend. I'm still angry with myself for having slept." —Stacy Schiff

"A character-driven 'page-turner' and a concisely definitive study of the 'actual' versus the 'virtual' as applied to relationships, language, poetry, experience."

—Tao Lin, *The Believer*

"Ben Lerner's *Leaving the Atocha Station* is a slightly deranged, philosophically inclined monologue in the Continental tradition running from Büchner's Lenz to Thomas Bernhard and Javier Marías. The adoption of this mode by a young American narrator—solipsistic, overmedicated, feckless yet ambitious—ends up feeling like the most natural thing in the world."

—Benjamin Kunkel, *New Statesman*'s Books of the Year 2011

A NOVEL

BEN LERNER

PICADOR FARRAR, STRAUS AND GIROUX NEW YORK

This is a work of fiction. All of the characters, organizations, and events portrayed in this novel are either products of the author's imagination or are used fictitiously.

www.picadorusa.com
www.twitter.com/picadorusa • www.facebook.com/picadorusa
picadorbookroom.tumblr.com

Picador® is a U.S. registered trademark and is used by Farrar, Straus and Giroux under license from Pan Books Limited.

For book club information, please visit www.facebook.com/picadorbookclub or e-mail marketing@picadorusa.com.

Grateful acknowledgment is made for permission to reprint the poem "Midsummer" by William Bronk. Copyright © 1955 by William Bronk. Reprinted with permission from the Trustees of Columbia University in the City of New York.

Owing to limitations of space, illustration credits can be found on page 245.

Designed by Jonathan D. Lippincott

The Library of Congress has cataloged the Faber and Faber edition as follows:

Lerner, Ben.
10:04: a novel / Ben Lerner.
p. cm.
ISBN 978-0-865-47810-7 (hardcover)
ISBN 978-0-374-71134-4 (e-book)
1. Writers—Fiction. 2. Mortality—Fiction. 3. Fatherhood—Fiction. 4. Man-woman relationship—Fiction. I. Title.
PS3612.E68 A33 2014
813'.6—dc23

2014004041

Picador Paperback ISBN 978-1-250-08133-9

Our books may be purchased in bulk for promotional, educational, or business use. Please contact your local bookseller or the Macmillan Corporate and Premium Sales Department at (800) 221-7945, extension 5442, or by e-mail at MacmillanSpecialMarkets@macmillan.com.

First published by Faber and Faber, Inc., an affiliate of Farrar, Straus and Giroux

First Picador Edition: October 2015

10 9 8

The Hassidim tell a story about the world to come that says everything there will be just as it is here. Just as our room is now, so it will be in the world to come; where our baby sleeps now, there too it will sleep in the other world. And the clothes we wear in this world, those too we will wear there. Everything will be as it is now, just a little different.

ONE

The city had converted an elevated length of abandoned railway spur into an aerial greenway and the agent and I were walking south along it in the unseasonable warmth after an outrageously expensive celebratory meal in Chelsea that included baby octopuses the chef had literally massaged to death. We had ingested the impossibly tender things entire, the first intact head I had ever consumed, let alone of an animal that decorates its lair, has been observed at complicated play. We walked south among the dimly gleaming disused rails and carefully placed stands of sumac and smoke bush until we reached that part of the High Line where a cut has been made into the deck and wooden steps descend several layers below the structure; the lowest level is fitted with upright windows overlooking Tenth Avenue to form a kind of amphitheater where you can sit and watch the traffic. We sat and watched the traffic and I am kidding and I am not kidding when I say that I intuited an alien intelligence, felt subject to a succession of images, sensations, memories, and affects that did not, properly speaking, belong to me: the ability to perceive polarized light; a conflation of taste and touch as salt was rubbed into the suction cups; a terror localized in my extremities, bypassing the brain completely.

I was saying these things out loud to the agent, who was inhaling and exhaling smoke, and we were laughing.

A few months before, the agent had e-mailed me that she believed I could get a "strong six-figure" advance based on a story of mine that had appeared in *The New Yorker*; all I had to do was promise to turn it into a novel. I managed to draft an earnest if indefinite proposal and soon there was a competitive auction among the major New York houses and we were eating cephalopods in what would become the opening scene. "How exactly will you expand the story?" she'd asked, far look in her eyes because she was calculating tip.

"I'll project myself into several futures simultaneously," I should have said, "a minor tremor in my hand; I'll work my way from irony to sincerity in the sinking city, a would-be Whitman of the vulnerable grid."

o

A giant octopus was painted on the wall of the room where I'd been sent the previous September for evaluation—an octopus and starfish and various gill-bearing aquatic craniate animals—for this was the pediatric wing and the sea scene was intended to calm and distract the children from needles or the small hammers testing reflex amplitude. I was there at the age of thirty-three because a doctor had discovered incidentally an entirely asymptomatic and potentially aneurysmal dilation of my aortic root that required close monitoring and probable surgical intervention and the most common explanation of such a condition at such an age is Marfan, a genetic disorder of the connective tissue that typically produces the long-limbed and flexible. When I met with a cardiologist and he suggested the evaluation I'd noted my excess proportion of body fat and conventional arm span and only slightly above average height, but he counter-noted my long, thin toes and mild double-jointedness and contended that I might well fall on the diagnostic spectrum. Most Marfanoids are diagnosed in early childhood, thus the pediatric wing.

If I had Marfan, the cardiologist had explained, the threshold of surgical intervention was lower (when the diameter of the aortic root reached 4.5 centimeters), was basically nigh (I was at 4.2 centimeters according to an MRI), because the likelihood of what they call "dissection," a most often fatal tearing of the aorta, is higher among Marfanoids; if I did not have an underlying genetic condition, if my aorta was deemed idiopathic, I would still probably require eventual surgery, but with a more distant threshold (5 centimeters), and the possibility of much slower progression. In either case, I was now burdened with the awareness that there was a statistically significant chance the largest artery in my body would rupture at any moment—an event I visualized, however incorrectly, as a whipping hose spraying blood into my blood; before collapse a far look comes into my eyes as though, etc.

There I was at Mount Sinai Hospital underwater in a red plastic chair designed for a kindergartner, a chair that had the immediate effect of making me feel ungainly, gangly in my paper gown, and thus confirming the disorder before the team of evaluators arrived. Alex, who had accompanied me for what she called moral support but was in fact practical support, as I had proved unable to leave a doctor's office with even the most basic recollection of whatever information had been imparted to me there, sat across from me in the lone adult chair, no doubt placed there for a parent, notebook open in her lap.

I'd been told in advance that the evaluation would be

conducted by a trio of doctors that would then consult and offer its opinion, which I thought of as a verdict, but there were two things about the doctors now entering with bright smiles that I was not prepared for: they were beautiful and they were younger than I. It was fortunate Alex was present because she would not have otherwise believed me that the doctors—all of whom appeared to be originally from sub-continental Asia—were themselves ideally proportioned in their white coats, with flawlessly symmetrical, high-boned faces that, no doubt through some deft application of shadow and gloss, glowed with almost parodic health even in hospital light, a dusky gold. I looked at Alex, who raised her eyebrows back at me.

They asked me to stand and proceeded to calculate the length of my arms and the curvature of my chest and spine and the arch of my feet, to perform so many measurements according to a nosological program mysterious to me that I felt as if my limbs had multiplied. That they were younger than I constituted an unfortunate milestone beyond which medical science could no longer stand in benevolent paternal relation to my body because such doctors would now see in my pathologized corpus their own future decline and not their past immaturity. And yet in this room outfitted for children I was simultaneously infantilized by three improbably attractive women in their mid- to late twenties while from the more than literal distance of her chair Alex looked on sympathetically.

It can taste what it touches, but has poor proprioception, the brain unable to determine the position of its body in the current, particularly my arms, and the privileging of flexibility over proprioceptive inputs means it lacks stereognosis, the capacity to form a mental image of the overall shape of what I touch: it can detect local texture variations, but cannot integrate that information into a larger picture, cannot read the realistic fiction the world appears to be. What I mean is that my parts were coming to possess a terrible neurological autonomy not only spatial but temporal, my future collapsing in upon me as each contraction expanded, however infinitesimally, the overly flexible tubing of my heart. Including myself, I was older and younger than everyone in the room.

o

Her support was moral and practical but also self-interested in that Alex had recently proposed impregnating herself with my sperm, not, she was at immediate pains to make clear, in copula, but rather through intrauterine insemination because, as she put it, "fucking you would be bizarre." The subject was broached at the Metropolitan Museum, which we often visited weekday afternoons, since Alex was unemployed, and I, a writer.

We had met each other in my freshman and her senior year of college in a dull class about great novels and felt an instant and mutual sympathy, but had not become best friends until we found ourselves almost neighbors in Brooklyn when I moved there a few years after graduation and we began our walks—walks through Prospect Park as light died in the lindens; walks from our neighborhood of Boerum Hill to Sunset Park, where we would watch the soft-winged kites at magic hour; nocturnal walks along the promenade with the looming intensities of Manhattan glittering across dark water. Six years of these walks on a warming planet, although walking wasn't all we did, had rendered Alex's presence inseparable from my sense of moving through the city, so that I intuited her beside me when she wasn't; when I crossed a bridge in silence, I often felt it was silence shared between us, even if she was visiting her parents upstate or spending time with a boyfriend, whom I could be counted on to hate.

Maybe she broached the subject at the museum and not over coffee or the like because in the galleries as on our walks our gazes were parallel, directed in front of us at canvas and not at each other, a condition of our most intimate exchanges; we would work out our views as we coconstructed the literal view before us. We did not avoid each other's eyes and I admired the overcast-sky quality of hers, dark epithelium and clear stroma, but we tended to fall quiet when they met. Which meant we'd eat a lunch in silence or idle talk, only for me to learn on the subsequent walk home that her mother had been diagnosed in a late stage. You might have seen us walking on Atlantic, tears streaming down her face, my arm around her shoulders, but our gazes straight ahead; or perhaps you've seen me during one of my own increasingly frequent lacrimal events being comforted in kind while we moved across the Brooklyn Bridge, less a couple than conjoined.

That day we were standing before Jules Bastien-Lepage's *Joan of Arc*—Alex looks a little like this version of her—and she said, apropos of nothing: "I'm thirty-six and single." (Thank god she had broken up with her latest, a divorced labor lawyer in his late forties who had done some work for the health clinic she'd codirected before it folded. After two glasses of wine, he invariably began regaling everyone within earshot with stories about his time undertaking suspiciously vague humanitarian labor in Guatemala; after three glasses of wine, the lawyer started in on his ex-wife's sexual repression and general frigidity; after four or five, he began to interweave these incommensurate discourses, so that genocide and his feelings of sexual rejection achieved implied equivalence within his slurred speech. Whenever I was around, I made certain his glass was full, hastening the relationship's demise.) "Not a day has gone by in the last six years when I haven't wanted a kid. I'm that cliché. I want my mom to meet my child. I have seventy-five weeks of unemployment benefits and insurance plus modest savings, and while I know that means I should be more afraid to reproduce than ever, what it actually makes me feel is that there will never be a good time, that I can't wait for professional and biological rhythms to coincide. We're best friends. You can't live without me. What if you donate the sperm? We could work out your level of involvement. I know it's crazy and I want you to say yes."

Three translucent angels hover in the top left of the painting. They have just summoned Joan, who has been working at a loom in her parents' garden, to rescue France. One angel holds her head in her hands. Joan appears to stagger toward the viewer, reaching her left arm out, maybe for support, in the swoon of being called. Instead of grasping branches or leaves, her hand, which is carefully positioned on the sight line of one of the other angels, seems to dissolve. The museum placard says that Bastien-Lepage was attacked for his failure to reconcile the ethereality of the angels with the realism of the future saint's body, but that "failure" is what makes it one of my favorite paintings. It's as if the tension between the metaphysical and physical worlds, between two orders of temporality, produces a glitch in the pictorial matrix; the background swallows her fingers. Standing there that afternoon with Alex, I was reminded of the photograph Marty carries in *Back to the Future*, crucial movie of my youth: as Marty's time-traveling disrupts the prehistory of his family, he and his siblings begin to fade from the snapshot. Only here it's a presence, not an absence, that eats away at her hand: she's being pulled into the future.

The presence of the future

The absence of the future

o

We were coconstructing a shoe-box diorama to accompany the book Roberto and I planned to self-publish about the scientific confusion regarding the brontosaurus: in the nineteenth century a paleontologist put the skull of a camarasaurus on an apatosaurus skeleton and believed he'd discovered a new species, so that one of the two iconic dinosaurs of my youth turns out not to have existed, a revision that, along with the demotion of Pluto from planet to plutoid, retrospectively struck hard at my childhood worldview, my remembered sense of both galactic space and geological time. Roberto was an eight-year-old in my friend Aaron's third-grade class at a dual-language school in Sunset Park. I had asked Aaron if there was some way I could be of use to one of his charges while also smuggling in occasional Spanish practice. Roberto was intelligent and sociable, but even more susceptible to distraction than the average child, and Aaron thought our working on a series of projects after school might trick him into, or at least model for him, modes of concentration. I had no official permission to be in the school, although Aaron had asked Roberto's mom—emphasizing that I was a published author—if she was comfortable with the prospect, and she was.

During our first session, Roberto had a nut-related allergic reaction to the granola bars I'd brought but failed to clear with Aaron and, as the boy crimsoned and wheezed, smiling all the while, I was seized with animal terror; I imagined having to open his windpipe with a pencil. Luckily, Aaron returned from his meeting in an adjacent classroom and calmed me down, explaining Roberto's allergy was minor and the reaction would soon pass, but that I should be careful in the future; he didn't know I was bringing a snack. The third or fourth week of tutoring, when Aaron was again out of the room, Roberto, without warning, mutinied, informing me he was going to find his friends and, since I wasn't his teacher, I couldn't stop him. He bolted down the hall and I walked quickly after him, cheeks burning with an embarrassment I feared any adult witnesses would confuse for a species of lechery. I eventually located him in the corner of the gym that was also the cafeteria, in a small circle of his classmates that had formed around a truly gargantuan water bug carcass, and I lured Roberto back to the classroom only by promising I'd let him play with my iPhone.

By now, the third month of tutoring, we were close friends: for snack I brought fresh fruit he never ate and Aaron had had Roberto's mom threaten the child about disobeying me. In the initial aftermath of my diagnosis, when every few minutes I believed I was dissecting, the time I spent trying to coax Roberto into focusing on the mythology of the kraken or recently discovered prehistoric shark remains was the only time in which I was myself distracted from the potentially fatal swelling at my sinus of Valsalva.

Thus only a few days after the Marfan evaluation I was again in a child-sized chair, cutting out with those awkward elementary school scissors various dinosaurs we'd printed off the Internet onto construction paper to serve as prey or companion for the apatosaurus in the diorama, no doubt anachronistically, as we hadn't the patience to determine which dinosaurs corresponded to what geological period, when Roberto returned to a subject that had entered his dreams since he'd watched a show on the Discovery Channel about the advent of a second ice age.

"When all the skyscrapers freeze they're going to fall down like September eleventh," he said in his typically cheerful tone, but more quietly, "and crush everyone." Roberto tended to modulate not tone but volume to indicate gravity and emotion.

"Maybe if it started getting really cold the scientists would figure out a new heating system for the buildings," I said.

"But global warming," he said, smiling and showing the gap where he was awaiting a mature incisor, but almost whispering, a sign of genuine fear.

"I don't think there will be another ice age," I lied, cutting out another extinct animal.

"You don't believe in global warming?" he asked.

I paused. "I don't think buildings are going to fall on anybody," I said. "Did you have another dream?"

"In my bad dream what happens is Joseph Kony is coming for me, and—"

"Joseph Kony?"

"The bad guy from Africa, from the movie."

"What do you know about Joseph Kony?"

"I saw a YouTube about him and about how he was killing all the people in Africa."

"Why would Joseph Kony come to Brooklyn? What's that have to do with global warming?"

"What happens in my bad dream is the buildings all freeze up after global warming makes an ice age and the prisons crack open too and then all the killers get out through the cracks and come after us and Joseph Kony comes after us and we have to escape to San Salvador but they have helicopters and night vision and anyway we don't have *papeles* so we can't get anywhere." He stopped cutting and put his chin on the table, then his forehead.

An increasingly frequent vertiginous sensation like a transient but thorough agnosia in which the object in my hand, this time a green pair of safety scissors, ceases to be a familiar tool and becomes an alien artifact, thereby estranging the hand itself, a condition brought on by the intuition of spatial and temporal collapse or, paradoxically, an overwhelming sense of its sudden integration, as when a Ugandan warlord appears via YouTube in an undocumented Salvadorean child's Brooklyn-based dream of a future wrecked by dramatically changing weather patterns and an imperial juridical system that dooms him to statelessness; Roberto, like me, tended to figure the global apocalyptically.

I asked him to look at me and then promised him in two languages the only thing I could: he had nothing to fear from Joseph Kony.

After I presented Roberto to his mother, Anita, in front of the school, first asking permission to buy us both churros from a silver-haired woman wrapped in a bright red blanket, one of the many vendors who appeared whenever the school day or the after-school sessions ended, selling churros in all weather and helado in warm, beautiful children swarming them, more material vibrancy and intergenerational exchange and linguistic diversity in this brief public than I had perceived during my entire childhood in Topeka, I did not, as was my habit, begin the long walk home, but instead reentered the building, drawn there by a subtle force. The school had emptied quickly; with the exception of a custodian and a superobese security guard with whom I exchanged a ritual nod, the only remaining inhabitants were a few teachers ensconced in their rooms, applying adhesive stars or planning lessons or replacing cedar shavings in wire cages, presences I could intuit as I began wandering the halls, running a hand along the construction paper autumnalia: foliage changing its Crayola, horns of plenty, turkeys whose bodies were formed by tracing multifingered extremities.

Do you know what I mean if I say that when I reached the second floor and disposed of the wax paper, I was in

Randolph Elementary School and seven, the wall hangings now letters addressed to Christa McAuliffe in exaggerated cursive, wishing her luck on the *Challenger* mission, which was only a couple of months in the future? I pass through Mrs. Greiner's door and find my desk, the chair no longer small for me, Pluto among the planets in the Styrofoam mobile suspended from the ceiling. My parents are at the Menninger Clinic; my older brother is in a classroom directly above mine; Joseph Kony is just coming to prominence as the leader of a premillennialist force; my aorta may or may not be proportional; the radiator sputters in the corner because November in the past is often cold. The classroom isn't empty, but its presences are flickering: Daniel appears at the desk beside mine, Daniel whose arms are always a patchwork of Peanuts Band-Aids and minor hematomas, who will go to the emergency room this spring for inhaling a jelly bean—on my dare—dangerously deep into his nose, who in middle school will become the first of us to smoke, but at the time is known for his habit of surreptitiously ingesting Domino sugar packets. It is sad work to build a diorama of the future with a boy you know will hang himself for whatever complex of reasons in his parents' basement at nineteen, but that work has been assigned, Mrs. Greiner standing over us to check our progress, the synthetic coconut odor of her lotion intermingling with the smell of rubber cement. I'll make Daniel's effigy and he'll make mine, but we'll co-construct the spacecraft, letting it dangle like a modifier from a string, perpetually disintegrating.

And I want to say something to the schoolchildren of America who were watching the live coverage of the shuttle's takeoff. I know it is hard to understand, but sometimes painful things like this happen. It's all part of the process of exploration and discovery. It's all part of taking a chance

Pulling us into the future

and expanding man's horizons. The future doesn't belong to the fainthearted; it belongs to the brave. The Challenger *crew was pulling us into the future, and we'll continue to follow them.*

o

An unusually large cyclonic system with a warm core was approaching New York. The mayor took unprecedented steps: he divided the city into zones and mandated evacuations from the lower-lying ones; he announced the subway system would shut down before the storm made landfall; parts of lower Manhattan might be preemptively taken off the grid. Some speculated that the mayor, having been criticized for his slow response to a record-setting snowstorm the previous winter, was strategically overreacting, making an exaggerated show of preparedness, but his tone at the increasingly frequent press conferences seemed to express less somber authority than genuine anxiety, as if he were among those he kept imploring to stay calm.

From a million media, most of them handheld, awareness of the storm seeped into the city, entering the architecture and the stout-bodied passerines, inflecting traffic patterns and the "improved sycamores," so called because they're hybridized for urban living. I mean the city was becoming one organism, constituting itself in relation to a threat viewable from space, an aerial sea monster with a single centered eye around which tentacular rain bands swirled. There were myriad apps to track it, the Doppler color-coded to indicate the intensity of precipitation, the same technology they'd utilized to measure the velocity of blood flow through my arteries.

Because every conversation you overheard in line or on the street or train began to share a theme, it was soon one common conversation you could join, removing the conventional partitions from social space; riding the N train to Whole Foods in Union Square, I found myself swapping surge level predictions with a Hasidic Jew and a West Indian nurse in purple scrubs. At Canal Street the three of us were joined by a teenager whose body seemed smaller than the cello case strapped to her back. She explained that the doomsday hype was designed to evacuate lower Manhattan so police could install bugs and other listening devices in every apartment. We stopped talking when a mariachi band composed of three men in their twenties, one of whom wore embroidered straight-cut muslin pants, struck up "Toda Una Vida." It was hard to tell if they played particularly well or if we passengers were, in the glow of our increasing sociability, particularly disposed to appreciate them, or music generally. Regardless, there was an unusual quantity of pathos in the song, applause, then an unusual quantity of currency in the hat.

Emerging from the train, I found it was fully night, the air excited by foreboding and something else, something like the feel of a childhood snow day when time was emancipated from institutions, when the snow seemed like a technology for defeating time, or like defeated time itself falling from the sky, each glittering ice particle an instant gifted back from your routine. Except now the material form of excitation wasn't ice: the air around Union Square was heavy with water in its gas phase, a tropical humidity that wasn't native to New York, an ominous medium. In front of the Whole Foods where Alex told me to meet her—it was a preposterous idea to shop at Whole Foods, given that it was always already mobbed, but they were the sole carrier of a tea on which Alex claimed to be dependent, one of her few indulgences—a reporter bathed in tungsten light was talking to a camera about a run on flashlights, canned food, bottled water. Children were darting back and forth behind her, stopping now and then to wave.

Alex greeted me and I noted to myself a difference in her appearance, an unspecifiable radiance, but, as we began to push our way as gently as possible through the crowds, I realized the alteration was most likely in my vision, because everything remaining on the shelves also struck me as a little changed, a little charged. The relative scarcity was strange to behold: in what were typically bright aisles of superabundance, there were now large empty spaces, especially among prepackaged staples, although plenty of outrageously priced organic produce still glistened in the artificial mist. Alex had some kind of list—storm radio, hand-crank flashlight, candles, various foodstuffs; they were out of almost everything on it at this point. We didn't care, and circulated through the vast store on the current of other shoppers, shoppers who seemed unusually polite and buoyant, despite the presence of police near the registers.

I want to say I felt stoned, did say so to Alex, who laughed and said, "Me too," but what I meant was that the approaching storm was estranging the routine of shopping just enough to make me viscerally aware of both the miracle and insanity of the mundane economy. Finally I found something on the list, something vital: instant coffee. I held the red plastic container, one of the last three on the shelf, held it like the marvel that it was: the seeds inside the purple fruits of coffee plants had been harvested on Andean slopes and roasted and ground and soaked and then dehydrated at a factory in Medellín and vacuum-sealed and flown to JFK and then driven upstate in bulk to Pearl River for repackaging and then transported back by truck to the store where I now stood reading the label. It was as if the social relations that produced the object in my hand began to glow within it as they were threatened, stirred inside their packaging, lending it a certain aura—the majesty and murderous stupidity of that organization of time and space and fuel and labor becoming visible in the commodity itself now that planes were grounded and the highways were starting to close.

Everything will be as it is now, just a little different—nothing in me or the store had changed, except maybe my aorta, but, as the eye drew near, what normally felt like the only possible world became one among many, its meaning everywhere up for grabs, however briefly—in the passing commons of a train, in a container of tasteless coffee.

Alex found her tea. We got one of the last cases of bottled water—Alex wanted to carry it because I'm not supposed to lift anything heavy enough to increase intrathoracic pressure, but I wouldn't let her—and then, since we were hungry, we went to the steaming buffets of prepared foods, on this night the least crowded part of the store, and piled high our plates with an incoherent mix of overpriced perishables: samosas, vegetarian chicken, chicken, various dishes involving quinoa, Caprese salad. We paid for these and our tea and coffee, exchanging jokes about our ill-preparedness with the teenager who checked us out, pink highlights in her black hair, then took the train back to our neighborhood, deciding by the time we got to our stop to head for Alex's apartment.

We turned onto her street and it started to rain, but it felt as if it had already been raining on her street and we'd walked into it, parting it like a beaded curtain. I might have mistaken my intensified attention to the wind for intensifying wind. We passed the community garden and saw two girls huddled together in some furtive effort. I thought they were trying to light a cigarette, but they separated and we could see the sparklers they held, brilliant white magnesium slowly phasing into orange. A small dog yapped at the leaping sparks as they moved around the garden describing circles, laughing, maybe writing their names. I felt acutely aware that nothing slowly flashed across the sky, that no one looked down on the city from above, banking hard on the approach.

In Alex's apartment we reheated the prepared foods on the stove while listening to the latest radio reports of the storm's progress—it was gaining strength—and we did most of the things we were told: filled every suitable container we could find with water, unplugged various appliances, located some batteries for the radio and flashlights. I was pleased to see Alex had a substantial cache of wine, most of it probably left behind by the lawyer, and I opened the bottle of red with the label displaying the most distant year, taking pleasure in the knowledge that its value would be lost on me. I poured myself a glass in a clean jam jar and, while Alex showered one last time before we had to fill the tub, I looked at the now no longer entirely familiar photographs on her fridge: here was Alex as a child—gingham and braids—with her mom and stepdad; here I was with Alex's little second cousin, whom she called her niece, at a party thrown last summer: I was placing a construction-paper crown on her head with mock solemnity, trick candles sparking in the cake beside her. Everything in the photograph was as it had been, only different, as if the image were newly indeterminate, flickering between temporalities. Then it wasn't. A schedule of unemployment benefits was affixed to the fridge with an NYU School of Public Service magnet.

It was only when we sat down to eat by the light—even though we still had power—of some votive candles Alex had discovered that the danger and magnitude of the storm felt real to us, maybe because our meal had the feel of a last supper, maybe because eating together produced a sufficient sense of a household against which we could measure the threat. The radio said the storm would make landfall around 4:00 a.m.; it was about ten now and the surges were already alarmingly high. How prepared are you, the radio asked, for days without running water? The food tasted better than it was, since it might be the best we'd have for a while, and Alex finished hers, whereas we almost always switched plates late in a meal so I could eat what she'd left over. She asked me not to get drunk as I finished the bottle, at least not until we knew how bad it was going to be. You don't want to be hung over without water, she said, gathering her brown hair into a high ponytail, and I'm not letting you drink up our supply.

Was I drinking quickly in part because I felt a little awkward about staying the night at Alex's, something I'd done countless times before? I was just uneasy about the storm, I said to myself, as I cleared the table and did the few dishes. As was our habit, we decided to project a movie on the bedroom wall; a former employer had given her an LCD projector into which she plugged her computer. Because the Internet could go out at any minute, we selected from the few disks she owned. *The Third Man* looked best to me, maybe because it's set in a ruined city, and I put it on while Alex changed into pajamas, then we got into bed together, although I remained in street clothes, storm radio and flashlight near me on the bedside table for whenever the power failed.

The shadows of the trees bending in the increasing wind outside her window moved over the projected image on the white wall, became part of the movie, as if keeping time to the zither music; how easily worlds are crossed, I said to myself, and then to Alex, who hushed me—I had a bad habit of talking over what we watched. We watched until Alex was asleep and Orson Welles was dead by a friend's hand in Vienna and I could hear rain intensifying on the little skylight I was worried might soon be shattered by flying debris. When the movie was finished I looked through the other discs and put on *Back to the Future*, which I'd found at some point on Fourth Avenue in a box of discarded DVDs, but I played it without sound, so as not to wake her. I plugged earbuds into the storm radio and put one in my left ear and listened to the weather reports while Marty traveled back to 1955—the year, incidentally, nuclear power first lit up a town: Arco, Idaho, also home to the first meltdown in 1961—and then worked his way back to 1985, when I was six and the Kansas City Royals won the series, in part because a ridiculous call forced game seven, Orta clearly out at first in replays. In the movie they lack plutonium to power the time-traveling car, whereas in real life it's seeped into the Fukushima soil; *Back to the Future* was ahead of its time. As I watched the silent film I began to worry about the Indian Point reactors just upriver.

Suddenly I became aware of a strange sensation: a faint echo of the radio in the unplugged ear. It took me a while to realize the downstairs neighbors were tuned to the same station. I turned to Alex and watched the colors from the movie flicker on her sleeping body, noted the gold necklace she always wore against her collarbone. I tucked a stray strand of hair behind her ear and then let my hand trail down her face and neck and brush across her breast and stomach in one slow motion I halfheartedly attempted to convince myself was incidental. I was returning my hand to her hair when I saw her eyes were open. It took all my will to hold her gaze as opposed to looking away and thereby conceding a transgression; there was only, it seemed, curiosity in her look, no alarm. After a few moments I reached for my jar of wine as if to suggest that, if anything unusual had happened, it was the result of intoxication; by the time I looked back at her face her eyes were closed. I put the jar back without drinking and lay beside her and stared at her for a long while and then smoothed her hair back with my palm. She reached up and took my hand, maybe in her sleep, and pressed it to her chest and held it there, whether to stop or encourage me or neither, I couldn't tell. In that position we lay and waited for the hurricane.

At some point I drifted off into strange dreams the radio penetrated and I woke with a start, convinced I'd heard shattering glass. It was 4:43 a.m. according to my phone, the menu screen of the DVD still on the wall, so we hadn't lost power. I focused on what the voice in my ear was saying: Irene had been downgraded before it reached landfall, moderate flooding in the Rockaways and Red Hook, the phrase "dodged a bullet" was repeated, as was "better safe than sorry." I got up and walked to the window; it wasn't even raining hard. The yellow of the streetlamps revealed a familiar scene; a few branches had fallen, but no trees. I went into the kitchen and drank a glass of water and glanced at the instant coffee on the counter and it was no longer a little different from itself, no longer an emissary from a world to come; there was disappointment in my relief at the failure of the storm.

I turned off the projector and Alex mumbled something in her sleep and turned over. I said, "Everything is fine, I'm going home now," said it just so I could say I'd said it in case she was upset later that I'd left without telling her. I thought about kissing her on the forehead but rejected the idea immediately; whatever physical intimacy had opened up between us had dissolved with the storm; even that relatively avuncular gesture would be strange for both of us now. More than that: it was as though the physical intimacy with Alex, just like the sociability with strangers or the aura around objects, wasn't just over, but retrospectively erased. Because those moments had been enabled by a future that had never arrived, they could not be remembered from this future that, at and as the present, had obtained; they'd faded from the photograph.

o

When we uncoupled I thought I saw Alena's condensed breath slowing in the air, but the apartment was too warm for that; regardless, her body returned to homeostasis, it seemed, much more rapidly than mine. She rose from the mattress and smoothed the dress she'd never taken off and I gathered myself and followed her onto the fire escape and took in the lights of the taller buildings that loomed around us, all of which were haloed now. She removed a cigarette from a pack that must have already been atop a sand-filled paint can and lit it by drawing a strike-anywhere match—whose provenance

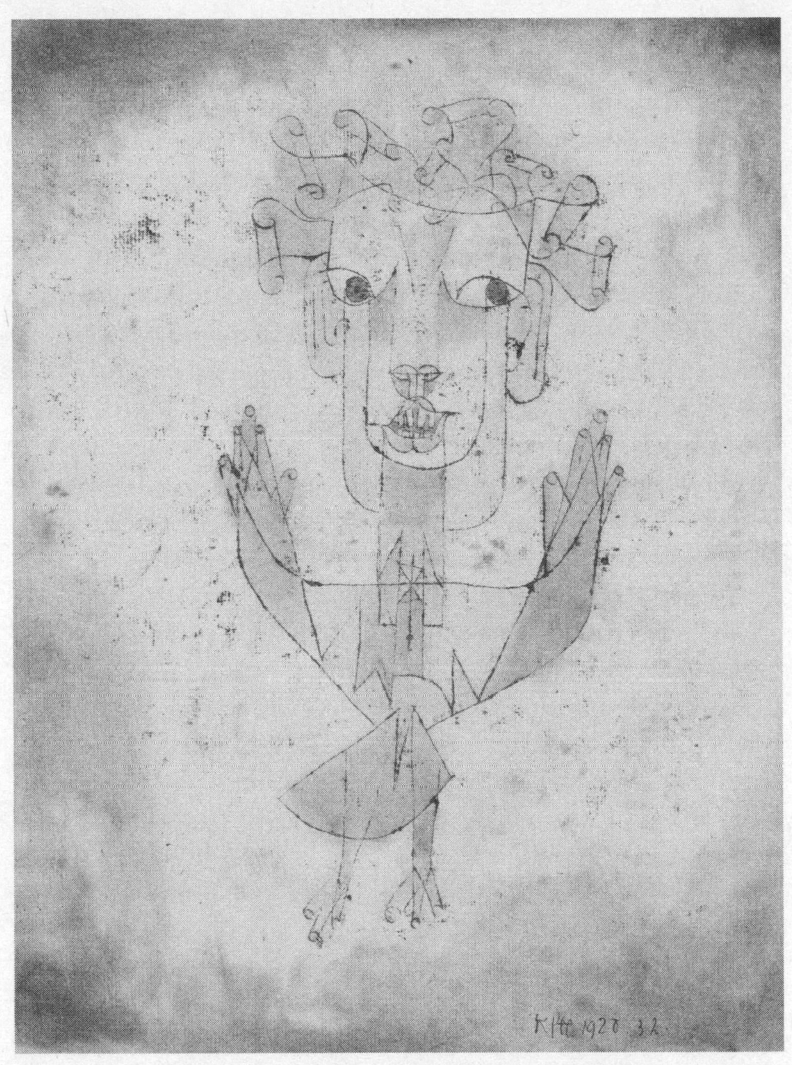

"The storm irresistibly propels him into the future to which his back is turned." —*Walter Benjamin*

was obscure to me—across the building's brick exterior. "Oh come on," I said, referring to her cumulative, impossible cool, and she snorted a little when she laughed, then coughed smoke, becoming real.

We chatted for the length of her cigarette about the show—the opening started in an hour or two—most of my consciousness still overwhelmed by her physical proximity, every atom belonging to her as well belonged to me, all senses fused into a general supersensitivity, crushed glass sparkling in the asphalt below. After she stubbed the cigarette out against the brick, a little shower of embers, I followed her back into the apartment, which was the gallery owner's pied-à-terre. Alena went to a bathroom without turning on a light and I listened as she pissed; she didn't flush, wash her hands, or, in that dark, consult the mirror.

We left the apartment together, but, by the time we reached the street, Alena had explained that she'd prefer to arrive at the opening separately, as a jealous ex would be there, and she didn't want to deal with the interrogation. I was a little stung, but, trying to mimic her nonchalance, said sure, that I'd planned to meet Sharon first at a café not far from the gallery anyway, then head over to the opening with her; we kissed goodbye.

Alena worked alongside Sharon and her husband Jon, two of my oldest New York friends, at a small production company that specialized in editing documentary film. It was a job Alena held part-time in order to support what she called her "artistic practice," a practice Sharon had had trouble describing and about which, because of the phrase "artistic practice," I'd had grave doubts. But it turned out Alena was serious, in spite of being hailed as a rising star by a postmedia art world that so often valorizes stupidity. Her current show, which, unable to do any of the heavy lifting,

I'd watched her hang, consisted of images and a few objects she had deftly aged: she'd painted a portrait from a contemporary photograph and then somehow distressed it—I couldn't understand her reluctant explanations of her process—so that it was networked with fine cracks, making it appear like a painting from the past. There was a painting based on an image downloaded from the Internet and then enlarged of a young woman whose eyes are lined with running shadow and upon whose face a man beyond the frame has ejaculated; she stares at the viewer as if from another century, the craquelure confusing genres and lending the image tremendous gravity; the title read: *The Picture of Sasha Grey*. Alena had painted several magnificent Abstract Expressionist imitations and then subjected them to her method; the Pollocks appeared compellingly unchanged, others seemed as if they'd been recovered from the rubble of MoMA after an attack or had been defrosted from a future ice age. There was a small self-portrait, also painted from a photograph, that had not been altered, had suffered no crazing, and the immediacy of its address in the context of the other work, I mean the directness of the sitter's gaze, was so powerfully located in the present tense that it was difficult to face.

Kissing Sharon hello at the café, I felt static as my lips brushed across her cheek, as if Alena and Sharon were coming into contact through me. Sharon ordered mint tea and I ordered what I thought was a simple drip coffee that turned out to be an exorbitantly priced single-origin Chemex affair. At the tiny table beside the window looking onto Houston, we split a large slice of chocolate bread. "It's Valrhona," Sharon said, which meant nothing to me; Sharon had a chocolatier's vocabulary—almost everything she ate, it seemed, involved chocolate. "Are you sleeping together yet?"

When we left the café and wandered south I could feel

the trains moving underground. I could feel, at least imagined that I felt, Sharon's pulse in her biceps, slightly faster than my own, as we walked—as we almost always walked—arm in arm. I looked up at an illuminated billboard on which nothing appeared but a violet wash, probably because a new advertisement was going up, and asked Sharon, who is colorblind, what she saw. Overhead the stars occluded by light pollution were presences like words projected through time and I was aware that water surrounded the city, and that the water moved; I was aware of the delicacy of the bridges and tunnels spanning it, and of the traffic through those arteries, as though some cortical reorganization now allowed me to take the infrastructure personally, a proprioceptive flicker in advance of the communal body. Sharon saw grays and blues, and as we crossed Delancey she described a movie she wanted to make about color-blind synesthetes who report that numbers are tinged with hues they otherwise can't perceive.

Soon we arrived at the packed gallery, where we'd planned to meet Jon, but he'd texted to say his cold had worsened. We made our way to the white wine on a table in the near corner. I saw Alena talking to two tall and handsome people across the space and I raised a hand awkwardly. She looked at me steadily while speaking to them but did not return my wave; I couldn't decide if her shadowed eyes were expressing perfect indifference or smoldering intensity, her signature form of ambiguity. I tried to turn from Alena's gaze to talk with Sharon as if I'd barely noticed the former's expression, but I spilled some of the wine as I lifted it to my lips. I glanced back at Alena, who was smiling slightly.

It was impossible, as at most openings, to look at the art; indeed, the opening as a form, insofar as I understood it, was a ritual destruction of the conditions of viewing for the artifacts it was meant to celebrate. Sharon and I tried to circulate a little, and, while the afterglow was slowly diminishing, I still experienced softly colliding with so many bodies as a pleasure, not an irritation; it was as if the crowd were a single, sensate organism. I said hello to a few people I knew from art magazines for which I'd written, but soon I could tell Sharon wanted to leave, and we began to swim our way to Alena, to congratulate her and move on to a drink.

Alena and Sharon kissed hello, but Alena and I didn't touch. I explained, trying to feign cool, that Sharon and I were going to catch up somewhere quiet, but that she should text me when things were winding down and I'd come back to help clean up. She said thanks, but she doubted she'd need help; her tone implied my offer presumed a greater degree of intimacy than our exchange of fluids warranted.

I was alarmed by the thoroughness of what I experienced as Alena's dissimulation, felt almost gaslighted, as if our encounter on the apartment floor had never happened. Here I was, still flush from our coition, my senses and the city vibrating at one frequency, wanting nothing so much as to possess and be possessed by her again, while she looked at me with a detachment so total I felt as if I were the jealous ex she'd wanted to avoid, a bourgeois prude incapable of conceiving of the erotic outside the lexicon of property. Maybe she'd separated from me only so she could reencounter me coolly, asserting her capacity to establish insuperable distances no matter our physical proximity. On the one hand, I felt a jealous anger rising within me, a desire for her to desire me, the only kind of desire, Alex had once told me during a fight, I was able to sustain. On the other hand, I frankly admired how she appeared capable of taking or leaving me, of taking and leaving me simultaneously, found it exciting, inspiring even, as if the energy we had generated were now free to circulate more generally, charging everything a little—bodies, streetlights, mixed media.

We walked west to a bar Sharon liked. It was lit in the

speakeasy fashion, dark wood and a tooled tin ceiling, no music. “Jon says she knows Krav Maga. Remember to agree on a safe-word.” It was quiet enough to hear the bartender shaking an artisanal cocktail.

“Why do you assume I’m the submissive?” The drinks involved gin and grapefruit and were served in Collins glasses.

“Because you’re a pussy.” Sharon desired to be vulgar with an earnestness that defeated vulgarity.

“I’m the one having casual sex in a stranger’s apartment with a mysterious woman who probably doesn’t care about me. You’re married.” I had officiated their wedding, first ordaining myself online.

“She cares about you, she just doesn’t attach.”

“When a male octopus ‘attacks’ in the attempt to mate, it uses its suckers to grapple with its target and insert the hectocotylus.”

“If Alena ever reproduces, it’s going to be through fission.”

“The breath-play thing,” I said with the help of my second cocktail, “makes me nervous.”

“What if you stopped worrying about protecting women from their desires?”

Now we were walking down Delancey, a gas I hoped was only steam rising from the street vent. “Maybe it’s how she grapples with and overcomes a fear of death.”

“Maybe it’s how she grapples with the threat of voicelessness.”

A passing ambulance threw red lights against us. “Or takes pleasure in making you confront the pleasure you take in those threats.”

“The flood of oxygen upon release.” We descended underground.

“A match burning in a crocus; an inner meaning almost

expressed," I quoted, but it was lost in the noise of the approaching train.

"Stand clear of the closing doors, please."

"We helped edit a film on bonobos for the BBC; they're our closest relative and have no concept of sexual exclusivity."

"They say monogamy is an effect of agriculture. Paternity only started to matter with the transmission of property."

"Get tested for HIV today," said the poster on the D.

"But they do eat the young of other primate species."

"So why did you get married if you don't want kids?" We emerged onto the Manhattan Bridge; almost everyone checked e-mail, texts.

"You left without saying goodbye," Alex's said.

"Shine bright like a diamond," Rihanna sang through the earbuds of the girl beside me, whose fingernails were painted with stars.

We were seated at a restaurant in Crown Heights, the penny-tile floor glowing in the candlelight. "I believe in promises. I believe in publicity."

"I promise to pass through a series of worlds with you," I remembered from her vows. I'd told the waiter I was only having wine, but ate half the spinach gnocchi off her plate, then paid for everything.

"She's going to get tired of you soon," Jon said. He was lying on the couch streaming *The Wire* on his laptop with two pink tissues issuing from his nostrils like a villain's mustache in an elementary school play. The coffee table was littered with used tea bags and copies of *Film Quarterly*. I rummaged in their kitchen but could only find warm gin.

"Why did you set us up, then?"

"She's smart and beautiful and nice and claims to like your poetry."

I walked home through the park. "You have failed to

reconcile the realism of my body with the ethereality of the trees," I said to the mist. Because the park is on the flight path, the city corrals and euthanizes geese. Which mate for life, I confirmed on Wikipedia. The glow of the screen seemed to come off on my hand. I looked up and saw the clouds as craquelure.

I poured myself a large glass of water that I forgot to bring to bed. "The little shower of embers," I texted Alena, then regretted it.

o

Out of Dr. Andrews's climate-controlled office on the Upper East Side, I walked into the unseasonably warm December afternoon, turned on my phone, and checked my e-mail to find a message from Natali, a mentor and literary hero of mine, about her husband, Bernard, for me an equally important figure:

> B fell in NYC and broke a vertebra in his neck. He had an operation and it went fine, and he is now out of immediate danger. But recovery is slow and I haven't been told when he might be able to be transferred back to Providence. Starting tonight I am staying at a hotel close to Mt. Sinai Hospital with uncertain Internet access. Below is my cell phone number but I am not quite competent in receiving messages. Some seem to vanish. Love, N.

As I read I experienced what was becoming a familiar sensation: the world was rearranging itself around me while I processed words from a liquid-crystal display. So much of the most important personal news I'd received in the last several years had come to me by smartphone while I was abroad in the city that I could plot on a map, could represent spatially, the major events, such as they were, of my early thirties. Place a thumbtack on the wall or drop a flag on Google Maps at Lincoln Center, where, beside the fountain, I took a call from Jon informing me that, for whatever complex of reasons, a friend had shot himself; mark the Noguchi Museum in Long Island City, where I read the message ("Apologies for the mass e-mail . . .") a close cousin sent out describing the dire condition of her newborn; waiting in line at the post office on Atlantic, the *adhan* issuing from the crackling speakers of the adjacent mosque, I received your wedding announcement and was shocked to be shocked, crushed, and started a frightening multiweek descent, worse for being embarrassingly clichéd; while in the bathroom of the SoHo Crate and Barrel—the finest semipublic restroom in lower Manhattan—I learned I'd been awarded a grant that would take me overseas for a summer, and so came to associate the corner of Broadway and Houston with all that transpired in Morocco; at Zuccotti Park I heard that my then-girlfriend was not—as she'd been convinced—pregnant; while buying discounted dress socks at the Century 21 Department Store across from Ground Zero, I was informed by text that a friend in Oakland had been hospitalized after the police had broken his ribs. And so on: each of these experiences of reception remained, as it were, in situ, so that whenever I returned to a zone where significant news had been received, I discovered that the news and an echo of its attendant affect still awaited me like a curtain of beads.

Neither Bernard nor Natali had ever seemed to exist in time, at least not in the same temporal medium I occupied; Bernard's wizardly beard and otherworldly learnedness had made him appear impossibly old when I first met him my freshman year of college, and it was only when I grew older that I was able to remember him as comparatively young; he was in his late sixties when I first attended one of his classes. And yet, precisely because he seemed beyond the reach of time, I could never imagine Bernard actually aging, and therefore his bodily fragility never seemed, in any particular present, real to me; in that sense he was forever young. Natali—the only person I knew who had read as much as Bernard, perhaps more, since she was fluent in several languages, having been born in Germany and having learned French as a child before becoming a major English-language poet—always seemed the same age to me, even in memory. This condition of temporal exception was in part the effect of a level of literary accomplishment that struck me as anachronistic: each was the author of more than twenty books in several genres; each had translated as many volumes; the small press they'd founded in the early sixties had published hundreds of books and pamphlets of experimental writing. Moreover, the house they inhabited in Providence—a house so full of books that it seemed built of books—also felt exempt from time. Bernard and Natali were always working and never working, that is, they were always reading and writing when they weren't hosting receptions for other writers; there was no division between labor and leisure; their days were not structured conventionally; the house was not subject to quotidian rhythms but to the strange duration of the literary.

All of this, I should say, initially made me intensely suspicious; they seemed too perfect, too open, pure, generous; how could they be involved with generations of authors—the offensive, the quick to take offense, the batshit crazy—without making a single enemy, unless they were secretly bland or intellectually inert or there were bodies decaying under the floorboards? The first time I was in their house I moved gingerly not only because I felt I was in a museum, terrified of breaking something, but also because I feared a trap.

As I reread Natali's message, I scrolled through memories of my first evenings in their house as my teenage years came to an end: spilling wine on hardwood and upholstery, Bernard and Natali patiently listening to my younger self as I affected literary seriousness, my speech no doubt a patchwork of interpretive clichés and errors of fact, their telling stories the import of which would often only occur to me years later. I remembered debating and/or flirting with other students and hangers-on, other young writers from whom I was desperate to distinguish myself, getting no help in that regard from either Bernard or Natali, since they treated everyone equally, infuriating me. But the memory that returned to me most vividly as I stood on East Seventy-ninth Street was of meeting their daughter, a young woman with whom I was for a time obsessed, and of whom I still occasionally think, despite having met her only once.

A distinguished South African writer had come that night to campus to read from his new novel, so I encountered the daughter at what was an unusually crowded gathering. It was perhaps the second or third time I'd been in the house, which meant I was still nervous, skeptical. I was standing in the dining room where food and wine and glasses had been laid out on the table, admiring a collage of Bernard's on the wall, when a woman—older than I was then, younger than I am now—identified the source of one of the collage's elements from behind me: a sliver of a movie poster for Murnau's *Sunrise*. I turned to face her and was, as they say, stunned—large gray-blue eyes, a full mouth, long and jet-black hair with a few strands of silver in it, and an immediately apparent poise and intelligence for which no catalog of features could account. Realizing that I was just staring at her, it finally occurred to me to speak, and I managed to say something about the rightness of fit between silent film and collage, mute media that depend on splicing for effect. Whatever its merit, she acted as though I'd contributed something intelligent, and electricity branched through me with her smile. I asked her if she was often at Bernard's and Natali's and she said, laughing, "I grew up here," and then I understood—her knowledge of the collage, her aura of brilliance, her obvious comfort in this hallowed space—that this gorgeous woman was their daughter.

We shook hands and said our names, but I was too overwhelmed by contact with the former to catch the latter, and before I could ask her to repeat it, she was taken away from me by a man, a distinguished professor of something, who wanted to introduce her to the distinguished writer. For the rest of the evening I milled around the reception waiting for an opportunity to insinuate myself back into her company, but somehow it never came, or I never had the nerve to act. Every time I heard her laugh or succeeded in picking out her voice from the general din or saw her move gracefully through a room, my whole body started, then I felt as if I were falling, a sensation akin to the myoclonic twitch that, just as you are drifting off to sleep, wakes you violently; standing there among the first editions, I was convinced it was the shudder of fate.

I found myself before the glass cases of curios and sculptures that lined one of the dining room walls and discovered that there was a small line drawing of the daughter in a silver frame, vaguely reminiscent of Modigliani in its elongation; I wondered if Bernard had composed the little unsigned portrait. By this point I'd outlasted most of the crowd. The wine gave me the courage to have another glass of wine, which in turn gave me the courage to take one of the now-available chairs in the living room and to listen along with the others to Bernard. He was telling the story, pausing every few minutes to stir the fire he was sitting beside, of a French author who, hard up for money, had fabricated letters to himself from famous interlocutors, then attempted to sell them to a university library. I glanced at Bernard's daughter furtively; in the firelight, she was dusky gold.

I did not say another word to her that evening. She would not, it appeared, be sleeping at the house. Soon after Bernard had finished his story—the forger was caught, but then published the letters as an epistolary novel to critical acclaim—the professor yawned to indicate his imminent departure and the daughter asked if she could have a ride. When they stood, everyone else in the living room stood, and I was fortunate enough to receive a kiss on my cheek from her, after she had kissed Bernard and Natali and one or two others goodbye. She said she hoped she would see me again, and the next thing I knew I was running through light snow back to my dorm, laughing aloud from an excess of joy like the schoolboy that I was. I had an overwhelming sense of the world's possibility and plentitude; the massive, luminous spheres burned above me without irony; the streetlights were haloed and I could make out the bright, crustal highlands of the moon, the far-sprinkled systems; I was going to read everything and invent a new prosody and successfully court the radiant progeny of the vanguard doyens if it killed me; my mind and body were as a fading coal awakened to transitory brightness by her breath when she'd brushed her lips against me; the earth was beautiful beyond all change.

I spent the next few months going to every reception and looking for the daughter, never having the guts to ask after her directly, or, that first year, to say much of anything to Bernard and Natali, although in their presence I was growing incrementally more relaxed, and whom now, more than ever, I wanted to impress. She would often appear in my dreams, at least one of which resulted in nocturnal emission, the last time I would experience that phenomenon, although most of them were chaste, clichéd—exploring Paris hand in hand, etc. She became a present absence, the phantom I measured the actual against while taking bong hits with my roommate; I thought I saw her in passing cars, disappearing around corners, walking down a jetway at the airport when I was heading home for winter break.

Finally I asked Bernard her name, her whereabouts, probably betraying desperation, at which point he gave me a quizzical look and explained: I have no daughter. I felt the world rearrange itself around me, that there had been a death. But the woman I had met with the distinguished professor, the one who said she'd grown up in the house, the one in the drawing, etc.? He had trouble recalling whom I meant. She must have intended "grown up here" in some other sense; perhaps, it occurred to me, she meant it was the place where she'd absorbed her education. He asked me to bring him the drawing and when he saw it he explained he'd found it at a garage sale in Michigan; tears, at least in my memory, started in my eyes.

Fifteen years had elapsed between my learning they were childless—of course they were childless; the house had no traces of a nuclear family's present or past—and my reading the message from Natali about Bernard's fall. Now, as I called Natali's cell phone, I again saw their daughter's face, felt the echo of desire, wanted to call her and talk about Bernard. In those fifteen years, I'd published Natali's and Bernard's work in magazines I'd edited, written essays about them, visited them frequently. Only recently had I come to Providence—at

Natali's request—and been asked to become their literary executor, a great honor and responsibility, a proposal to which, after reminding them in a long and wine-soaked speech about my myriad insufficiencies, and noting my diagnosis, I agreed.

Natali picked up the phone, although "picked up" is an anachronistic phrase; she sounded the same as ever. I asked what I could do. The answer was basically nothing, though I was welcome to visit as soon as tomorrow morning. Perhaps I could bring some poems, as she was reading a little to Bernard when he wasn't sleeping.

I took the 5 train back to Brooklyn, undercooked and ate spaghetti, and then started to pace my apartment, trying to decide what poetry to bring. Four hours later it looked as though my apartment had been ransacked or had endured a seismic event. I'd pulled dozens of books from the unfinished pine shelves, stirring up dust, and then discarded them in piles on the floor, either because the book in question was a gift from Bernard or Natali, or a book they had published, or a book they'd written, and so it seemed a failure of imagination to select it, or because I knew or feared it was a poet they didn't like, or because the poems were too elegiac, or too long to be read to Bernard in his condition. I was growing increasingly desperate, my worry about Bernard now compounded by the ridiculous worry that bringing the wrong book would somehow invalidate their trust in me as their executor, expose me as unworthy. Added to that was the shame I began to feel when I realized that, if I were in Bernard's position, I wouldn't even think about literature, would just be asking for morphine and distracting myself, if possible, with reality TV, a line of thought that then led me to imagine recovering, or failing to recover, from open-heart surgery.

I lay on the floor and watched the slow rotation of the

ceiling fan and found it a little difficult to breathe as all the temporal orders broke over me: Bernard and Natali were succumbing to biological time; they had asked me and my aorta to conduct their writing into the future, a future I increasingly imagined as underwater; none of the past was usable—I couldn't find, in my apartment full of books, a single page of it to bring to the same hospital where they'd measured my limbs and, depending on insurance, might inseminate my friend.

Then out of nowhere, as if descending from the ceiling, the right poet came to me: William Bronk. I remembered how Bernard had told me he'd met Bronk just once, and neither had said much; they'd had lunch or coffee in congenial if mildly awkward silence. Bernard believed Bronk was one of the great and underappreciated poets of the second half of the twentieth century. A decade later, after Bronk's death, Bernard had told me, he met a graduate student who had been a distant relation or family friend of Bronk's and had gotten to know the poet in his later years. The graduate student was always talking about Bronk as if Bernard and Bronk were dear friends, as if they'd known each other since childhood, which Bernard found a little puzzling. After the fifth or sixth conversation in which the student tried to reminisce with Bernard about Bronk, about the kind of man he was, Bernard felt it necessary to explain to the student that, while he admired the poetry tremendously, he'd only met Bronk once, and briefly, that he had no sense of him as a person. The student was shocked: But he always spoke about you, he said to Bernard, about how you'd sought him out, about how well you got along, the understanding between you, etc. One of the main reasons I came here to study with you was because of your relationship. I imagine Bernard saw the world rearrange itself around the student.

Wallace Stevens, I remember Bernard telling me on another occasion, had heavily influenced two poets Bernard particularly loved: Ashbery, whom everyone rightly celebrated, and Bronk, who was largely unknown. Ashbery wrote in color, Bernard said, whereas Bronk wrote in black and white; Ashbery embraced Stevens's lushness, whereas Bronk stripped it down, as if Stevens were being translated into a limited vocabulary. As a result, Bronk's poetry was suspended between philosophical heft and an almost autistic linguistic simplicity, a combination that, I must say, had never really worked for me: I'd read all his books out of a sense of duty, but I was usually bored or unconvinced by the affect of profundity. But now, when I found Bronk's selected poems on one of the shelves and opened the book at random, the power of it was all finally there, finally real for me:

MIDSUMMER

A green world, a scene of green deep
with light blues, the greens made deep
by those blues. One thinks how
in certain pictures, envied landscapes are seen
(through a window, maybe) far behind the serene
sitter's face, the serene pose, as though
in some impossible mirror, face to back,
human serenity gazed at a green world
which gazed at this face.
And see now,
here is that place, those greens
are here, deep with those blues. The air
we breathe is freshly sweet, and warm, as though
with berries. We are here. We are here.
Set this down too, as much

as if an atrocity had happened and been seen.
The earth is beautiful beyond all change.

This was what I brought to the hospital the next morning, along with some quinoa salad and dried mangoes for Natali. I just caught the elevator as the doors closed, and hit the button for the seventh floor, but the number didn't light up. Still, the elevator started to ascend, stopping on every floor. I was the only one in the elevator and its erratic behavior was making me nervous, so I got out on the fourth floor and walked. Later I would learn that this was a Sabbath elevator—an elevator that operates automatically in order to circumvent the Jewish law requiring observers to abstain from operating electric switches on Shabbat.

Bernard looked tiny in the hospital bed, his neck in a brace, but he also seemed like himself; the first thing he said to me, his voice raspy because of damage to his larynx, was that he was sorry he hadn't had a chance to read my novel, but he'd been detained. It smelled like a hospital room smells, like sanitizer and urine, but it was otherwise okay. A paper curtain offered privacy to or from the other patient in the room, who must have been asleep.

I entertained Natali and Bernard, trying to ignore the beeping of the machines to which he was attached, by recounting in comical terms my anxiety about what to bring, how I knew this had all been arranged as a secret test for me. When I presented them with the Bronk, I believed that Natali was touched, that it was exactly the right book, that it proved I had been listening with care all these years, but I might have imagined that response. Bernard started to retell the story about the graduate student, but it required too much effort, and he let it go. I changed the topic to their "daughter"—only now did I really feel the kinship between the stories—but Bernard didn't seem to remember what I was talking about, even though we'd laughed about it together many times before.

Despite the bright hospital lighting, emerging onto the street felt like crossing from night into day, or from a darkened theater, a matinee, into sunlight, or, I imagined, like surfacing in a submarine—the threshold between the hospital and its outside was like a threshold between worlds, between media. Have you seen people pause in revolving doors like divers decompressing, transitioning slowly so as to prevent nitrogen bubbles from forming in the blood, or noticed the puzzled look that many people wear—I found a bench across Fifth Avenue and sat and watched—when they step onto the sidewalk, as if they've suddenly forgotten something important, but aren't sure what: their keys, their phone, the particulars of their loss? Terrible to see them recall it a second later; as I observed the hospital from a safe distance, I thought back to the weeks I'd spent sleeping on the futon at Alex's after an SUV struck a friend of hers in Chelsea, how some mornings Alex, who tended to get out of bed before she was fully awake, would be halfway to the kitchen to put on the water for her tea before she remembered that Candice was dead. (I don't know how I knew she briefly didn't know, or how I could tell when the fact returned to her consciousness.) If you want to pick out the devastated or soon-to-be-devastated from the stream of people leaving Mount Sinai, I decided, don't look for frank expressions of sorrow or concern, look for people whose faces resemble those of passengers deplaning after a long flight—a blank expression as the body begins adjusting to a new time zone and ground speed.

"Ground speed"—I sat, my back to the park, waiting for the city to reabsorb me, holding my breath until the exhaust from a passing bus dissipated. The beeping of a reversing FedEx truck became Bernard's heart monitor. I began to say the words aloud, joining the thousands of people in the city talking to themselves at that moment, repeating the phrase until *ground* began to sound like the past participle of *grind*—as if velocity could be powdered, pulverized. It made me think of instant coffee.

o

There were still piles of books on my apartment floor when the protester arrived the following week to use my shower. He was a few years younger than I and taller, so much taller—easily six-foot-three—that he made the building feel smaller; he had to duck so as not to hit his head on the landing as he followed me up the stairs to my third-floor apartment. Was he Marfanoid? He set his oversized climbing backpack beside the door and sat on the top stair to take his shoes off before entering although I told him it wasn't necessary, and while he did so I could smell a variety of odors: sweat, tobacco, dog, the must of his socks. I asked him how long he had been sleeping in the park and he said a week, but that he'd been at one encampment or another across the country for more than six weeks. He'd been picked up at his door in Akron—he had been living in his parents' basement—by a caravan of protesters he'd made contact with on craigslist, just as craigslist was being used to connect protesters with people in the city who would let them use their bathrooms. He smiled his disarming smile without interruption. Did I go to Zuccotti a lot? he asked me.

It was eight or so, the time I normally had dinner, and I asked if he was hungry, explained that I couldn't really cook, but was going to make some sort of stir-fry, and he said sure. It was only when I got the towels that I'd washed for him out of the dryer—my apartment had a small washer-and-dryer unit in the closet—that I thought to ask, a little embarrassed by the luxury, if he wanted to wash any clothes. Definitely, he said, and I showed him how it worked; he got his backpack and emptied the clothes it contained into the washer, but wore what he had on into the bathroom.

When I started chopping vegetables I realized I wasn't really hungry, had probably thought to cook just to have something to offer and because I wanted some activity to undertake while my bathroom was occupied. I opened a bottle of the lawyer's wine; Alex had given me several. I put on red quinoa to boil and found some tofu in the back of the fridge that looked okay and added it to the broccoli and squash while the garlic and onions simmered in the oil. From the kitchen I could see steam escaping from the bathroom door. I put my phone into the little speaker dock and instructed it to play *The Very Best of Nina Simone*—I wanted to drown out any sounds he might make before showering that could embarrass us.

While I stirred the vegetables I realized with slowly dawning alarm that I couldn't remember the last time I'd cooked by myself for another person—I could not, in fact, ever remember having done so. I'd cooked *with* people plenty, usually acting as a dazzlingly incompetent sous chef for Alex or Jon or other friends or family. On various occasions I'd said to a woman I was interested in, "I would invite you to dinner, but I can't cook," at which point I would hope she'd say, "I'm a great cook," so I could ask her to come over and teach me; then we'd get drunk in the kitchen while I displayed what I hoped was my endearing clumsiness, never learning anything. Excepting the sandwiches I had made for Alex when she had mono—and even those I tended to buy and not prepare—I simply could not recall a single instance in which I had by myself constructed a meal, however rudimentary, for another human being. The closest memory I could summon was of scrambling eggs on Mother's or Father's Day as a child, but the uncelebrated parent, as well as my brother, always assisted me. Conversely, there was simply no end to the number of meals I could recall other people making for me, thousands upon thousands of meals, a quantity of food that would have to be measured in tons, dating from my mother's milk to the present; just that week Aaron had roasted a chicken for our monthly dinner to catch up and discuss Roberto; Alena had made some kind of delicious trio of Middle Eastern salads the night before; in neither meal had I lent a hand, although I'd cursorily offered. Typically my contribution was just wine, itself the carefully aged work of others. Surely there were instances I was forgetting, but even assuming there were, they were exceedingly rare.

I would like to say my recognition of this asymmetry led me to meditate—as I added soy sauce and pepper to what was destined to be a meal of prodigious blandness—on the pleasure I was taking in cooking for my fellow man as he bathed, but I was aware at that point of no pleasure. I would like to say that, at the very least, I resolved to cook henceforth for my friends, to be a producer and not a consumer alone of those substances necessary for sustenance and growth within my immediate community. I would like to say that, as the protester finished his shower, I was disturbed by the contradiction between my avowed political materialism and my inexperience with this brand of making, of *poeisis*, but I could dodge or dampen that contradiction via my hatred of Brooklyn's boutique biopolitics, in which spending obscene sums and endless hours on stylized food preparation somehow enabled the conflation of self-care and political radicalism. Moreover, what did it mean to say that Aaron or Alena had prepared those meals for me, when the ingredients were grown and picked and packaged and transported by others in a system of great majesty and murderous stupidity? The fact is that realizing my selfishness just led to more selfishness; that is, I felt lonely, felt sorry for myself, despite the fact that I was so often cooked *for*, because, as I stood there in my little kitchen stirring vegetables, stood there at the age of thirty-three, I was crushed to realize nobody depended on *me* for this fundamental mode of care, of nurturing, nourishing. "Don't leave me," Nina Simone begged in French, and, for the first time I could remember—whether or not the desire was a non sequitur—I wanted a child, wanted one badly.

Then I recoiled at the thought, wanted one not at all. So this is how it works, I said to myself, as if I'd caught an ideological mechanism in flagrante delicto: you let a young man committed to anticapitalist struggle shower in the overpriced apartment that you rent and, while making a meal you prepare to eat in common, your thoughts lead you inexorably to the desire to reproduce your own genetic material within some version of a bourgeois household, that almost caricatural transvaluation of values lubricated by wine and song. Your gesture of briefly placing a tiny part of the domestic—your bathroom—into the commons leads you to redescribe the possibility of collective politics as the private drama of the family. All of this in the time it took to prepare an Andean chenopod. What you need to do is harness the self-love you are hypostasizing as offspring, as the next generation of you, and let it branch out horizontally into the possibility of a transpersonal revolutionary subject in the present and coconstruct a world in which moments can be something other than the elements of profit.

The food was okay, but the protester kept saying it was awesome. He had put his dirty clothes back on but looked and smelled refreshed. He drank only water, but the food made him voluble, and, as his clothes banged around in the dryer, he talked to me about his travels, how more than anything else—debating everybody about everything, getting kettled and beaten by police on the Brooklyn Bridge, learning to wire generators, quitting drinking—his experiences in what he called the movement had helped him chill out, as he put it, about men. I thought he was embarking on a story of sexual awakening, but he meant something more general: instead of assuming that every male stranger past puberty was a physical and psychosocial threat, he was now open to the possibility of their decency. For as long as I can remember, he said, whenever I walk past a guy on the street or see a guy in another car or the halls of a building, what I'm thinking to myself, consciously or not, is: Can I take him, who would win the fight? Almost every man thinks that way, the protester said, and I agreed, even though my awareness of that line of thinking had diminished steadily if incrementally since I was a teen, replaced now with my awareness that a blow to my aorta could kill me. When I'd opened the door for the protester, though, and sized up his height, had my chances in a fight occurred to me? Probably. But I don't think that way anymore, the protester said, not after so many experiences like this, referring, I supposed, to my letting him shower, sharing food.

We talked about the latest NYPD brutality for a while and then he said, You know how when you're a kid and you go to the bathroom with other boys, I mean you're standing side by side pissing—I was a little worried where the protester was going with this—the big thing was looking at the other kid's dick out of curiosity, and as you got older that became more and more of an offense, could get you called a faggot or whatever, and so that stops at some point, unless you're cruising maybe, I don't know. But then sometime in middle school or maybe for some people it's high school there is this kind of performance that starts when you take your dick out of your pants to piss in a urinal, you start bending at the knees just a little, or otherwise making a show as if you were lifting some kind of weight.

I was laughing because I did know what the protester was talking about, knew exactly, but had somehow never noted the widespread practice consciously. Countless instances flashed before my eyes—in locker rooms in Kansas as a kid, more recently in airports all over the country and in large restaurants, two of the only institutions where I now urinated in company, because at school I always entered a stall; many men, maybe the majority, would act, as they took themselves in hand, as if they were grasping, at the minimum, a heavy pipe, and others as though they were preparing themselves for a feat of superhuman strength, often then making a show of supporting their back with the free arm if they held their penis with one hand, or grasping their member with two hands, as if either of those postures were required by the weight. I tried to recall if I'd seen this in other countries. Regardless, we were both laughing by this point, laughing as hard as I'd laughed in a long time, because now the protester stood and started miming perfectly there in my dining room the midwestern man's premicturition ritual display.

I saw my dad do it and my coaches and my friends and I did it basically without knowing it, had done it all my life, the protester said, catching his breath, and then the other day we were in the McDonald's bathroom by the park where the manager lets us go and my friend Chris was just like, When are you going to quit acting like it weighs so much, man? Do you need help with that or something? And that was the first time I even realized I was doing it, realized that all these men were always doing it, and I just stopped. I mean, I know it's not the point of Occupy, but I'm telling you that now I don't size men up in terms of fights all the time and I don't act like my cock weighs a ton and it does make me see the world a little differently, you know?

After we cleaned up together we walked to the train; I was meeting Alex at Lincoln Center. Before he got off at Wall Street, I told him to text me if he or a friend needed to shower again and that I was sure I'd see him at the park regardless, that I was often at the People's Library, but I never did. It felt strange and unsettling to stay on the train as the protester got off and the doors closed, to continue uptown toward a center for the performing arts, but I never considered altering my plan.

Alex and I found each other in the relatively short line on Sixty-second Street for Christian Marclay's *The Clock*. The twenty-four-hour video work was running continuously for one week. Wait times were unpredictable; we'd met in and abandoned the line twice before when the estimated wait was two hours or more; now it didn't look so bad, probably because it was a work night. Alex and I hadn't seen each other in a few days and could catch up while we waited side by side.

She had been to see her mother in New Paltz and, while her mom had looked unchanged since the last visit a month before—frail, but no more frail—much of her talk now was frankly about death, indiscriminate cytotoxins circulating through her. It's not that she thinks she's dying tomorrow or has given up on trying to live for many years, Alex said, but she clearly thinks of her remaining time as the prolongation of the illness and not its outside. Alex's mother, a sociologist who taught at the state university in New Paltz, had raised her largely on her own; Alex's father, who was from Martinique, was never married to her mother, and Alex had no clear memory of him. Her stepfather, also a professor at SUNY New Paltz, had been around since she was six; he was gentle, attentive, and, Alex reported, increasingly, if quietly, desperate now.

"Meanwhile," Alex said, clearly wanting to change the subject, "I learned today that I have to get my fucking wisdom teeth removed."

"I thought you did that as a kid."

"I had two out but they left two on top they thought weren't going to cause problems and now they're 'impacted' and have cavities because I can't reach them when I brush."

"When are you going to do it?"

"Soon, before my health insurance runs out. It will still cost me at least a thousand dollars, by the way, because of how bad my dental is."

"Shit. I'm sorry. Let me know when you schedule it and I'll go with you. I'll make you soup. I've been working on my cooking."

"You'll like this: the receptionist says I can either just do local anesthetic or a heavier IV thing and I'm supposed to choose which one to do. The dentist says just to do local but almost nobody I know has just done local."

"What did you do as a kid?"

"That's the thing—I can't remember. I asked my mom and she said she thought I did something heavier. Apparently if you do the IV sedation it induces amnesia. That's why so many people have trouble remembering what they did. The difference isn't really in how much pain you experience but in whether you remember it."

"I wouldn't want them working on me when they know I won't remember what they're doing."

"I'll probably just do local."

I thought about offering to pay for whatever her insurance wouldn't cover, and worried she was leaning toward local only because it was cheaper, but I wasn't sure if she'd appreciate the gesture, so I let it go.

I told her about the protester, hoping to cheer her up with the whole pissing-contest thing, and the line moved or seemed to move quickly; we'd waited well under an hour when we were let in. *The Clock* is a clock: it's a twenty-four-hour montage of thousands of scenes from movies and a few from TV edited together so as to be shown in real time; each scene indicates the time with a shot of a timepiece or its mention in dialogue; time in and outside of the film is synchronized. Marclay and a team of assistants spent several years sifting through a century of film for possible footage for their collage. When we found our seats it was 11:37; the tension of imminent midnight was palpable, the twenty-three and a half hours of film that preceded us building inexorably to that climax. (I had wanted to arrive by 10:04 to see lightning strike the courthouse clock tower in *Back to the Future*, allowing Marty to return to 1985, but Alex couldn't get a train back from her mother's in time.) Now the actors in each scene, no matter how incongruous, struck me as united in anticipation of that threshold. Even though we had arrived only twenty-three minutes before the end of the day, we were immediately riveted. Several consecutive people on the screen were on the phone begging for stays of execution.

When the hour arrived, Orson Welles fell from the clock tower in *The Stranger*; Big Ben, which I would come to learn appears frequently in the video, exploded, and people in the audience applauded; some kind of zombie woman emerged from a grandfather clock and everybody laughed. But then, a minute later, a young girl awakes from a nightmare and, as she's comforted by her father (Clark Gable as Rhett Buttler), you see Big Ben ticking away again outside their window, no sign of damage. The entire preceding twenty-four hours might have been the child's dream, a storm that never happened, just one of many ways *The Clock* can be integrated into an overarching narrative. Indeed, it was a greater challenge for me to resist the will to integration than to combine the various scenes into coherent and compelling fiction, in part due to Marclay's use of repetition: at 11:57 a young woman tries to seduce a boy; at 1:19 they reappear, sleeping in separate beds; what has passed between them? It was impossible not to speculate on what had transpired in the interval, in that length of fictional time synchronized with nonfictional duration, the beating of a compound heart.

Scores of people left the theater after midnight. We remained for exactly three hours; strangely, even though you knew you'd walk out on the film eventually, it felt disrespectful to leave in the middle of an hour. I would return at different times in subsequent days and come to love how, as you spend time with the video, you develop a sense of something like the circadian clock of genre: the hour of 5:00 to 6:00 p.m.—rumored to be the first hour Marclay had completed because there are so many scenes of people "watching the clock" in that interval—was dominated by actors leaving work; around noon you could expect an uptick in westerns, in shoot-outs; etc. Marclay had formed a supragenre that made visible our collective, unconscious sense of the rhythms of the day—when we expect to kill or fall in love or clean ourselves or eat or fuck or check our watch and yawn.

At some point in the second hour of watching with Alex, I noticed she had drifted off, and I surreptitiously checked the time on my phone. Half an hour or so later, I did it again, realizing only then that the gesture was absurd: I was looking away from a clock to a clock. I was a little embarrassed to realize how ingrained this habit of distraction was for me, but decided it revealed something important about the video that I'd forgotten it was telling me the time.

I'd heard *The Clock* described as the ultimate collapse of fictional time into real time, a work designed to obliterate the distance between art and life, fantasy and reality. But part of why I looked at my phone was because that distance hadn't been collapsed for me at all; while the duration of a real minute and *The Clock*'s minute were mathematically indistinguishable, they were nevertheless minutes from different worlds. I watched time in *The Clock*, but wasn't in it, or I was experiencing time as such, not just having experiences through it as a medium. As I made and unmade a variety of overlapping narratives out of its found footage, I felt acutely how many different days could be built out of a day, felt more possibility than determinism, the utopian glimmer of fiction. When I looked at my watch to see a unit of measure identical to the one displayed on the screen, I was indicating that a distance remained between art and the mundane. *Everything will be as it is now*—the room, the baby, the clothes, the minutes—*just a little different*.

Now I think it was while looking from *The Clock* to my cell phone and back again that I decided to write more fiction—something I'd promised my poet friends I wasn't going to do—and over the next week I began to work on a story, outlining much of it in my notebook while sitting in the theater. The story would involve a series of transpositions: I would shift my medical problem to another part of the body; replace astereognosis with another disorder, displace Alex's oral surgery. I would change names: Alex would become Liza, which she'd told me once had been her mother's second choice; Alena would become Hannah; Sharon I'd change to Mary, Jon to Josh; Dr. Andrews to

Dr. Roberts, etc. Instead of becoming a literary executor, and so confronting the tension between biological and textual mortality through that obligation, the protagonist—a version of myself; I'd call him "the author"—would be approached by a university about selling his papers. Just like the French writer in the story Bernard had recounted the night I met his daughter, "the author" would plan to fabricate his correspondence. That's the prose I generated first, the kernel of the work, and I believed it was viable. I wrote:

> The author would go back later and make sure he wasn't overusing the signature words of the author he was imitating . . . He would reread the one or two matter-of-fact messages they had actually exchanged, look again at his *Selected Letters*.
>
> All this was changing as the technology changed. If an author left no electronic archive, so there was no record of what e-mails you might have sent to him or her, and if you did receive some e-mails from the author in question, and so possessed the relevant address, a plausible sense of when the message might have been sent, then you could write yourself from the backdated vantage of the dead, claim to have printed it out years ago.
>
> Here's a message from a novelist you did in fact meet, verifiably had dinner with around some Festschrift, recounting and expanding on the talk you never had about your novel, then in an embryonic stage. Here a critic responds at length to the input on an essay you never gave. Then the debates with poets over edits you might have suggested, leading some major writers to make some major statements.
>
> It was not only the historical moment in which

> the technological transition made such forgery practicable, he reasoned, but it was also the moment in which, if one got caught, the crime could largely be described as gestural, falling somewhere between performance art and political protest. Especially if one donated whatever money the library paid to, say, the People's Library at Occupy Wall Street.

The story came quickly, almost alarmingly so—I had a draft finished within a month—and I sent it to my agent, who sent it to *The New Yorker*, which had expressed interest to her about my writing after the unexpected critical success of my first novel. To my surprise, they wanted it, but they also wanted a major cut: to get rid of the stuff about the fabricated correspondence, the section I considered the story's core. The editors argued it overwhelmed what was otherwise an elegant meditation on art, time, mortality, and the strange nature of literary reception. But I wasn't going to be one of those people, I insisted to myself, who lets *The New Yorker* standardize his work; I wasn't going to make a cut whose primary motivation was, on some level, the story's marketability. Although I'd felt a small frisson when *The New Yorker* had accepted it—my parents would be exceedingly proud of me—and although I wanted the approximately eight thousand dollars, I also relished the opportunity to turn *The New Yorker* down, to be able to tell the story of my story as evidence of my vanguard credibility. I wrote a hasty and, I later realized, typo-filled message to the magazine, cc'ing my agent, explaining that I was withdrawing the piece, that the change they were demanding—I would later realize they'd never even implied it was an ultimatum—violated the integrity of my writing.

I shared the story and this backstory with Natali during

one of my visits to the hospital. While Bernard slept beside us, she read it and said simply: I think they're right about the edit. I showed it to another writer friend and he agreed. Then I showed it to my parents, who thought I was crazy; what the editors were asking for was clearly an improvement.

Finally I showed it to Alex. Her reaction to the piece in which she figured was understandably complicated—Alex wanted to be left out of my fiction—but about the fabrication question, she had no doubt: the story was better without it. Since I'd stolen the wisdom tooth trouble from her life and put it in the story, she joked, maybe I should pay what insurance wouldn't cover with money from the magazine, assuming they'd take me back. I saw the joke as an opportunity and I begged her to let me do just that: Then I can tell myself I'm apologizing to them to help a friend, I explained, not because I'm an idiot; besides, it's a nice crossing of reality and fiction, which is what the story is about in the first place. She was quiet for a minute and then said, "No way," but in a manner we both knew was just a moment in the dialectic of her yes.

The next day my agent helped me word my mea culpa, no doubt back-channeling with the editors about how all of this was new to me, that I was mainly a poet unused to being edited, that my apparent impertinence was the issue of inexperience, etc. The magazine was gracious and decided to run the revised story quickly—so quickly, in fact, that, a few weeks later, I could read it in the doctor's office while I waited for Alex to emerge from her extractions.

TWO

THE GOLDEN VANITY

The author waited for the librarian in the coffee shop on the little commercial strip across from the campus. He sat by the window facing the Gothic stone buildings and watched the students walk head down against the wind.

Someone said his name because his coffee was ready. He approached the counter and collected the giant cappuccino, noting the flower pattern in the foam. As he started the walk back to his table, the coffee shop door opened, admitting cold air and a middle-aged woman, surely the librarian; she recognized him and waved.

His problem was that the coffee required two hands, or at least he had taken it with two hands, one on cup and one on saucer, so as not to spill coffee or upset foam; he couldn't return her wave. He felt himself scowling at this situation, realizing too late she'd think he was scowling at her. His solution was to look at the cup with exaggerated intensity, in the hope that she would understand his dilemma. He walked slowly, eyes fixed on the dissolving flower, to the seat beside the window, having ruined everything.

But he remembered Dr. Roberts's idea. Roberts had said that when the author found himself in one of these "false predicaments," and he began to draw shorter and shorter breaths, he should just describe whatever little crisis he'd manufactured, what he was feeling, to whomever he was meeting in the same "winning and humorous way" he recounted it after the fact to Roberts.

The librarian was at the table she'd inferred was his destination by the time he reached it. He set down the cup and saucer with excessive care. She had a lot of curly hair he only now saw as auburn. He shook the hand she extended and said:

"I wanted to wave to you when you came in but I had this coffee in my hands and I was afraid I'd spill it and then I was afraid that by failing to wave I appeared unpleasant and then I felt myself scowling at appearing unpleasant and then realized I must really seem unpleasant and so had already made a disastrous impression."

She laughed as though this were indeed winning, and said, "You sound like your novel." The anxiety dissipated, but into flatness. He spilled some of the coffee lifting it to his lips.

The year before, they'd found cavities in the author's wisdom teeth; they needed to come out. He could elect IV sedation ("twilight sedation") or just local anesthetic, as the dentist suggested. They'd taken a panoramic X-ray of his head, chin on a little stand while a camera whirred and clicked around him, and then scheduled the extractions for the following month, when the dentist was back from vacation. There was no rush. It would be a few days of unpleasantness, that's all. Let the office know twenty-four hours in advance if you want the IV, said the receptionist, whose fingernails were painted with stars.

He learned from the Internet that the difference between

twilight sedation and local anesthesia was not primarily a difference in the amount of pain but in the memory of it. The benzodiazepines calm you during the procedure, yes, but their main function is to erase your memory of whatever transpires: the dentist getting leverage, cracking, a sudden jet of blood. This helped explain why the people he asked were fuzzy regarding the details of their own extractions, often unsure if they'd been sedated or not.

That October his ruminations about twilight sedation dominated his walks with Liza. They would meet at Grand Army Plaza in the late afternoon and head into the Long Meadow of Prospect Park, then wander along the smaller trails as the light died in the trees. Finally, it was the last walk before he had to call if he wanted the IV.

The unusual heat felt summery, but the light was distinctly autumnal, and the confusion of seasons was reflected in the clothing around them: some people were dressed in T-shirts and shorts, while others wore winter coats. It reminded him of a doubly exposed photograph or a matting effect in film: two temporalities collapsed into a single image.

"I don't want them working on me when they know I won't remember what they're doing," he said.

"We are not talking about this again," Liza said. It was characteristic of Liza to begin an activity by claiming she'd have no part in it. "We're not having Thai food" meant that she'd come around to the idea; "We're not seeing that movie," that he could buy tickets.

"But more than that," he said, ignoring her, "I can't figure out if abolishing the memory of pain is the same thing as abolishing the pain."

"And who knows," Liza said, quoting him from previous walks, "if the memory is really abolished or just repressed, distributed differently."

"Right. And that could be worse," he said, as if this were an original idea. "A trauma cast out of time, experienced continuously, if unconsciously, instead of as a discrete event."

"So many of these people," Liza proclaimed gravely, making a sweeping gesture that included couples on benches, families playing in the grass, and a group of women practicing Tai Chi, "are living lives ruined by repressed trauma surrounding their wisdom teeth."

"If I take the drugs, it's like dividing myself into two people." He ignored her again. "It's a fork in the road: the person who experienced the procedure and the person who didn't. It's like leaving a version of myself alone with the pain, abandoning him." They turned south onto the path that would eventually take them to the lake.

"And then you meet him one day in a dark alley. And he wants to settle the score."

"I'm serious."

"Or he starts inserting himself into your life, sabotaging your relationships, causing scandals at your work. You'd have to kill him, kill yourself."

"And what kind of precedent am I establishing, exactly, if I deal with a difficult experience by inducing amnesia?"

"You already have amnesia. We have this conversation every day."

"Look, I have to decide tomorrow. One business day before the procedure."

"What do you want me to say? I'd do local if the dentist says that's sufficient, and save the three hundred dollars you'll have to pay out of pocket for the IV. But I'm a lot tougher than you are." She was. "You're going to do the twilight-sedation thing because you're a weakling. It's a sure sign that you're going to do it that you keep worrying about it."

They walked in silence until they reached the lake. On the near shore, a group of teenage girls, maybe Mexican, were dressed in white, practicing a dance involving paper streamers, tinny music issuing from a portable stereo. The softening sky was reflected in the water. Airplanes moved slowly toward LaGuardia; a few swans moved slowly across the surface of the pond. Everything suddenly complied, corresponded: the pink paper streamer in a girl's hand echoing the rose streak of cloud that was echoed in the water. He felt the world rearrange itself around him.

"I'm just doing local," he resolved.

"The sublimity of the view has lent the young man courage," Liza said, deepening her voice.

"Shut up," he said.

"Napoleon alone on the eve of battle communing with the Alps, receiving their silent counsel."

"Shut up," he said, laughing.

When he woke up the next morning, he called the dentist's office and told the receptionist he wanted the IV. Then he called Liza and said he'd changed his mind and would she go with him Monday because they won't let you leave unaccompanied with all those drugs in your system. She sighed theatrically and said sure.

That night he was going on a date. Or at least he was meeting his friends Josh and Mary for drinks, and they'd invited a woman, Hannah, they thought he might like, who might like him. It was the only kind of first date he could bring himself to go on, the kind you could deny after the fact had been a date at all.

Since late the previous spring, when he'd published his novel to unexpected praise, the women his friends attempted to set him up with had invariably read his book, or had at least glanced, in advance of their meeting, at those preview pages available online at Amazon. This meant that instead of the conventional conversations about work, favorite neighborhoods, and so on, he'd likely be asked what parts of his book were autobiographical. Even if these questions weren't posed explicitly, he could see, or thought he saw, his interlocutor testing whatever he said and did against the text. And because his narrator was characterized above all by his anxiety regarding the disconnect between his internal experience and his social self-presentation, the more intensely the author worried about distinguishing himself from the narrator, the more he felt he had become him.

He spent most of the afternoon at the little drafting desk beside the window, answering e-mails from the college, where he was on leave from teaching, and failing to answer interview questions for a small magazine in England, worrying about his teeth. He did laundry—there was a small washer-and-dryer unit in a closet—and he paced the eight hundred square feet of his third-floor apartment distractedly, opening a book at random, reading a page, returning it to the pine shelf without knowing what he'd read. He showered, stood naked in front of the full-length mirror on the inside of the laundry-closet door, and considered his unfortunate body, how it might appear to Hannah, whoever she was, how he might compensate for its many flaws through strategic angling and flexing.

They were meeting at a bar in Dumbo far from any train. When the sun had set, he decided to take a long walk, eventually make his way there. It was still unseasonably warm but there was now an implication of winter in the air. Lights and voices looked and sounded different within it, sparkled more, carried farther. He turned left onto Atlantic from

Fourth Avenue, the *adhan* issuing from the mosque's crackling speakers, and slowly walked the mile and a half to the Promenade. He leaned against the iron railing; the intensities of Manhattan loomed across the water.

Eventually he turned from the river and wandered back through Brooklyn Heights. On a small cobblestone street that dead-ended unexpectedly, some conspiracy of brickwork and chill air and gaslight gave him the momentary sense of having traveled back in time, or of distinct times being overlaid, temporalities interleaved. No: it was as if the little flame in the gas lamp he paused before were burning at once in the present and in various pasts, in 2012 but also in 1912 or 1883, as if it were one flame flickering simultaneously in each of those times, connecting them. He felt that anyone who had ever paused before the lamp as he was pausing was briefly coeval with him, that they were all watching the same turbulent point in their respective present tenses. Then he imagined his narrator standing before it, imagined that the gaslight cut across worlds and not just years, that the author and the narrator, while they couldn't face each other, could intuit each other's presence by facing the same light, a kind of correspondence.

Reggaeton from a passing car returned him to himself. He checked his phone for the time and directions to the bar and walked underneath the roaring bridges into Dumbo, his hands cold with anxiety as the meeting place drew near. He was late enough now that he assumed Hannah would have already joined Josh and Mary. He found the address—no sign, just a single exposed bulb near the door—touched his face to see if it was greasy, would be shiny, but found it dry. Then he located the little packet of breath strips in his coat pocket. When he tried to place one on his tongue, he realized he'd accidentally removed several mentholated strips at once; they congealed into a gummy mass, which he spat onto the sidewalk.

The bar was twilit in the speakeasy fashion, dark wood and a tooled tin ceiling, most of the seating in paneled booths, no music. It was quiet enough that he could hear the bartender shaking one of the artisanal cocktails whose prices he was resolved not to complain about aloud, and he immediately saw Josh, whose face was at this point mainly beard, and Mary, who was wearing a hat, a cloche he'd already decided was a mistake, in a corner booth across the room. He couldn't see Hannah, who was behind a panel, but inferred her presence from Josh and Mary's postures, the nature of Josh's wave, maybe the number of glasses on the table.

Would you know what he meant if the author said he never really saw her face, that faces were fictions he increasingly could not read, a reductive way of bundling features in the memory, even if that memory was then projected into the present, onto the area between the forehead and chin? He could, of course, enumerate features: gray-blue eyes, what they call a full mouth, thick eyebrows that she was probably careful to have threaded, a small scar high on the left cheek, and so on. And sometimes these features did briefly integrate into a higher-order unity, as letters integrate into words, words into a sentence. But like words dissolving into sentences, sentences into paragraphs and plots, combining these elements into a face required forgetting them, letting them dematerialize into an effect, and that somehow never happened for long with Hannah, whom he was now beside.

Who was in profile three drinks later, laughing at Josh's high-pitched imitation of their boss, petty tyrant of the production company where they edited film. He watched her tuck strands of black hair behind her ear, noted its pointed helix, only now perceiving her nose ring, silver but appearing rose gold in that light. Then, Josh and Mary gone, they were side by side in the booth, leaning against each other a little more with each drink, and he was saying these things about faces to her, how it's important for a writer to be "bad with faces," and she asked if he had ever seen the satellite image of that rock formation on Mars—one of those standard textbook images used to illustrate *pareidolia*, a term he'd never heard. It's when the brain arranges random stimuli into a significant image or sound, she explained: faces in the moon, animals in clouds. She took out her phone and Googled it, and he used the excuse of looking together at the little glowing screen to press more closely against her.

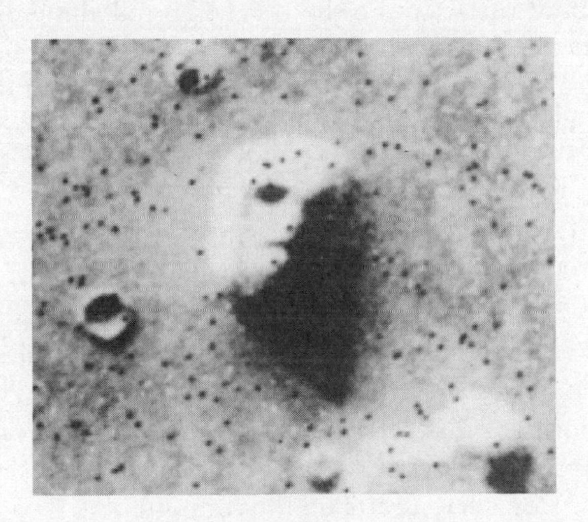

On the wall behind Dr. Roberts hung a tactically inoffensive abstract painting, rhythmic brushstrokes in lavender, blue, green—very competently executed visual Muzak. If you asked the author what Roberts looked like, he would conjure the painting rather than the face.

Roberts said, "I understand your writing has garnered some attention, but how exactly would you, in your early thirties, have any papers that a university library would be interested in collecting?"

The author said he shared Roberts's surprise and paraphrased the special-collections librarian: because he'd been "particularly precocious," her phrase, and because in his twenties he had co-edited a small and now-defunct but influential literary magazine, they suspected he might already be in possession of a "mature archive." Moreover, collecting practices were changing, and papers were now often sold in increments. They'd buy, let's say, a third of the author's papers now, then acquire the other two installments across the years. Since he would presumably want all his papers in one place, there was an institutional interest in establishing a relationship early, to invest in him. The author pronounced "papers" in a way that made it clear he was placing the word in quotes.

"And do you have a 'mature archive'?" Roberts asked. He seemed to like the phrase.

"No," he said. "Almost all the correspondence about the magazine was e-mail, and I had a different e-mail account for much of that time. I never printed anything. What I do have is boring, logistical. And in terms of my own work"—he was trying not to place "work" in quotes—"I don't write by hand and don't save drafts on the computer."

"What do you have?"

"Oh, massive and obsessive electronic correspondence with my best writer friends that's poorly written and full of gossip and shit-talking and divulges all manner of embarrassing information. I have a folder full of postcards from authors, some of them famous, politely thanking me for sending them my book."

"Do libraries buy e-mails?"

"Apparently they're starting to. Electronic archives. She said everything is changing as the technology changes. But they wouldn't want anything I have. And I wouldn't want anyone to see it, even after I'm dead."

Roberts made a pause that italicized the author's last four words, silence that had the same effect as repetition.

"A year ago, this would have been weird and silly and flattering, their interest, and now it seems like some institutional premonition that I'm going to die."

"There is no evidence that your condition is going to worsen," Roberts repeated, without impatience, for the thousandth time.

"I'm also surprised to find," the author said, ignoring him, "that I want to have 'papers,' want to leave and be left those traces, that it would authenticate me."

Roberts made the pause that meant "Go on."

He had told the story so many times that slight variations crept in. He couldn't recall the exact sequence of events. For instance, had he found a message the day after the extractions saying he should call the dentist as soon as possible, or did he answer a call directly from the dentist that afternoon? Either way, the day after the procedure, a week before his scheduled follow-up, he was standing beside the window, staring at the clock tower on Hanson Place, cell phone to his ear, listening to the dentist say there was a problem with his X-ray. "There is a problem with my X-ray," he repeated with his sore mouth. The dentist said he happened to be reviewing the file and there was an area that concerned him. "You are concerned about my teeth," the author confirmed. "I want you to see a neurologist," the dentist replied.

There was a full beat before the dentist said, "Everything will be fine, I think."

There was a poster of Picasso's dove in the first neurologist's waiting room, watercolors of Manhattan sunsets where they sent him for blood work, photographs of orchids where he waited for his CAT scan, his MRI.

Finally he got in to see Dr. Walsh, famous in his field. Silver hair, rimless glasses, a purple tie under the white coat. He was always almost smiling, at least the corners of his mouth were slightly upturned, because his blue eyes were narrowed in a perpetual squint, enabling him to express a kind of optimistic concentration without seeming patronizingly upbeat.

When Dr. Walsh told him the findings, the author was looking at a print of a painting of a beach scene: two empty white wooden chairs facing the sea, a small sailboat in the middle distance. He had a "mass," what is called a meningioma, located in his cavernous sinus; it appeared benign.

"Who chooses this art?" the author wanted to ask.

"The art?" Dr. Walsh would further narrow his eyes.

"Do you choose this stuff or does the hospital buy it in bulk? Where does it come from?"

Dr. Walsh would swivel in his chair to see the image the author was staring at, then turn back to the author, but not speak.

"I understand the desire to have some decorations that indicate this isn't just a hospital room, that a patient isn't just a pathologized body, that this isn't purely the realm of science. I understand that the exclusive criterion you or the institution would have for selecting an appropriate image would be that it's inoffensive—if not actively calming, at least not agitating. It's supposed to prove that you are neither a machine nor an eccentric because it nods blandly to established cultural modes, the medium of painting and the cliché instance of it. They are images of art, not art."

"Three doctors at the hospital share this consultation room," Dr. Walsh might respond, adjusting his wedding band.

"Let's try to stay focused," Liza would say if she were there, placing a hand on his shoulder.

"But the problem, one of the problems"—cold spreading through him, as when they'd injected him with contrast dye—"is that these images of art only address the sick, the patients. It would be absurd to imagine a doctor lingering over one of these images between appointments, being interested in it or somehow attached to it, having his day inflected by it or whatever. Apart from their depressing flatness, their interchangeability, what I'm saying is: we can't look at them together. They help establish, deepen, the gulf between us, because they address only the sick, face only the diagnosed."

Instead, he'd asked, a tremor in his voice, "Am I going to be okay?"

"It is entirely possible that the tumor will never grow larger and that it will remain asymptomatic," Dr. Walsh explained.

"Is there a surgical option?" he heard himself say.

"You could consult with a surgeon, but I don't believe so. No." Dr. Walsh stood, walked to the adjacent wall, and slipped an X-ray onto the illuminator, which he switched on. "I believe the location of the neoplasm rules that out."

"So what do I do?" He could not make himself join Dr. Walsh at the illuminator, would not look at the cross-section of his skull.

"Well, we don't really do anything right now." Dr. Walsh sat back down. "Except follow you closely. We will develop a strategy if and when symptoms present."

Headaches, disordered speech, weakness, visual disturbances, nausea, numbness, paralysis. Prosopagnosia, pareidolia. The softening sky reflected in the water. Silver but appearing rose gold in that light. The momentary sense of having traveled back in time.

Say they join his family—parents, brother and sister-in-law, and their boys, two and five—on Sanibel Island, off the Gulf Coast of Florida, for the winter holidays.

It's dark when they arrive at the rented beach house, turning onto a gravel drive. The warm air is redolent of jasmine, the surf audible, a sound he's always found alien. He tries to remember the light snow that morning in New York, beads of precipitation on the oval window streaking as the plane took off.

The author carries his younger nephew, Theo, into the house, which smells vaguely of sunscreen, citrusy disinfectant. He walks with Theo, who has one thumb in his mouth and his free hand down the author's shirt, up to the watercolors of seashells and starfish, recalling his confrontation with Dr. Walsh about medical art as though it had happened.

Theo finds and squeezes his nipple, which makes the author start and laugh; since Theo began to be weaned, he goes after the breast of anyone who carries him. He gives Theo a raspberry on his neck, which causes him to shriek with laughter, then puts him down and watches him waddle away toward his mother, who's just entering with more bags, screen door slamming behind her. On the porch, Hannah is showing Cyrus her thumb trick.

Hannah goes upstairs to unpack, his brother and sister-in-law to establish the kids in their room. He sits with his parents drinking the Coronas the previous guests left in the refrigerator, his dad playing the cheap guitar he travels with.

"Have you been able to do any writing lately?" his dad asks, playing the chords of "The Golden Vanity," a song he'd sung the author as a child.

"Just this."

"I wouldn't be able to write anything right now, either, if I were you," his mom says. "With so much stress. But I really think you're going to be okay." The author looks at her. "I really do."

He used to cry at the end of "The Golden Vanity," when the boy who has managed to sink an enemy ship is left to drown in the ocean by a double-crossing captain, so his dad would improvise additional stanzas for the ballad in which the boy was rescued by a benevolent sea turtle and deposited safely on an island.

His nephews come running down the stairs in their pajamas, hair wet from the bath. His dad starts up a song about his two grandsons and their magical airplane pj's.

His brother and sister-in-law follow. "Maybe your uncle will tell you a story," his brother says, opening a beer.

"I know a story about the world's biggest shark," the author says. His sister-in-law had told him about Cyrus's most recent obsession. "But I don't know if the boys like sharks." The boys insist loudly that they do.

The boys' room is empty save for a rickety bunk bed on the off-white carpet, a large red suitcase open on the floor. He hears Hannah showering in the adjacent bathroom. The window is open; he smells the jasmine again. He lies down in the bottom bunk with Theo and stares up at Cyrus's mattress. Cyrus is sucking audibly on the leg of the small stuffed "piggy" he still won't sleep without. It takes the author a while to pick up the sound of the surf.

He tells the boys to listen for the waves and then to imagine that this bunk bed is a ship at sea in search of the world's largest and most vicious shark. What does vicious mean, Cyrus stops sucking long enough to ask. It means mean and ready to eat people up. The moon is high in the sky and you can see its light on the water. We have to be very, very quiet because we don't want the shark to hear us. We're sailing out to sea to capture this shark and so we have to look very carefully in the moonlight for its fin. Its dorsal fin, Cyrus contributes from his bunk. That's right, its dorsal fin, the author whispers, Theo's hand searching in his shirt.

I see it, the author quietly exclaims, but then he encounters a problem with his tense. He doesn't know how to continue the story in the present, at least not in a way that would put the boys to sleep as opposed to enlisting their participation in a kind of game. To his surprise, he feels the onset of panic, cold spreading through him. The particularly precocious author can't handle the formal complexity of the bedtime story. He takes a long pull on the beer, which doesn't help. The author is having difficulty ordering his speech.

He takes four deep, deliberate breaths, counting them out as Roberts suggests. Theo imitates him, inflating his little chest. This happens to him several times a day, this sudden fear that symptoms are presenting. Now that we've spotted the shark, the author resumes, let's put down the anchor of our boat and I'll tell you all about him. He's reassured by the sound of his own voice—no audible tremor. There once was a shark named Sam, who was thought vicious but ultimately proved to be brave and kind when he saved a family whose ship was sinking, et cetera. And he led the family to a sunken treasure, although Theo was asleep by then.

The author opened the door to his room. Hannah was towel-drying her hair in front of a long mirror, the reflection of her face blocked by her body, though she could see him. "I'll be right down," she said.

Downstairs he found the last Corona and joined the others. He was surprised to feel drunk already.

"We're thinking of going to the beach," his brother said.

"The old folks are going to bed," his dad said. His mom was already in their room. He had no idea what time it was.

"Come with us," his sister-in-law said.

He yelled up to Hannah to join them when she could. His brother found a bottle of red wine in a kitchen cabinet. They opened it and walked out back and across the moonlit gravel to a path that led around another bungalow and down to the beach. The path was covered in crushed shells and surrounded by low trees, mangroves probably. Small things fled their steps in the dark, lizards or insects. Then they emerged onto the beach and he was stunned by the panoramic sky, the impossible number of stars. The sand was brighter than he expected, glowing, and they walked midway to the water and sat down on it, passing the bottle between them.

There were a few small fires along the beach where people were camping. They tried to remember the last time they'd been on a beach together. Had it been ten years ago in Barcelona? No, there had been a wedding in L.A.

Then his brother asked, "Where's Ari? Did she go to bed already or is she coming?" They heard what could have been the slamming of a screen door in the distance, and his brother said, "That must be her."

But the author said, "She isn't in this story." He thought his speech sounded a little slurred, his voice issuing from far away. He heard laughter, and turned and saw the embers of cigarettes on the balcony of one of the beachfront condos.

"Why not?" his sister-in-law asked with disappointment.

He picked up the bottle his brother had screwed into the sand and drank. It took him a long time to say he didn't know how to explain it, that if he knew how to explain it she would be walking toward them now, not Hannah. I've divided myself into two people. A cut across worlds. Footfall on gravel, then crushed shells, silence when she reached the sand.

There was the sound of clapping from the condo, and he turned back to see that someone had launched a balloon from the balcony. No, a lantern, an illuminated red paper globe, probably a threat to sea life. It floated slowly past them and out over the water. From their respective present tenses, they all watched the same turbulent point.

The day of the extractions, he had taken the train with Liza to the office on Madison Avenue near Central Park. They rode the elevator to the twenty-eighth floor. He signed in with the receptionist, and he and Liza hung up their coats and sat down in the cramped waiting room. He was embarrassed to admit how nervous he was, but Liza knew it, and reassured him by making gentle fun of him, asking if he had any manuscripts she should burn if he didn't "pull through."

It wasn't long before a nurse called his name and he passed through the door beside the receptionist and was led to a windowless room. He tried to make himself comfortable in the chair as the nurse took his blood pressure and remarked on the weather and then placed some kind of monitor on his ankle. Soon a muscular male nurse in purple scrubs entered with an IV stand, untangled and attached various wires, and cleaned his arm with alcohol. The dentist appeared, smiled at the IV, and said in his Romanian accent, "Do I really scare you that much." The male nurse finished setting up the IV, left, and returned with a stand of tools that he wheeled in front of the dentist. The author looked away while the first nurse sank a needle into his vein.

He was in the middle of asking the dentist how long the procedure would take when he realized he was hearing his voice from far away; he left the question unfinished. That was because he was also walking with Liza in the park explaining how he had been right to elect the twilight sedation, late light filtering through the lindens. He knew he was still in the chair and at one point heard the dentist ask, pausing the drill, if he was okay, heard himself grunt affirmatively, but he was also explaining to his mom on the phone that the procedure had turned out to be a nonevent. He was suffused with warmth; the universe was benevolent, the lamp positioned to shine into his mouth was the nourishing sun. He knew it wasn't but it also was, and then the dentist was saying, "All done." He had no idea if five minutes or an hour had passed. He realized the first nurse was giving him instructions and he became aware of gauze in his mouth when he said, "Yes, yes." Then he followed her to the waiting room without feeling the floor beneath him and watched but did not listen as she repeated the instructions to Liza, who thanked her and helped him into his coat.

The dazzling sun cleared his head a little, and by the time they were in a cab his sense of time had stabilized, but he was still so thoroughly suspended in the warm glow of the drugs that he experienced the sudden starting and stopping of the taxi while they inched their way east as a gentle rocking motion. He felt no pain, and only the awareness that his tongue was numb was vaguely uncomfortable, reminding him of the wounds packed with gauze. Had Liza been talking this whole time? He turned and faced her as they merged onto the FDR Drive, and she looked beautiful, her arms raised to pull her light brown hair into a ponytail; he watched her chest rise and fall as she breathed, saw the thin gold necklace she always wore against her perfect collarbone. Then without transition he was looking at the skyline of lower Manhattan, the buildings growing larger and more detailed as the taxi approached, though he was not aware of moving. Then he was aware of moving at an impossibly smooth rate, and there was the Brooklyn Bridge, cablework sparkling. Liza was cursing at the little touch-screen television in the taxi, which she couldn't seem to turn off, and he reached out a hand to help her and experienced contact with the glass as a marvel, like encountering solidified, sensate air. Then he was smoothing her hair back and she was laughing at this uncharacteristic intimacy, something he'd done only a few times in their six years. Now the view again, and it occurred to him with the force of revelation:

I won't remember this. This is the most beautiful view of the city I have ever seen, the most perfect experience of touch and speed, I've never felt so close to Liza, and I won't remember it; the drugs will erase it. And then, glowing with the aura of imminent disappearance, it really was the most beautiful view, experience. He wanted badly to describe this situation to Liza but couldn't: his tongue was still numb; he couldn't even ask her to remind him of what the drugs would erase. While he was distantly aware that Liza would tease him for it later, that he was being ridiculous, he felt tears start in his eyes as they merged onto the bridge and he watched the play of late October sunlight on the water. That he would form no memory of what he observed and could not record it in any language lent it a fullness, made it briefly identical to itself, and he was deeply moved to think this experience of presence depended upon its obliteration. Then he was in his apartment; Liza gave him a couple of pills, put him to bed, and left.

He woke around midnight and felt like himself. His jaw ached a little. He pissed, changed the russet-colored, saturated gauze, and took another painkiller with a full glass of water. He texted Liza and also Josh, who had asked how it all went. He smiled at how much time he'd wasted ruminating about the extractions; it was nothing. He streamed an episode of *The Wire* on his laptop and fell asleep.

When he got out of bed late the next morning and had his coffee—iced so as not to disrupt the clotting—he realized: I do remember the drive, the view, stroking Liza's hair, the incommunicable beauty destined to disappear. I remember it, which means it never happened.

THREE

I arrived at NewYork-Presbyterian Hospital in a cold sweat, could actually feel the urea and salts emerging from my underarms and trickling down my ribs. I had been worrying about this appointment for well over a month—ever since it had been scheduled—had worried about it so much and so vocally that Andrews had offered to medicate me; every few minutes riding the train uptown, I patted the inside pocket of my coat to confirm the presence of the pill.

The glass doors slid open to admit me and I walked through the atrium past the Starbucks kiosk to the elevators, which I took to the seventh floor. The reception area into which I emerged was unusually luxurious, more like what I imagined the office of a major executive would look like than what I'd come to expect from medical suites. The series of abstract prints on the wall—faint grids in different colors, Agnes Martin knockoffs—was merely anodyne, but the framing was museum-quality. The receptionist I approached had an easy smile I felt was a little misplaced—the smile of a woman who sold expensive jewelry, as if I were shopping for an engagement ring; there was nothing medical about it. I gave her my name and she entered it into a computer and then printed out a form she told me to take to the floor above me; "They'll take care of you there."

Before I pressed the up button on the elevator, I saw my reflection in the shiny metal doors and said to myself, maybe even mouthed some of the words: "Take the elevator back down and leave this building and never return; you don't have to do this." But of course I took the elevator up to what was a much more conventional medical floor, where lab work was done and patients were physically examined, not just consulted about options and their pricing in and out of network.

The receptionist I handed my form to was a young woman—she looked eighteen to me, though surely she was older—who could have been a swimsuit model or hired to dance in a club in the background of a music video. She was not unusually beautiful, but her proportions, visible through her black pantsuit even while she sat, were consistent with normative male fantasy. I thought it was inappropriate to cast her in this role, whoever in human resources was doing the casting, but then felt as awkward about that thought as I did about automatically taking in the dimensions of her body. I found it difficult to meet her eyes and I tried not to blush. To my knowledge, I almost never blush, almost never visibly redden from embarrassment or shame, but trying not to blush is a distinct, involuntary activity for me: pressing, for whatever reason, my tongue against the roof of my mouth, clenching my jaw, shortening my breath—which might, it has occurred to me, cause me to redden just perceptibly. I handed the receptionist the credit card; my exorbitantly priced insurance didn't cover anything.

She gave me a second piece of paper to which she had stapled my receipt and told me to wait until I was called. I managed to look her in the eyes as I thanked her, but the knowledge in hers was terrible, as if to say: Take a good look, pervert. When I sat down, I took the pill from my pocket and was about to ingest it, but then wondered—although it would be unlike Andrews to make this kind of mistake—if it might alter the sample. I was turning it over in my fingers when a nurse called my name and asked me to follow her.

She led me to a separate room and said on its threshold that the only thing I needed to remember was to wash my hands carefully and not to touch anything that could be potentially contaminating. She handed me a small plastic container labeled with my name and various numbers and repeated slowly, as though to a man-child: Make sure your hands are very clean, or you'll have to do it over, and then told me what to do with the container when I finished. She smiled at me without any embarrassment or awkwardness, a charity, and disappeared around the corner. I entered the room and shut the door behind me.

On the one hand I was being medicalized, pathologized, broken into my parts, each granted a terrible autonomy; on the other hand I felt trace amounts of what could only be described as excitement, reminiscent of the first time Daniel lent me, at age eleven, a *Playboy*; the combination made me a little nauseated.

I hung my coat on the metal coat hanger and looked around me. In the middle of the room was something like a dentist's chair, peach-colored plastic upholstery and a strip of medical paper down its middle that the good nurse must replace between patrons, patients; I was not sitting in that chair. In front of the chair was a television with a DVD menu on the screen. Wireless headphones I resolved not to use were on top of the TV. Toward the back of the room was a sink with a dispenser of liquid soap and a little placard reminding me to wash my hands thoroughly. On the back wall was a contraption, vaguely reminiscent of one of those drive-through bank deposit boxes, where I could submit the container, transferring it to technicians on the other side of the wall, who could thereby receive it without our having to face one another. Bank, medical office, pornographic theater—it was a supra-institution. It took me a minute to realize I could hear voices through the wall, make them out clearly: a woman was talking about her daughter's boyfriend, how he was a keeper; a man was on the phone ordering lunch in Spanish, something with white rice, black beans. If I could hear them, surely they could hear me; I resolved to use the headphones.

I went to the sink and washed my hands, then washed them again. Then I walked to the chair, took the remote control from the armrest, and started looking at the menu on the screen. The TV was hooked up to some sort of service where you could select from a huge number of movie titles organized alphabetically, but also by ethnicity: *Asian Anal Adventures*, *Asian Persuasion*, *Asian Oral Fetish*, etc.; *Black Anal Adventures*, *Black Blowjobs*, *Black Cumshot Orgy*, etc., although after the ethnically specific menu you had the option of searching compilations by activity alone: *Best of* whatever. *The Picture of Sasha Grey* flashed before me. I was surprised by the extremity of some of the videos, and surprised to see them indexed racially; I guess I had expected magazines. I was embarrassed to choose, but was not in a position to deny that audiovisual assistance would expedite the process. I looked down at the remote control to see how it worked, exactly, and then remembered: I'm not supposed to touch anything that could contaminate the sample. What could be more contaminating than this remote control, which had been in how many sullied hands?

After a few seconds of panicky deliberation, I just pressed play—which started *Asian Anal Adventures*, even though that's not at all my thing; *not* choosing seemed less objectionable somehow than having to express a positive preference among the available categories—and put the remote control and the plastic container down and walked back to the sink and washed my hands. Then I returned to the screen and undid my jeans and was about to get the whole thing going when I realized my pants were even more potentially contaminating: I'd been on the subway for an hour; I couldn't remember the last time I'd laundered the things. I shuffled back to the sink with my pants and underwear around my ankles and began to worry about how long I was taking, if there was a time limit, if the nurse was going to knock on the door at some point and ask me how it was going or tell me it was the next patient's turn. I did the shuffle back to the screen and hurriedly donned the headphones, but then it occurred to me: contact with the headphones was no different than contact with the remote control. I thought about putting an end to this increasingly Beckettian drama and just trying to go on, but then I imagined getting the call that the sample wasn't usable, and so again shuffled—now wearing the headphones, now hearing the shrieks and groans of the adventurers—back to the sink to wash my hands once more. Above the sink there was mercifully no mirror.

Why, I wondered as I dispensed yet more soap, would my hands compromise the sample anyway; it's not as though I'm going to be touching the actual sperm; surely I can just be careful not to introduce my hand in any deleterious way. At this point it was academic: I was finally in a position to proceed directly from cleansing my hands to deploying them—after basically hopping back to the console—onanistically.

It was time to perform, a performance about which I had more anxiety than any actual sexual encounter, which was why Andrews had given me Viagra, which, at that moment, I wished I'd taken. It was too late now; he said it could require hours to take effect and, besides, there was my fear, probably ridiculous, of some sort of chemical contamination. And wasn't it bad for people with cardiac conditions; had he failed to think of that as well? Doesn't it induce vasodilation? I felt angry, like an angry old man. But rage at Andrews wasn't going to help my situation—his face (or his tactically inoffensive abstract painting) wasn't the right mental image to be conjuring now.

I dreaded the prospect of abandoning the masturbatorium and having to tell the nurse after twenty minutes of self-pollution that I just couldn't do it, but that dread was of course nothing compared to telling Alex. What would happen then? I would either have to reschedule, the pressure doubled, or back out of the whole project, straining, if not ruining, our friendship, or be forced to have them extract it through some horrible procedure, assuming that's something they can do. For six weeks I'd talked about my performance anxiety with Jon and Sharon and Alena and they'd laughed at me, assured me I'd be fine. For several days before providing the sample, abstinence was required; during that period Alena, through a carefully calculated configuration of double entendres and supposedly incidental contact and theatrical smoking, had tried to ensure that I was, as she put it, "primed."

And, thankfully, I was: the whole thing was over with almost comical speed, the brief experience dominated by the involuntary afterimage of the young receptionist, as the receptionist had, I believed, foreseen. The relief was profound. I dressed and delivered the sample to the other side of the wall and fled the institution as quickly as possible.

Walking west with the park in mind, I tried to imagine

the process I'd begun: the lab would evaluate volume, liquefaction time, count, morphology, motility, etc., and report back to me about my viability as a donor. The fertility specialist Alex had consulted had suggested we just skip this part, that, since sperm was specially prepared for IUI, and since we had no particular reason to believe my sperm was abnormal, excepting the fact that I'd never to my knowledge impregnated anyone despite high-risk behavior, we should just proceed to IUI and see if it was successful. But I hadn't really decided if I was prepared to be a donor or a father, especially since Alex and I were still trying to figure out how much I'd be merely the former or the latter, and this test seemed like it might help the conversation, either by ending it (if my sperm was so dysfunctional as to require male fertility treatments I wasn't willing to do, for example, or as to render IUI unbearably protracted—it only had around a 10 percent success rate in any particular instance to begin with, given Alex's age), or by demystifying some of the steps. Trivial as it may sound, I had been so allergic to the idea of actually delivering the sperm that I thought forcing myself to go through the semen analysis would rob that dimension of the process of its psychological significance. I didn't want to say no to Alex just because I couldn't face the prospect of jacking off to porn in a medical office. While I tried to figure out if I thought completing the test had actually changed any part of my thinking, I was almost struck by a downtown bus at the intersection of Sixty-eighth and Lexington.

Eventually I reached the park and walked into it only far enough to find a bench and sit down and watch the nannies, all of whom were black or brown, push around white kids in expensive strollers. I imagined trying to explain all of this to a future child, whom I pictured as Alex's second cousin: "Your mother and I loved each other, but not in the way that makes a baby, so we went to a place where they took part of me and then put it in part of her and that made you." That sounded okay. I pictured myself beside her bed, stroking her brown hair. "Really," I would explain, "everyone gets help making a baby, it's never just a mom and dad, because everybody depends on everybody else. Just think of this apartment where we are now," I'd say—although I probably wouldn't live in the same apartment as the child. "Where did the wood come from and the nails and the paint? Who planted the trees and cut them down and shipped the wood and built the apartment, who paid for those things and how did the workers learn their skills and where did the money come from, and so on?" I could have that conversation, I assured myself, as I watched a Boston terrier (originally bred for hunting rats in garment factories, only later bred for companionship) tree a squirrel: I'll narrate our mode of reproduction as a version of "It takes a village." But then my voice went on speaking to the child without my permission: "So your dad watched a video of young women whose families hailed from the world's most populous continent get sodomized for money and emptied his sperm into a cup he paid a bunch of people to wash and shoot into your mom through a tube."

"Wasn't the tube cold?" I heard in Alex's cousin's voice.

"You'd have to ask her."

"Why didn't you two just make love?"

"Because that would have been bizarre."

"Can IUI be used for gender selection?" Now she sounded like a child actress.

"Sperm can be washed or spun to increase the odds of having male or female offspring, but we didn't do that, sweetie; we wanted it to be a surprise."

"How much does IUI typically cost?"

"Great question. According to the rate sheet, and because they recommended some injectable medications for your mom, and because we did some ultrasounds and blood work, probably five thousand a pop." I regretted saying, even though I hadn't said anything, "a pop."

"What was the annual per capita gross national income of China at the time of ejaculation?"

"Four thousand nine hundred and forty U.S. dollars, but I think that's an unreliable measure of quality of life and I'd dispute the relevance of the fact, Camila." I had always liked the name Camila.

"What if you have to do IVF to make me?"

"That's more like ten thousand."

"Average annual cost of a baby in New York?"

"Between twenty and thirty thousand a year for the first two years, but we're going to live lightly."

"After that?"

"I don't know. Ask your phone." A teenager had sat down on the bench beside me and was texting; I absorbed her into the hypothetical interrogation.

"How are you going to pay for all of this?" she asked me.

"On the strength of my *New Yorker* story. You're over-focused on the money, Rose." It was my maternal grandmother's name.

"Is that why you've exchanged a modernist valorization of difficulty as a mode of resistance to the market for the fantasy of coeval readership?"

"Art has to offer something other than stylized despair."

"Are you projecting your artistic ambition onto me?"

"So what if I am?"

"Why didn't Mom just adopt?"

"Ask your mother. I guess because that's equally or more ethically complicated most of the time and because, independent of culturally specific pressures, some women experience a biological demand."

"Why reproduce if you believe the world is ending?"

"Because the world is always ending for each of us and if one begins to withdraw from the possibilities of experience, then no one would take any of the risks involved with love. And love has to be harnessed by the political. Ultimately what's ending is a mode."

"Can you imagine the world if and when I'm twenty? Thirty? Forty?"

I could not. I hoped my sperm was useless.

"Cutting and other forms of self-harm and parasuicidal behavior are endemic in my age group." I pictured the teenager pulling up her sleeve, showing me the red crosshatching.

"You're misusing *endemic*."

"The average cost for a month of inpatient treatment is thirty thousand." This observation was in Dr. Andrews's voice.

"She will be surrounded by love and support."

"How will you work out your level of involvement so that neither I nor Mom resents you for it?" The teen.

"As we go along."

The conversation didn't stop so much as recede beneath the threshold of perceptibility. Maybe to distance myself from the morning's anxiety, I removed the blue pill from the inside pocket of my coat and tried to crush it, which I couldn't do, but with two hands I succeeded in breaking it in half. I absentmindedly tossed the halves onto the sidewalk in front of me, at which point a nearby pigeon approached it, no doubt accustomed to being fed by tourists from this bench. What is the effect of sildenafil citrate on stout-bodied passerines? I stood and tried to shoo the bird away; it startled, but then turned back and quickly ate a half before I managed to intervene.

o

Two days after providing a sample of my reproductive cells for analysis, I was in the basement of the Park Slope Food Coop bagging the dried flesh of a tropical stone fruit, trying not to listen to one of my louder coworkers as she explained her decision to pull her first-grader out of a local public school and, despite the cost and the elaborate application process, place him in a well-known private one.

The Park Slope Food Coop is the oldest and largest active food cooperative in the country, as they tell you at orientation. Every able-bodied adult member works at the co-op for two hours and forty-five minutes every four weeks. In exchange you get to shop at a store with less of a markup than a normal supermarket's; prices are kept down because labor is contributed by members; nobody is extracting profit. Most of the goods are environmentally friendly, at least comparatively, and, whenever possible, locally sourced. Alex had been a member when I moved to Brooklyn and it wasn't too far from my apartment so I'd joined. Despite being frequently suspended for missing shifts while traveling, and despite complaining all the while about the self-righteousness of its members, its organizational idiocy, and the length of its checkout lines, I'd remained a member. Indeed, for most of the members I knew except Alex, who rarely complained about anything ("You do my complaining for me"), insulting the co-op was a mode of participation in its culture. Complaining indicated you weren't foolish enough to believe that belonging to the co-op made you meaningfully less of a node in a capitalist network, that you understood the co-op's population was largely made up of gentrifiers of one sort or another, and so on. If you acknowledged to a nonmember that you were part of the co-op, you then hurried to distinguish yourself from the zealots who, while probably holding investments in Monsanto or Archer Daniels Midland in their 401(k)'s, looked down with a mixture of pity and rage at those who'd shop at Union Market or Key Food. Worse: *The New York Times* had run an exposé about certain members sending their nannies to do their shifts, although the accuracy of the reporting was disputed. The woman now holding forth about her child's schooling was almost certainly a zealot.

And yet, although I insulted it constantly, and although my cooking was at best inept, I didn't think the co-op was morally trivial. I liked having the money I spent on food and household goods go to an institution that made labor shared and visible and that you could usually trust to carry products that weren't the issue of openly evil conglomerates. The produce was largely free of poison. The co-op helped run a soup kitchen. When a homeless shelter in the neighborhood burned down, "we"—at orientation they taught you to utilize the first-person plural while talking about the co-op—donated the money to rebuild it.

I worked in what was known as "food processing" on every fourth Thursday night: in the basement of the co-op, I, along with the other members of my "squad," bagged and weighed and priced dry goods and olives; we cut and wrapped and priced a variety of cheeses, although I tended to avoid the cheese, as it required some minimum of skill. In general the work was simple: the boxes of bulk food were organized on shelves in the basement. If dried mangoes were needed upstairs, you found the ten-pound box, opened it with a box cutter, and portioned the fruit into small plastic bags you then tied and weighed on a scale that printed the individual labels. Then you took the food upstairs and restocked the shelves on the shopping floor. You were required to wear an apron and a bandanna in addition to your plastic gloves. Open-toed shoes were prohibited, but I'd never owned a pair of open-toed shoes. For better or for worse, most people were sociable and voluble, like the woman talking now—this seemed to make the shift go faster for my comrades; for me, the talk often slowed time down.

"It just wasn't the right learning environment for Lucas. The teachers really tried and we believe in public education, but a lot of the other kids were just out of control."

The man working on bagging chamomile tea immediately beside her felt obliged to say, "Right."

"Obviously it's not the kids' fault. A lot of them are coming from homes—" The woman who was helping me bag mangoes, Noor, with whom I was friendly, tensed up a little in expectation of an offensive predicate.

"—well, they're drinking soda and eating junk food all the time. Of course they can't concentrate."

"Right," the man said, maybe relieved her sentence hadn't taken a turn for the worse.

"They're on some kind of chemical high. Their food is full of who knows what hormones. They can't be expected to learn or respect other kids who are trying to learn."

"Sure."

It was the kind of exchange, although *exchange* isn't really the word, with which I'd grown familiar, a new biopolitical vocabulary for expressing racial and class anxiety: instead of claiming brown and black people were biologically inferior, you claimed they were—for reasons you sympathized with, reasons that weren't really their fault—compromised by the food and drink they ingested; all those artificial dyes had darkened them on the inside. Your child, who had never so much as sipped a high-fructose carbonated beverage containing phosphoric acid and E150d, was a more sensitive instrument: purer, smarter, free of violence. This way of thinking allowed one to deploy the vocabularies of sixties radicalism—ecological awareness, anticorporate agitation, etc.—in order to justify the reproduction of social inequality. It allowed you to redescribe caring for your own genetic material—feeding Lucas the latest in coagulated soy juice—as altruism: it's not just good for Lucas, it's good for the planet. But from those who out of ignorance or desperation have allowed their children's digestive tracts to know deep-fried, mechanically processed chicken, those who happen to be, in Brooklyn, disproportionately black and Latino, Lucas must be protected at whatever cost.

Noor interrupted my reverie of disdain: "Remind me, do you have kids?"

"No." Noor was bagging the mangoes. I was tying, weighing, and labeling the bags.

"I couldn't," she said, "deal with navigating New York schools."

How would Alex, or Alex and I, deal with it, if we reproduced? If I had enough money for private school, was I sure I wouldn't be tempted? I was eager to change the subject. "Did you eat junk food growing up?"

"Never in the house, but with my friends—all the time."

"What did you eat at home?" Noor was from Boston and was in graduate school now, I'd learned on our previous shift.

"Lebanese food. My dad did all the cooking."

"He was from Lebanon?"

"Beirut. Left during the civil war."

"And your mom?" I realized I'd been labeling the mangoes incorrectly, had entered the wrong code into the electric scale. I had to do them over.

"She was from Boston. My family on that side is Russian, Jewish, but I never knew those grandparents."

"My girlfriend's mom is Lebanese," I said for some reason, perhaps to distance myself mentally from Alex and the topic of fertilization. Alena's mother was also from Beirut, but who knew if Alena was my girlfriend. "Do you still have a lot of family in Lebanon?"

She paused. "It's a long story. I have a kind of complicated family."

"We have more than two hours," I exclaimed with mock desperation, but, because Noor looked upset, or at least grave, I moved on quickly: "Nobody in my family could cook, so we—" But then she did begin to speak, both of us keeping our eyes on our work. She spoke quietly enough that we wouldn't be overheard by the others, who were now discussing the merits of Quaker pedagogy.

My dad died three years ago from a heart attack and his family is largely still in Beirut, Noor said, although not in these words. I've always thought of myself as connected to them, even though I barely saw them growing up. My dad had a really strong sense of Lebanese identity and I did too. They tried to raise me bilingually. He was a very secular Muslim, as much a Marxist as anything else, and one of his parents had been Christian, but in the U.S., maybe as a reaction against all the racism and ignorance, he decided to join a mosque in Boston—really it was more of a cultural center than a mosque. I grew up going there a lot and developed a sense of difference from most of the kids I knew. In high school and then in college I was active in Middle Eastern political causes and majored in Middle Eastern studies at BU. I was involved with the BU Arab Student Association, although that could be complicated sometimes since my mom's family was Jewish, even if not at all religious, and regardless, it was often tense with my mom because she felt I was only interested in my dad's history, had identified with him at her expense. Anyway, about six months after my dad died, my mom started dating—*dating* was the word she used—an old friend of hers named Stephen, some kind of physicist at MIT, who I'd always known a little because we'd played with his kids occasionally when we were younger; he'd since been divorced. My mom told my brother and me about Stephen at dinner one night, said she knew it was going to be hard for us, but hoped we'd understand. We said we understood, although we were both weirded out, and my brother in particular was furious it was so soon, although I think he only expressed his fury to me.

I wasn't living at home, Noor said, I was a senior in college and lived with friends, so I didn't see Stephen very much, but my brother said Stephen was coming around all the time, and my brother and I were both pretty upset at the speed. We were both suspicious—how could we not be?—that their romance had a history, that it must have started when my dad was still alive. I told my brother that the relationship was probably just mom's way of trying to deal with her grief, probably wasn't serious, but every time I talked to my mom she seemed to be with Stephen. Well, about a year after my dad died I was planning to go to Egypt for three months because I'd been offered this fellowship at the American University in Cairo for recent Arab-American graduates, and I was also planning to visit Lebanon. A few days before my flight my mom called me and asked if I could meet her for lunch. It was immediately obvious to me from her tone that she was going to tell me she was remarrying, I knew it right away, and I knew she wanted to tell me in a public place because she thought it might temper my initial reaction, and then she would ask that I help her tell my brother, who was going to freak. I was surprised that I wasn't angry, maybe in part because my parents had so clearly been estranged in the last years of their marriage, but I felt sad and a little sick and we met at some overpriced French place in the Back Bay.

At this point in Noor's story, a voice came over the PA asking if dried mangoes were out of stock—"are we out of dried mangoes?"—or could somebody from food processing bring some up. This was unavoidably my job, no matter how reluctant I was to interrupt her narrative. I told Noor I would be right back, made a kind of pouch out of my apron that I filled with some of the small, labeled bags, and took them upstairs. As always, I was embarrassed to emerge into the semipublic space of the shopping floor with a bandanna in my hair and sporting a pastel apron. The aisles were mobbed—the co-op had fifteen thousand active members and a shopping area of six thousand square feet, not to mention a checkout system of radical, willful inefficiency—and I had to fight my way to the bulk section, where I deposited the mangoes. I didn't get cell phone service in the basement, and now my phone vibrated in my back pocket, indicating I'd received a text, a one-word query from Alex: "Results?"

Back in the basement I saw another member had usurped my place beside Noor; he must have finished whatever he was bagging and then taken over my job. I was usually quiet and accommodating in the co-op, however critical my internal monologue, but this time I said: Excuse me, but I'd like to have my job back so I can continue my conversation with Noor. He said sure without a trace of resentment, and I resumed tying, labeling, weighing. The problem was that my butting in had drawn a few other members' attention, and Noor wasn't going to resume her story if they were listening. We worked in silence, which communicated to others that we knew they were listening, which further piqued their interest. An excruciating ten minutes passed in which Noor was quiet and I imagined possible conclusions to her story: Stephen turned out to be a virulent Islamophobe, and/or he worked for the FBI and tried to use her to infiltrate the BU Arab Student Association, or maybe the Lebanese part of her family had cut everybody off out of rage that her mom had plans to remarry.

When our coworkers had finally struck up their own conversations and forgotten about us, Noor picked up her narrative without my having to ask: So there we were at this French restaurant. As soon as the waiter had taken our order, Noor said to me, I said to my mom: You're going to marry Stephen, aren't you? and she laughed nervously and said that Stephen and she had in fact discussed marriage, that maybe that could happen someday, but that wasn't why she had asked me to lunch, at which point I assumed that she was going to tell me she had cancer or something. But instead she said to me: Noor, your father and I made a decision when you were a baby and I've always wondered if it was the right decision but your father was sure and insisted that we had an agreement but since he's died I've been thinking it over and now I feel that we were wrong. Your father, my mom said to me, Noor said, although not exactly in these words, was not your biological father. I got pregnant by another man but your father and I were in love and he wanted a child and so we got married, deciding that we would raise you as our child and that's what we did and your father as you know loved you tremendously and thought of you as his own child always. There had been so much turmoil and cutoff and exile in his family I just think we wanted you to feel like you were fully our child, fully in your home. We fought a lot when you were in elementary school because I regretted not telling you, but at that point his position was that it was too late even if we had initially been wrong because you would feel betrayed and confused and it would be psychologically damaging. But in the last year I have been thinking about this constantly, Noor's mother said to her, and thinking about my own mortality, and I just feel I have to tell you however disturbing this news might be. Also, I've been in therapy with someone who has helped me understand that telling you this is important for our own relationship. What I want to be clear about is that your father loved you as much as any father could love a daughter and whatever decision we made, rightly or wrongly, we made out of a sense of what would be best for you. She'd clearly memorized, Noor said to me, the last part of her speech.

"Jesus," I said.

It gets crazier, Noor said, smiling. A waiter put a salad in front of me and I remember staring into the salad trying to take in what my mom had said as she waited for me to respond. I remember we were both sitting there in silence not eating, waiting for my response to form. I felt like I was bracing for some impact because I simply couldn't feel anything and then my mom went on: Noor, she said, now more quietly, I imagine your first question is going to be who your biological father is—which actually was not my first question, Noor said to me—and part of why I wanted to tell you all of this, part of why it felt absolutely necessary, and part of why I've been so involved again, I think, with Stephen—

"Jesus," I repeated. I was working as slowly as possible so as not to let finishing the mangoes interrupt the story again. Noor slowed down the rhythm of her work along with me, which led to her slowing down the story.

Right, Noor said to me. It's because, my mom said, Stephen is your real dad, and then corrected herself: your biological father. I had dated him before I met your father and although it was clear to both of us that our relationship, at least our romantic relationship, wasn't going to last, and even though we were being careful, I got pregnant and your father, I mean Nawaf—Nawaf was the name of the man I considered my father, Noor said to me, and it was horrible to hear my mom say his name, since she'd always said "your father" or "dad"—Nawaf wanted a child badly, Noor's mother said to her, and we were falling in love and so we decided to get married and have a family. We told Stephen our plan and Stephen at that point in his life didn't want anything to do with a child and he said he would respect our decision and that he wouldn't ever say anything. And Stephen, as you know, eventually had his own family. It's funny, Noor said to me, I still didn't feel anything; I put my hands on the table on either side of my plate and I remember waiting and waiting for the impact and the only thing that happened is my hands seemed to fade.

"Fade?"

"I mean they started to pale," Noor said, raising her gloved hands from her work as if to show me. "I had always thought of my skin as dark because my father's skin was dark, because I took after him, because I was Arab-American, and as I sat there looking at my hands, without feeling anything, it was like I could see my skin whitening a little, felt color draining from my body, which it probably was because I was in shock, but I mean I started seeing my own body differently, starting with my hands."

"What did you say to your mom?" I asked. Noor was olive-skinned. Did she look different to me now than earlier in our shift?

"I said that I had to go to the bathroom and just walked right out of the restaurant. It was kind of funny," Noor laughed, "that I told her I had to go to the bathroom, since she could just see me walk right out of the front door, it wasn't like she thought I was coming back. Anyway"—Noor's tone shifted a little, indicating she was going to draw her story to a close—"you had asked me about my family in Lebanon—it's complicated now because I don't know if I can call them my family, exactly."

"Do they know the story?" I asked.

"Not unless my dad told them, which I can't imagine him doing. My mom doesn't think so."

"Did you see them when you were living in Cairo?"

"I didn't end up going anywhere. I spiraled into a big depression and when I finally climbed out of it I applied to grad school and moved here."

"Do you"—I wasn't sure how to put the question—"do you still consider yourself Arab-American?"

"When I'm asked, I say that my adoptive father was Lebanese. Which I guess is true. I still believe all the things that I believed; it hasn't changed my sense of any of the causes. But my right to care about the causes, my right to have this name and speak the language and cook the food and sing the songs and be part of the struggles or whatever—all of that has changed, is still in the process of changing, whether or not it should. Like, somebody wanted me to give a talk at Zuccotti Park about Occupy's relation to the Arab Spring and I didn't feel qualified, so I said no. There are a lot of people I haven't been able to bring myself to tell because, even if they don't want to, they'll treat me differently—*I* treat me differently."

"I can't imagine what any of this must have felt like, must feel like," I said. I wanted to say that it's not the sperm donor that matters, that the real father is the man who loved and raised her, but before I could figure out how to articulate my position tactfully, I was distracted by a vision of Alex in the future, falling in love with someone, maybe moving out of the city with "our" child. Would I be thought of as the father? Just a donor? Not at all?

Since she'd fallen quiet, and I felt I should fill the silence, I opted to say something vague about the connection between storytelling and manual labor, how the latter facilitates the former, the work creating a shared perceptual pattern, but the way she nodded indicated she'd ignored me.

"A lot of the time I still feel like I'm waiting for the impact, feel the same way I felt at the restaurant. My mom and Stephen live together now, by the way. They didn't marry. We're all trying to work things out. What I would say is that it's a little like—have you ever kept talking to somebody on your cell phone not realizing the call was dropped, gone on and on and then felt a little embarrassed?"

I said that I had.

"I have a friend who was really wronged by his older brother but had never confronted him about it. The details don't matter. But one day he got the courage to do it, to confront him on the phone. He'd been building up the courage for years. And he called his brother up and he said: I just want you to listen. I don't want you to say a word, just listen. And his brother said okay. And my friend said what it had taken him such a long time to say, was walking back and forth in his apartment and saying what had to be said, tears streaming down his face. But then when he finished talking, only when he finished talking, he realized his brother wasn't there, that the call had been lost. He called his brother back in a panic and he said, How much of that did you hear? and his brother said: I heard you say you wanted me to listen and then we got disconnected. And my friend for whatever reason just couldn't do it again, couldn't repeat what he had said. My friend told me this and told me that now he felt even more confused, more alone, because he'd had this intense experience of finally confronting his brother, and that experience changed him a little, was a major event in his life, but it never really happened: he never did confront his brother because of patchy cell phone service. It happened but it didn't happen. It's not nothing but it never occurred. Do you know what I mean? That's kind of what it felt like," Noor said, "except instead of a phone call it was my whole life up until that point that had happened but never occurred."

Although I felt Noor had been speaking for hours, only forty-five minutes of our shift had passed. As we bagged the last of the mangoes, someone came from checkout and asked if anybody had ever worked at the register; one of the cashiers had had to go home early and they needed another person. Noor said she had done checkout before and discarded her gloves and bandanna and apron and, after smiling goodbye to me, went upstairs. I spent the rest of the shift bagging dates and trying not to look at the clock.

When my shift was over I left the co-op, buying a couple of bags of mango first, and, since it was unseasonably warm, decided to take a long walk. I walked on Union Street through Park Slope and my neighborhood of Boerum Hill and through Cobble Hill and beyond the BQE until I reached Columbia Street, a walk of a couple miles. I turned right on Columbia—the water was on my left—and walked until it became Furman and then continued a mile or so until I could descend into Brooklyn Bridge Park, which, except for a few joggers and a homeless man collecting cans in a shopping cart, was empty. I found a bench and looked at the magnificent bridge's necklace lights in the sky and reflected in the water and imagined a future surge crashing over the iron guardrail. I thought I could smell the light, syrupy scent of cottonwoods blooming prematurely, confused by a warmth too early in the year even to be described as a false spring, but that might have been a mild olfactory hallucination triggered by memory—or, I found myself thinking, a brain tumor. Across the water, a helicopter was lowering itself carefully onto the downtown heliport by South Street, a slow strobe on its tail.

I breathed in the night air that was or was not laced with anachronistic blossoms and felt the small thrill I always felt to a lesser or greater degree when I looked at Manhattan's skyline and the innumerable illuminated windows and the liquid sapphire and ruby of traffic on the FDR Drive and the present absence of the towers. It was a thrill that only built space produced in me, never the natural world, and only when there was an incommensurability of scale—the human dimension of the windows tiny from such distance combining but not dissolving into the larger architecture of the skyline that was the expression, the material signature, of a collective person who didn't yet exist, a still-uninhabited second person plural to whom all the arts, even in their most intimate registers, were nevertheless addressed. Only an urban experience of the sublime was available to me because only then was the greatness beyond calculation the intuition of community. Bundled debt, trace amounts of antidepressants in the municipal water, the vast arterial network of traffic, changing weather patterns of increasing severity—whenever I looked at lower Manhattan from Whitman's side of the river I resolved to become one of the artists who momentarily made bad forms of collectivity figures of its possibility, a proprioceptive flicker in advance of the communal body. What I felt when I tried to take in the skyline—and instead was taken in by it—was a fullness indistinguishable from being emptied, my personality dissolving into a personhood so abstract that every atom belonging to me as good belonged to Noor, the fiction of the world rearranging itself around her. If there had been a way to say it without it sounding like presumptuous co-op nonsense, I would have wanted to tell her that discovering you are not identical with yourself even in the most disturbing and painful way still contains the glimmer, however refracted, of the world to come, where everything is the same but a little different because the past will be citable in all of its moments, including those that from our present present happened but never occurred. You might have seen me sitting there on the bench that midnight, my hair matted down from the bandanna, eating an irresponsible quantity of unsulfured mango, and having, as I projected myself into the future, a mild lacrimal event.

o

"It's always a projection back into the past, the idea that there was a single moment when you decided to become a writer, or the idea that a writer is in a position to know how or why she became a writer, if it makes sense to think of it as a decision at all, but that's why the question can be interesting, because it's a way of asking a writer to write the fiction of her origins, of asking the poet to sing the song of the origins of song, which is one of the poet's oldest tasks. The first poet in English whose name is known learned the art of song in a dream: Bede says that a god appeared to Caedmon and told him to sing 'the beginning of created things.' So while I assume I was asked to talk about how I became a writer with the idea that my experience might be of some practical use to the students here, I'm afraid I have nothing to offer in that regard. But I can tell you how, from my current vantage, I have constructed the fiction about the origins of my writing, such as it is.

"In the story I've been telling myself lately, I became a poet, or became interested in becoming a poet, on January twenty-eighth, 1986, at the age of seven. Like most Americans who were alive at that time, I have a clear memory of watching the space shuttle *Challenger* disintegrate seventy-three seconds into flight. There had been, as many of you probably know, unusual excitement about this mission because one of the seven crew members was a teacher named Christa McAuliffe. She was selected from I don't know how many applicants to be the first teacher in space, also the first civilian, part of a program called the 'Teacher in Space Project,' which would be canceled a few years after her death. McAuliffe was selected in part to represent 'ordinary Americans' and so we ordinary Americans were particularly interested in this mission. Millions of schoolchildren were being taught curricula related to the program and were looking forward to the launch. My third-grade class wrote her letters expressing our pride and wishing her luck. I remember Mrs. Greiner trying to explain the word *Godspeed*.

"Can I ask you, by a show of hands, to indicate if you watched the *Challenger* disaster live? Right. The majority of Americans who are over thirty years old today remember watching the shuttle crumble on live TV. It's consistently noted as the dawning of our era of live disasters and simulcast wars: O. J. Simpson fleeing in the white Bronco, the towers collapsing, etc., although there had of course been other televised traumas before. I don't have a single friend who doesn't remember watching it as it happened—not as a replay later when you knew the shuttle was doomed, but when you expected the shuttle to disappear successfully into space and instead saw it engulfed in a giant fireball, saw the branching plumes of smoke as its components fell back to earth. I remember a moment of incomprehension, trying to imagine that what I'd witnessed was part of the plan, some kind of timed separation of one part of the shuttle from the other, and then, with a terrible sinking feeling, realizing, even as a seven-year-old, that that wasn't possible.

"The thing is, almost nobody saw it live: 1986 was early in the history of cable news, and although CNN carried the launch live, not that many of us just happened to be watching CNN in the middle of a workday, a school day. All other major broadcast stations had cut away before the disaster. They all came back quickly with taped replays, of course. Because of the Teacher in Space Project, NASA had arranged a satellite broadcast of the mission into television sets in many schools—and that's how I remember seeing it, as does my older brother. I remember tears in Mrs. Greiner's eyes and the students' initial incomprehension, some awkward laughter. But neither of us did see it: Randolph Elementary School in Topeka wasn't part of that broadcast. So unless you were watching CNN or were in one of the special classrooms, you didn't witness it in the present tense.

"What many of us did watch live was Ronald Reagan's address to the country later that night. I knew everybody in my family hated Reagan, but I could tell that even my parents were moved by the speech. At the time I didn't know that politicians' speeches were written by other people, but I did know—because it was discussed in my favorite movie, *Back to the Future*, which had come out the previous year—that Reagan had been a Hollywood actor. Reagan's speech was written by Peggy Noonan and is widely considered one of the greatest twentieth-century presidential addresses.

Noonan would go on to write a bunch of memorable Republican catchphrases—'read my lips: no new taxes'; 'a thousand points of light'; 'a kinder, gentler nation.' (She would also, by the way, become a consultant for the television program *The West Wing*.) The speech was only four minutes long. And the ending—one of the most famous conclusions of any presidential speech—entered my body as much as my mind: *We will never forget them, nor the last time we saw them, this morning, as they prepared for the journey and waved goodbye and 'slipped the surly bonds of earth' to 'touch the face of God.'*

"The prosody of that last part of the sentence, the way the iambs offered both a sense of climax and of closure, the way the alternating stresses lent the speech a sense of authority and dignity, of mourning and reassurance—I felt it in my chest; the sentence pulled me into the future. I had no idea what *surly* meant then, and it's an awkward modifier in this phrase, since you usually see it in contexts like 'a surly waiter,' meaning uncivil; a 'surly sky' is threatening or ominous. It's hard for me to apply it to a 'bond,' although I see how it does elegiac work by helping us think of the astronauts as having escaped a threat as opposed to having succumbed to one—they are in a better place now, etc. (Bede says: 'By his verse the minds of many were often excited to despise the world.') But the meaning of the words was nothing compared to that first experience of poetic measure—how I felt simultaneously comforted and stirred by the rhythm and knew that all across America those rhythms were working in millions of other bodies too. Let me allow the preposterousness of what I'm saying to sink in: I think I became a poet because of Ronald Reagan and Peggy Noonan. The way they used poetic language to integrate a terrible event and its image back into a framework of meaning, the way the transpersonality of prosody constituted a community: poets were the unacknowledged legislators of the world, it seemed to me.

"Had I seen a transcript of the speech, I would have seen that 'slipped the surly bonds of earth' and 'touch the face of God' were in quotation marks. They weren't Reagan's words, and they weren't Noonan's: they were taken from a poem by John Gillespie Magee entitled 'High Flight.' Magee—an American pilot in the Royal Canadian Air Force—died at nineteen in a midair collision during World War II and on his gravestone near where he died in Lincolnshire the first and last lines of 'High Flight' are engraved: 'Oh! I have slipped the surly bonds of earth / Put out my hand and touched the Face of God.' 'High Flight' is a very famous poem and it's not so surprising Noonan had it on hand. It's the official poem, whatever that means, of the Royal Canadian Air Force. It's on a lot of stones in military cemeteries. When I learned these facts while writing a term paper in high school, I didn't feel as though I'd been cheated: I loved the idea that a poem written by a young man weeks before his fiery death would be quoted by a speechwriter and read by a president and felt in the chests of a million American children in the wake of another aerial disaster. It showed poetry's power to circulate among bodies and temporalities, to transcend the contingencies of its authorship.

"While preparing these remarks, I was reading up a little on Magee—by which I mean, why hide the fact, that I was reading his Wikipedia entry—when I noted a section called 'Sources of Inspiration for *High Flight*.' 'Sources of Inspiration' is an understatement, a euphemism; if Magee were a student of mine and showed me a poem with this number of 'sources,' I'd either say it was a work of collage or an act of plagiarism. The last line of 'High Flight'—'And touched the face of God'—also concludes a poem by a man named Cuthbert Hicks, a poem that was published three years before Magee's in a book called *Icarus: An Anthology of the Poetry of Flight*. Hicks's poem ends: 'For I have danced the streets of heaven, / And touched the face of God.' What's more, *Icarus* contains a poem called 'New World' by one G.W.M. Dunn, which includes the (unfortunate) phrase 'on laughter-silvered wings,' which Magee stole for the second line of 'High Flight.' Moreover, the penultimate line of 'High Flight'—'The high, untrespassed sanctity of space'—sounds an awful lot like a line from a poem in *Icarus* by someone known by the initials C.A.F.B., 'Dominion over Air,' a poem that had previously been published in the *RAF College Journal*: 'Across the unpierced sanctity of space.' Reagan's unattributed quotation provided by Noonan was taken from a poem that was cobbled together by a young poet out of an anthology of other young poets enthralled by the power of flight, which cost many of them their lives—unless someone made this all up on Wikipedia, which is possible; I didn't have time to track down a copy of *Icarus*. I find this less scandalous than beautiful: a kind of palimpsestic plagiarism that moves through bodies and time, a collective song with no single origin, or whose origin has been erased—the way a star, from our earthly perspective, is often survived by its own light.

"I want to mention another way information circulated through the country in 1986 around the *Challenger* disaster, and I think those of you who are more or less my age will know what I'm talking about: jokes. My brother, who is three and a half years older than I, would tell me one after another as we walked to and from Randolph Elementary that winter: Did you know that Christa McAuliffe was blue-eyed? One blew left and one blew right; What were Christa

McAuliffe's last words to her husband? You feed the kids—I'll feed the fish; What does NASA stand for? Need Another Seven Astronauts; How do they know what shampoo Christa McAuliffe used? They found her head and shoulders. And so on: the jokes seemed to come out of nowhere, or to come from everywhere at once; like cicadas emerging from underground, they were ubiquitous for a couple of months, then disappeared. Folklorists who study what they call 'joke cycles' track how—particularly in times of collective anxiety—certain humorous templates get recycled, often among children. When the IRA blew up a fishing boat with Admiral Mountbatten on it in 1979, the year of my birth, people told the same dandruff joke. When an actor named Vic Morrow died in a helicopter crash in 1982, there was the joke again—head and shoulders. (Procter & Gamble developed the shampoo in the 1950s.) The *Challenger* joke cycle, which seemed to exist without our parents knowing, was my first experience of a kind of sinister transpersonal syntax existent in the collective unconscious, a shadow language to Reagan's official narrative processing of the national tragedy. The anonymous jokes we were told and retold were our way of dealing with the remainder of the trauma that the elegy cycle initiated by Reagan-Noonan-Magee-Hicks-Dunn-C.A.F.B. (and who knows who else) couldn't fully integrate into our lives.

"So at the beginning of my story of origins is a false memory of a moving image. I didn't see it live. What I saw was a televised speech that wasn't written by anyone, but that, through its rhythmic structure, was briefly available to everyone; the next day I went to school and another powerfully unoriginal linguistic practice enveloped me, an unsanctioned ritual of call-and-response that was, however insensitively, a form of grieving. If I had to trace my origins as a poet to a specific moment, I'd locate it there, in those modes of recycling. I make no claims for 'High Flight' as a poem—in fact, I think it's a terrible poem—and Ronald Reagan I consider a mass murderer. I don't see anything formally interesting about the *Challenger* jokes; I can't find anything to celebrate there; they weren't funny even at the time. But I wonder if we can think of them as bad forms of collectivity that can serve as figures of its real possibility: prosody and grammar as the stuff out of which we build a social world, a way of organizing meaning and time that belongs to nobody in particular but courses through us all. Thank you."

I thought the applause for my remarks was enthusiastic, but I might well have been mistaken, because almost none of the questions in the ensuing conversation was addressed to me; the other two writers on the panel were much better known. I sat in a modernist leather chair on the stage at Columbia's School of the Arts, unable to see the audience clearly because of the tungsten lights, a distinguished professor of literature moderating, and mainly listened to the distinguished authors—so distinguished I'd often thought of them as dead—talk about the origins of their genius. (Would you believe me if I said that one of the distinguished authors was the same South African man I'd observed from across the room at Bernard and Natali's fifteen years before?) There were the usual exhortations to purity—think of the novel not as your opportunity to get rich or famous but to wrestle, in your own way, with the titans of the form—exhortations poets don't have to make, given the economic marginality of the art, an economic marginality that soon all literature will share.

But at the elegant dinner the distinguished professor had arranged for us after the panel, all the initial small talk was about money: had you heard about X's advance, how much money Y received when her aggressively mediocre book was optioned for film, and so on. After two quick glasses of Sancerre, the distinguished male author started holding forth, periodically tugging at his salt-and-pepper beard, his signature gesture, moving from one anecdote about a famous friend or triumphant experience to another without pausing for the possibility of response, and it was clear to everyone at the table who had any experience with men and alcohol—especially men who had won international literary prizes—that he was not going to stop talking at any point in the meal. Unless he dissects, I thought. When a young Latino man tried to refill his glass of water from a pitcher, the distinguished male author snapped in Spanish, without looking at the man, that he was having sparkling water, and then switched back into English without missing a beat. The distinguished professor was sitting immediately across from the distinguished male author and seemed more than happy to receive his logorrhea; a younger woman—probably also an English professor, but too young to be distinguished—was sitting beside him, smiling bravely, realizing her evening was doomed.

I was on the other side of the table sitting across from the distinguished female author, enjoying how the crispness and lightness of the wine had a rightness of fit with the restaurant's pear-wood paneling and bright terrazzo floors. Seated to my right was a well-dressed graduate student about my age who was plainly starstruck by the distinguished female author, perhaps the subject of his dissertation. To the distinguished female author's left was her husband, probably also distinguished in some way, who had the look of many husbands: eyebrows perpetually raised a little in a defensive mask of polite interest, signifying boredom. I was unsure if I should say *gracias* or thank you to the man refilling my water glass. Even here, where a meal for seven would cost at least a thousand dollars, much of the work was done by a swift underclass of Spanish-speaking laborers. I thought of Roberto, of his terror of Joseph Kony. I tried to picture, as I looked around the restaurant, those towns in Mexico in which almost all of the able-bodied men were gone, employed now in New York's service industry.

"I enjoyed your story in *The New Yorker*," the distinguished female author said to me. It seemed that the story—which was in part the result of my dealing with the reception of my novel—had been much more widely read than the novel itself.

"Thank you," I said. And then I said, although I had only read one of her books and it hadn't made much of an impression on me, "I've long been an admirer of your work." She smiled with only the left side of her mouth in a way that doubted the statement; I found the expression winning.

"Do you have a brain tumor?" she asked. I was impressed less with her frankness than with the fact that it appeared she'd actually read the story.

"Not that I know of."

"Is it part of a longer work?"

"Maybe. I think I might try to make it into a novel. A novel in which the author tries to falsify his archive, tries to fabricate all these letters—mainly e-mails—from recently dead authors that he can sell to a fancy library. That idea was the origin of the story."

"Why does he need the money? Or is the money what he wants?"

"I think it's more a response to his own mortality—like he's trying to time-travel, to throw his voice, now that he's dealing with his own fragility. It starts off as a kind of fraud but I imagine he might really get into it, might really feel like he and the dead are corresponding. Like he's a medium. But you wouldn't know, even at the novel's end, if he really planned to sell the letters or if he was just working on an epistolary novel of some sort. And he could meditate on all the ways that time is monetized—archival time, a lifetime, etc." I was trying to sound excited about the project I was describing, but felt, despite the wine, dispirited: another novel about fraudulence, no matter the bruised idealism at its core.

I ordered an appetizer of charred shrimp with puntarelle, whatever that was, and seared scallops for my main course. I was told by the waiter that my choices were excellent. The distinguished female author said she'd also have the scallops, and that felt somehow like a gesture of fellowship.

The graduate student asked the distinguished female author what she was working on. "Absolutely nothing," she said, with utter seriousness, and, after a brief interval of silence, we all laughed. Then she said to me, "Whom would he correspond with, what dead people?" The frustrated graduate student—he didn't want to hear more about me—and the bored husband tried to make conversation. I could hear the distinguished male author droning on in the distance.

"Primarily poets, I guess. Poets I corresponded with a little—mainly for the magazine I used to edit and that the protagonist will have edited—and whose tone I know how to imitate. Robert Creeley comes to mind."

"I used to know Creeley pretty well." She sipped her wine. "Would you include real correspondence, too—I mean, do you have actual letters you received that you'll insert into the fiction?"

"No," I said. "Almost all the correspondence about the magazine was e-mail, and I had a different e-mail account for much of that time. I never printed anything. What I do have is boring, logistical."

"I could write you a letter for it—he could falsify one from me but I could write it."

"That would be great." I loved the idea.

"You should really try it." I thought she meant try to write the novel, but: "You should try to pass off letters you've written to an archivist. That's how you'd know if the fiction was plausible." I laughed.

"I'm serious. I can put you in touch with the appraiser I worked with when I thought about selling my papers to the Beinecke."

"I don't have the courage," I said. Was she serious? One waiter materialized to refill our wine, another placed my appetizer before me. Puntarella was a green with dandelion-shaped leaves.

"Well, put the stuff about the shuttle in there somehow. I liked that. When you talked about the kids watching the explosion, the nervous laughter—that reminded me of something I hadn't thought of for a long time, but that I used to think about constantly."

"These are amazing," I said, referring to the shrimp, which were. "You've got to try a bite," I said, and she reached across the table with her fork.

"When I was in the first year many centuries ago, our teacher, Mrs. Meacham, lost her daughter." I guessed first grade was called "first year" in Britain. "Nobody told us, of course. We had a substitute for a few days, were informed that Mrs. Meacham was mildly ill, and then there she was again, maybe a little more distant than usual, but basically unchanged. It must have been a week or two after she'd been back, we were doing recitation exercises, and she called on me to read a passage from the textbook—I remember it as a passage from the Bible, but that seems unlikely. Anyway, she called on me and I read a few lines and then she stopped me. She looked straight at me and she said, her voice frighteningly calm: 'You look just like my daughter, Mary.' I remember the name clearly. The class was completely silent, we'd never heard Mrs. Meacham say anything off script. Then she said, slowly: 'My dead daughter, Mary. You look just like my daughter, who is dead.' She said it like it was some sort of grammatical demonstration." The graduate student was trying to listen while still facing the husband, who was talking about a recent trip to India. Our glasses were unobtrusively refilled. "We were all shocked," she continued. "I remember looking down at my book and feeling tremendous shame, as though I'd been reprimanded. Then I looked up at Mrs. Meacham, who was staring at me, and I heard this terrible laughter."

"Laughter?"

"*My* laughter. I heard it before I recognized it as issuing from my body. It was completely involuntary. It was a profoundly nervous response. For a few seconds only I was laughing, and then everybody started laughing. Everybody in the classroom erupted into loud, hysterical laughter, and Mrs. Meacham, in tears, fled the room. And as soon as she fled the room, the laughter stopped. It stopped all at once, like a disciplined orchestra that has received a sign from the conductor. And we just sat there in silence, ashamed and confused." She took another bite of my appetizer, which I hadn't touched while she'd been speaking.

"And then Mrs. Meacham came back into the classroom," she said when she'd swallowed the food, chasing it with wine, "and resumed her position at the front of the class, and called on me again to read the passage. And I read the passage and the school day continued, and then the school year, as if nothing had happened. I thought of it because you mentioned both the nervous laughter and the jokes, I suppose. Children trying to process a death."

We drank in silence for a minute and I ate the last shrimp and asked, "Do you have kids?"

"No."

"Did you want them?" I tried to check in with myself about whether I was mistaking my mild inebriation for an easy sympathy between us.

"At times I have, but most times I haven't."

"You never tried?" I'd decided I didn't care about the sympathy-and-wine calculus.

"I had a surgery to remove a fibroid when I was in my twenties and the scarring made it impossible. That used to happen more in those days."

"I'm sorry," I said.

She shrugged. "I think on balance I didn't want kids anyway. Do you have children?"

"No, but my best friend wants me to help her get pregnant. I mean, we're thinking of doing IUI. But"—and this was certainly only sayable because of the wine—"my sperm is a little abnormal." The graduate student involuntarily turned and faced me.

The distinguished female author laughed, not at all unkindly, and asked, "How so?"

"Apparently, every man has a lot of abnormal sperm—sperm that are shaped wrong or something and so aren't going to fertilize an egg. But I have more abnormal sperm than is normal, so they said it might be harder for me to get someone pregnant."

"But not impossible."

"No. But it could take a really long time and my friend is already thirty-six. And they might recommend going straight to IVF, which I don't think she'd want to do."

"So you're off the hook? Do you want to be off the hook?"

"I don't know. They want me to repeat the test—this one could have been off. And regardless, I think Alex—my friend—is still going to want me to try for a while. Try the IUI thing, I mean."

"Isn't this all terribly expensive?"

"Yeah, and Alex is between jobs. But my agent thinks I can get a big advance for a second novel. On the strength of the story. And I teach."

"Falsifying his archive to subsidize fertility treatments; faking the past to fund the future—I love it. I'm ready to endorse it sight unseen. What else happens?"

There was one other story I knew I would tip in, a story I'd only recently heard from Alex's stepfather. "I'm not sure how this will fit, exactly, but the protagonist had—will have had—a relationship when he was younger that I think will form an important part of his history and relate to his inclination toward fabrication. He's in college and falls in love with this woman, Ashley, a couple of years his senior who, about six months after they first get together, comes back from the doctor in tears and tells him she's been diagnosed with cancer."

"That young?"

"It happens, right? Say they find it somehow during a routine examination. At first it looks like she's going to drop out and go live with her family during treatment, but then she decides—in part because she's in love with him, in part because her relationship with her parents is difficult—to undergo it there, at a hospital not far from campus. This is the first romantic relationship either has ever been in where one partner really has to care for the other, not just try to impress the other; it's his first serious relationship away from home and it's developing in the shadow of death. There's no surgery, but then—worse—there's radiation and chemo; he drives her to the hospital in her car for each treatment, dropping her off because, for whatever complex of reasons, she doesn't want him there, asks that he respect the intimacy of her relationship to her oncologist, a woman with whom she feels close. He waits in the parking lot or drives around smoking, listening to music. She loses weight, hair; there is a lot of weeping and courageous resolve; he learns to cook meals rich in bioflavonoids for immune support; he leads conversations about their future in which he insists he wants kids—which he doesn't—in order to insist on futurity in general. Imagine a year of this," I said to the distinguished female author. "He's a boy pretending to be a man losing his partner; he's making occasional love to an emaciated young woman who might have a terminal condition, while their peers are eating ecstasy and going to parties or whatever; he's ghostwriting her papers, e-mailing her professors to request extensions, and so on. And then one night, let's say it's New Year's Eve, they're watching a movie in bed, say it's *Back to the Future*, and she says to him:

" 'I want to tell you something, but I want you to promise you won't be mad.'

" 'Okay, I promise,' he promises.

" 'I'm not sick.'

" 'What do you mean?'

" 'I don't have cancer,' she says.

" 'You're in remission,' he confirms.

" 'No, I've never had it,' she says.

" 'Go to sleep, baby.'

" 'No, I'm serious—I've never had it. I wanted to tell you, but things got out of hand.'

" 'Hush,' he says, a strange feeling coming over him.

" 'I'm serious,' she says, and something in her voice asserts that she is.

" 'And you've been faking your treatment,' he says sarcastically.

" 'Yes,' she says.

" 'You get chemo for a fake diagnosis.'

" 'No, I sit in a bathroom stall.'

" 'And Dr. Sing,' he says, forcing himself to laugh.

" 'That was the name of my doctor in Boston.'

" 'This isn't funny, Ashley. You sound crazy. You've lost thirty pounds.'

" 'I make myself throw up. I have no appetite.'

"He begins to feel desperate. 'Your hair.'

" 'I shave it. At first I pulled out patches.'

" 'The pills.' He's stood up. He's standing in his underwear by the bed."

" 'I have Zoloft. I have Ativan,' " the distinguished author said, role-playing Ashley. " 'I have large blue vitamins I put in the old bottles.' "

"Right. He doesn't want to ask why, to concede the possibility of her lie, but: 'Why?' "

" 'I felt alone. Confused. Like something *was* wrong with me.' "

" 'The lie described my life better than the truth,' " I added. " 'Until it became a kind of truth.' " I drained my drink. " 'I would have done the chemo if they'd offered it to me.' "

The distinguished female author looked at me, perhaps trying to figure out if the story was lifted from my life. "Yes," she decided, "you should put that in the novel."

A rectangular plate bejeweled with diver scallops was placed before each of us simultaneously. There were tiny slices of what looked like green apple, fine pieces of what was probably an exotic celery. A new wine was being served. The distinguished female author and I were now unabashedly getting drunk. As we ate, I told her the story of my visit to the masturbatorium, and I had her cracking up; we were laughing loudly enough to draw some stares from other tables. For dessert we shared a chocolate tart and each had a large Armagnac.

Outside the restaurant in the false spring air everyone shook everyone's hand with the particular awkwardness of people who had eaten together but had not spoken. The distinguished male author said to both of us with affected gravity that he was deeply sorry he hadn't had the chance to ask after our current projects, which he was sure were splendid. With even greater solemnity, I responded, "I've long admired your work"; the distinguished female author had to cough away her laughter. Then she and I embraced one another and she said to me, "Just do it all." When I asked, "Do what?" she just repeated, "Do it all," and we hugged one another again and then I headed south toward the subway as she and her exhausted-looking husband hailed a cab to take to the East Side. I walked past Lincoln Center, where the well dressed were filtering out of the opera, milling about the illuminated fountain. At Fifty-ninth I took the D back to Brooklyn, repeating to myself in time with the rhythm of the train: Do it all, do it all.

When I got out of the train I walked to Alex's apartment and rang the bell, which I almost never did—normally I'd just text her that I was downstairs—and she descended to let me in. She was a little dressed up, either because she'd had a job interview earlier that day or because she'd been on a date, and she looked particularly pretty to me in her liquid satin and Venetian wool; I said hello and focused on appearing sober as we ascended the stairs. When we got inside the apartment she asked me how the event was and, instead of answering, I wrapped my arms around her and drew her against me and kissed her on the mouth and tried to find her tongue. She pushed me away hard, laughing, coughing, wiping her mouth, and said: "What the fuck are you doing? Are you drunk?" "Of course I'm drunk," I said, and tried to approach her again, but she held out her arms to stop me. "Seriously, what are you doing?"

"I'm doing it all," I said meaninglessly, and then I said: "I'm not going back there to jack off into a cup every month for two years. Okay, so my sperm are a little abnormal, but it doesn't mean I can't get you pregnant."

"What do you mean, your sperm are abnormal?"

"It's normal to have abnormal sperm," I said, as if she'd insulted me, and she laughed. I sat down on the futon and beckoned for her to join me there and thought: This is going to be fine; after all, we made out a few times in college. She did come toward me, but only to pick up one of the embroidered Indian pillows from the futon, which she swung into my face. "Go to sleep, you fucking idiot, we are not having sex." Stunned, I opened my mouth to say a lot of things—about joke cycles, the origins of poetry, correspondences—but instead I stretched out and, placing the pillow over my head, not under it, said: Good night. Later she told me I'd kept her up by trying to recite "High Flight."

o

Dear Ben, I put down, *I too found it a pleasure meeting you, albeit briefly, in Providence, though in such a crowd little conversation was possible. But to put a face to the name, as they say, if they still say that, and I hope there will be another occasion soon to be in each other's company.*

I deleted the "I too," just made it "It was a pleasure," and started a new paragraph: *I remember writing William Carlos Williams in, what, 1950, and feeling the letter was very much an intrusion. I don't mean to imply that I'm to you what Williams was to me then, only to sympathize with, to remember how I shared, the worry you expressed that reaching out might be construed as overreaching. But it isn't, and you're certainly not, and anyway how else is one to find one's contemporaries, form a company? How else to locate the writers with whom one corresponds, both in the sense that we are corresponding now, and in that more general sense of some kind of achieved accord, the way we speak of a story corresponding with the facts? You no doubt know Jack Spicer's use of that term in all its weird possibility, how he corresponded with the dead, took dictation. And of course we have Baudelaire's sense of "Correspondances."*

The author could go back later and make sure he wasn't overusing Creeley's signature words. I'd reread the one or two matter-of-fact messages we had actually exchanged, would look again at his *Selected Letters.*

I also recall here that letter sent in my midtwenties because I was writing like you about starting a little magazine, articulating insofar as I could its "general program," which of course involved expressing my discontent with the magazines then current. You ask if "we need another," a good question, but I wonder how much the "we" should be its subject. Of course the magazine is a thing one hopes has its circulation, however small, has its influence, however hard to measure, but it is also the instrument through which your own sense of the possibilities of the art will be forged, tested. It seems to me now evident that the best magazines come from editors who themselves "need" the thing to exist, and out of the singularity of that need a magazine of some possible public use arises.

The card of the special collections librarian and the card of the archival appraiser she had recommended would hang above the author's desk, a silver thumbtack in the plaster. As he worried about the growth of a tumor, as I worried about the dilation of my aorta, the letters would accumulate, expanding the story into a novel.

Attached to this e-mail are four recent poems I would be pleased, indeed, to have appear in your inaugural issue, to appear if they appeal. Their immediate occasion is a visit last summer to Lascaux . . .

I clicked send, transmitting the proposal to my agent, mild pain shooting through my chest, no doubt psychosomatic, and left to meet Alena at her apartment on the Lower East Side.

Along with an artist friend of hers, Peter, who also had a law degree, Alena had been working on a project—*not* an art project, she kept insisting—that she'd often described to me, but which I'd always largely dismissed as fantasy: she and Peter were in the process of trying to convince the largest insurer of art in the country to give them some of its "totaled" art. When a valuable painting is damaged in transit or a fire or flood, vandalized, etc., and an appraiser agrees with the owner of a work that the work cannot be satisfactorily restored, or that the cost of restoration would exceed the value of the claim, then the insurance company pays out the total value of the damaged work, which is then legally declared to have "zero value." When Alena asked me what I thought happened to the totaled art, I told her I assumed that the damaged work was destroyed, but, as it turned out, the insurer had a giant warehouse on Long Island full of these indeterminate objects: works by artists, many of them famous, that, after suffering one kind of damage or another, were formally demoted from art to mere objecthood and banned from circulation, removed from the market, relegated to this strange limbo.

Ever since Peter—who had a friend at the insurance company—had arranged a tour of the warehouse for Alena, she was obsessed with the idea of acquiring some of these supposedly valueless works, many of which she considered to be more compelling—aesthetically or conceptually—than they had been prior to sustaining damage. Her plan, which I'd thought sounded naïve, had been to tell the insurer that she and Peter had founded a nonprofit "institute" for the study of damaged art and to encourage the company to make a donation. They wrote up a mission statement which I copyedited, informally affiliated themselves with a nonprofit arts organization run by one of Alena's friends, dressed up like responsible adults, and got a meeting with the head of the insurance company, who, it turned out, was also a painter. They charmed her. The head of the company agreed these totaled artworks were of both aesthetic and philosophical interest and—to Alena and Peter's surprise—was open to the idea of donating a selection for small-scale exhibition and critical discussion, assuming the details could be worked out. Peter spent a few months drafting an appropriately official-sounding agreement with the insurer (no personal details about the parties involved in the claim would be divulged, etc.) and Alena looked into various spaces where they could display the objects and host discussions about these no-longer-artworks and their implications for artists, critics, theorists. In the end, and to my shock, the insurer agreed to donate a gallery's worth of "zero-value" art to Alena's "institute," and even covered the cost of shipping.

That morning I'd received a text from Alena that she and Peter would like me to be the first visitor to the "Institute for Totaled Art."

Alena buzzed me in and I climbed the four flights of stairs to her apartment. She lived in a giant rent-controlled loft in a former commercial building; an uncle was on the lease. It had one room that served as Alena's studio and then a vast open space into which you could have fit at least two of my apartments. Sometimes Alena's younger brother—a student at NYU—lived in the apartment with her, although he hadn't been around in recent months. Almost all the furniture was easily movable and so the room was arranged a little differently each time I visited, which made me feel crazy; the black couch was no longer against the wall, but now the record player was; the drafting table was in a different corner; and so on. I kissed Alena and hugged Peter and sat on an empty crate and asked them where the institute was housed. You're in it, she said, and disappeared into her studio. Shut your eyes, she yelled back to me.

I shut my eyes—whenever I shut my eyes in the city I become immediately aware of the wavelike sound of traffic—and then I heard her bare feet on the hardwood as she approached me. Put out your hands, she said, and I did. She dropped what felt like a series of porcelain balls or figurines into them. Now open them, she said: what I was holding were the pieces of a shattered Jeff Koons balloon dog sculpture, an early red one. It was wonderful to see an icon of art world commercialism and valorized stupidity shattered; it was wonderful to touch the pieces with their metallic finish, to see the hollow interior of a work of willful superficiality. It probably wasn't originally worth that much money by art world standards—somewhere between five thousand and ten thousand dollars, between one and two

IUIs, a year or two of Chinese labor—but it had been worth enough money to charge the experience of holding its ruins with a frisson of transgression. Besides, somebody would probably pay a lot of money for the remnants even if the rubble had legally been declared worthless. Alena and Peter started laughing at my stunned silence and Alena picked up one of the smaller fragments from my hand and hurled it onto the hardwood, where it shattered. "It's worth nothing," she basically hissed. She looked like a chthonic deity of vengeance. Not for the first time, I wondered if she was a genius.

Dazed, I walked into her studio. There was more than one gallery's-worth of artworks stacked against the wall, laid out on the kitchen island she'd installed as a work surface, or resting on the floor. Some were by artists I recognized, most were not. Some were obviously compromised—badly torn or stained. So many of the paintings had sustained water damage that I felt as though I'd been transported into a not-so-distant future where New York was largely submerged, where you could look down from an unkempt High Line and see these paintings floating down Tenth Avenue. Why aren't you touching anything, Alena said, you can touch them now, and she took my hand and pushed it against what either still was or had once been a painting by Jim Dine. "Since the world is ending," Peter quoted from behind us, "why not let the children touch the paintings?"

But it was not the slashed or burnt or stained artworks that moved me the most, that made me feel that Peter and Alena were doing something profound by unearthing the living dead of art. To my surprise, many of the objects were not, at least not to my admittedly inexpert eye, damaged at all. Here was an unframed Cartier-Bresson print under a pile of other photographs on the island. I held it up to the pale light streaming in through the studio window but perceived no tears, scratches, fading, stains. I asked Peter and Alena to show me the damage, but they were equally baffled. Here was an abstract diptych by a well-known contemporary artist in what seemed to us perfect condition; Alena consulted the paperwork—heavily redacted by the insurer—and found that it was missing a panel, that it was in fact a triptych, but the two panels in her possession were uncompromised.

I sat on the makeshift daybed Alena had constructed for her studio out of cinder blocks and an old mattress—a mattress I'd checked more than once for the russet traces of bedbugs—and studied the Cartier-Bresson. It had transitioned from being a repository of immense financial value to being declared of zero value without undergoing what was to me any perceptible material transformation—it was the same, only totally different. This was a reversal of the kind of recontextualization associated with Marcel Duchamp, still—unfortunately, in my opinion—the tutelary spirit of the art world; this was the opposite of the "readymade" whereby an object of utility—a urinal, a shovel—was transformed into an object of art and an art commodity by the artist's fiat, by his signature. It was the reversal of that process and I found it much more powerful than what it reversed because, like everyone else, I was familiar with material things that seemed to have taken on a kind of magical power as a result of a monetizable signature: that's how branding works in the gallery system and beyond, whether for Damien Hirst or Louis Vuitton. But it was incredibly rare—I remembered the jar of instant coffee the night of the storm—to encounter an object liberated from that logic. What was the word for that liberation? *Apocalypse? Utopia?* I felt a fullness indistinguishable from being emptied as I held a work from which the exchange value had been extracted, an object that was otherwise unchanged. It was as if I could register in my hands a subtle but momentous transfer of weight: the twenty-one grams of the market's soul had fled; it was no longer a commodity fetish; it was art before or after capital. Not the shattered or slashed works to which Alena thrilled, but those objects in the archive that both were and weren't different moved me: they had been redeemed, both in the sense that the fetish had been converted back into cash, the claim paid out, but also in the messianic sense of being saved from something, saved for something. An art commodity that had been exorcised (and survived the exorcism) of the fetishism of the market was to me a utopian readymade—an object for or from a future where there was some other regime of value than the tyranny of price. I looked up at Peter and Alena, who were waiting for me to speak, but could only manage: "Wow."

Although I knew it wouldn't last, as I walked back to Brooklyn from Alena's apartment across the Manhattan Bridge, everything my eye alighted on seemed totaled in the best sense: complete in extent or degree; absolute; unqualified; whole. It was still fully afternoon, but it felt like magic hour, when light appears immanent to the lit. Whenever I walked across the Manhattan Bridge, I remembered myself as having crossed the Brooklyn Bridge. This is because you can see the latter from the former, and because the latter is more beautiful. I looked back over my shoulder at lower Manhattan and saw the gleaming, rippled steel of the new Frank Gehry building, saw it as a standing wave; I looked down at the water to see a small boat slowly pass; the craquelure of its wake merged with the clouds reflected there and I briefly saw the vessel as a plane. But by the time I arrived in Brooklyn to meet Alex, I was starting to misremember crossing in the third person, as if I had somehow watched myself walking beneath the Brooklyn Bridge's Aeolian cables.

Our world

The world to come

I wandered on Henry Street through Brooklyn Heights. Alex and I were meeting for a drink at a place just across Atlantic, although Alex wasn't drinking. She had started a new job for which she was radically overqualified and underpaid; she was basically tutoring kids at an after-school program in Carroll Gardens, but she felt it would be best to apply for other jobs while employed and she wanted the structure and welcomed whatever money. I ordered something with bourbon and mint and a sparkling water for Alex and took our drinks to one of the wooden booths. The carefully selected ephemera on the walls dated from before the Civil War; there seemed to be a competition among hip bars to see who could travel back in time the furthest. We sipped our drinks under Edison bulb sconces.

"Are we going to talk about your very clumsy effort to seduce me?" I'd written Alex an e-mail about my semen analysis but we hadn't really talked about my trying to do it all. She wanted us to go in and talk to the fertility specialist in detail about the results.

"I was amazed you could resist my charms—I even recited poetry."

"I'm serious."

"It was stupid and I'm sorry. I was, as you know, very drunk."

"That was the problem. That's what you should be sorry for."

"Okay. But why?"

"Because if we're going to try to make a baby, however we try to make one, I don't want it to be one of the things you get to deny you wanted or deny ever happened."

"What do you mean?"

"'It was the only kind of first date he could bring himself to go on, the kind you could deny after the fact had been a date at all.'"

"That's fiction and we're not talking about a first date."

"What about the part about smoothing my hair in the cab? The part that's based on the night of the storm. The alcohol is a way of hedging. So that whatever happens only kind of happened." I made myself not take a drink.

"Okay, but your whole plan only kind of involves me—my level of involvement to be determined, whether I'm a donor or a father. You're asking me to be a flickering presence. I give reproductive cells and then the rest we figure out as we go along."

"Yes, but that's because it's up to you. As I've said since

the beginning, if you want to fully coparent, whatever that would mean, I would do that with you. I wouldn't have asked you otherwise. I would prefer to do that with you, in fact. If you want to try to have sex as part of a reproduction strategy"—I involuntarily raised my eyebrows at the phrase "reproduction strategy"—"or whatever you want to call it, I'm open to that, too. We'd have to talk more about it. You would have to stop sleeping with Alena, at least during that time. That would be too strange."

I drained my glass. "What, we'd be a couple? Are you proposing?"

"No. People do this. It would be like we were . . . amicably divorced." We both laughed. We had no idea how it would work. But I knew how we could pay for it: I told her I'd sent off the proposal, described my plan to expand the story.

She was quiet for half a minute, then: "I don't know." I'd expected her to say it sounded brilliant, which was what she normally said whenever I ran a literary idea by her—an adjective she'd never applied to any of my nonliterary ideas.

"What don't you know?"

"I don't want what we're doing to just end up as notes for a novel."

"Nobody is going to give me strong six figures for a poem."

"Especially a novel about deception. And it sounds morbid to me. I feel like you don't need to write about falsifying the past. You should be finding a way to inhabit the present." I remembered the sensation in my chest when I'd sent off the proposal, as if that way of dilating the story was linked to the dilation of my aorta. "And anyway, you shouldn't be writing about medical stuff."

"Why?"

"Because you believe, even though you'll deny it, that writing has some kind of magical power. And you're probably crazy enough to make your fiction come true somehow."

"I don't believe that."

"How often have you worried you have a brain tumor?"

"Not once," I laughed, lying.

"Liar. Remember what happened with your novel and your mom."

In my novel the protagonist tells people his mother is dead, when she's alive and well. Halfway through writing the book, my mom was diagnosed with breast cancer and I felt, however insanely, that the novel was in part responsible, that having even a fictionalized version of myself producing bad karma around parental health was in some unspecifiable way to blame for the diagnosis. I stopped work on the novel and was resolved to trash it until my mom—who was doing perfectly well after a mastectomy and who, thankfully, hadn't had to do chemo—convinced me over the course of a couple of months to finish the book.

"Do you know what I realized the other day," I said, "while being interviewed by somebody from the Netherlands over Skype about that novel, which just came out in Dutch? I realized how the lie about his mom is really about my dad."

"How?"

"Or about my dad's mother, my grandma, whom I never met; she died when he was twenty. I don't know if you want to hear a story about mothers and cancer right now."

"I would like to hear the story."

"My dad told me all of this when I flew home from Providence for Daniel's funeral my freshman year of college. He picked me up at the airport and we started driving back to

Topeka and I was so upset I could barely speak. I remember we were moving slowly because there was a light but freezing rain. The first part of the story I'd already heard: the day his mother died from breast cancer—'cancer' was never said in the family, but everybody knew, even the kids—he called up his girlfriend, Rachel, who was soon to become his first wife, a marriage that lasted all of a year, and before he could say anything, he realized that she was crying and that he could hear weeping, no, wailing in the background. Before he could share the news about his own mom, before he could even ask what happened, Rachel said: My father died. Rachel's father, a well-known businessman in D.C., where my dad lived and was now in college, had been perfectly healthy, as far as anybody knew. But on the same morning my dad's mom died after a multiyear struggle with a terrible illness, he just dropped dead at his office from a coronary."

"That's insane."

"Or maybe he dissected, I don't know. Rachel told my dad that the funeral would be in Albany, where her father was from, and that she hoped he would go up with her the next day and he said sure and hung up the phone without ever telling her about his mom. Meanwhile, my dad's own mom wasn't being mourned properly at all. My grandfather was either in denial or involved with someone else, but either way, my dad and his younger siblings were being served frozen dinners and left to watch *Gunsmoke* or whatever and there was no service planned of any sort. So my dad just said that Rachel's dad had died and he was going to Albany for the funeral and my grandfather said, without asking any questions: Fine. He took the train to Albany with Rachel, who wept the whole time—he never talked about his mom—and they eventually arrived at the family home, where the more Jewish side of the family was constantly praying and would be sitting shiva for seven days after the burial. It was a giant house and he was given a guest room and he sat up all night staring at the ceiling with occasional bouts of weeping from other parts of the house still audible late into the night as he tried to imagine where his mother's body was, although I might be making that detail up." I raised my hand to get the waitress's attention from across the bar and then raised my empty glass.

"Guess what his job was the next day at the funeral? They gave him smelling salts and he was supposed to go around and revive any of the women who passed out or got weak from weeping. My dad, at twenty, secretly mourning his mother, walking around a funeral, which his mother would not have, dry-eyed and holding some kind of chemical compound under the noses of people whose ululations were causing them to swoon. I had heard this part of the story before, although it had never struck me so powerfully as it did that night as we drove home through the sleet for Daniel's funeral, but then my dad started to tell me the part he'd never told me before." My drink had arrived and I tried it; it was sweeter this time. Alex expressed the intensity of her attention by not touching her water. She had an ability to hold herself so still that it became a form of gracefulness.

After the funeral, when I left the family to sit shiva in that giant house in Albany, my dad told me, I had to take a train to Penn Station and then another train to D.C. I arrived at Penn Station without incident, although it was snowing heavily, but then in Penn Station there was some kind of problem with the train, no doubt due to the weather. I remember how cold I was: I was wearing my one suit, which I'd worn to the funeral, but my winter coat didn't go with a suit, so I'd left it at home. There was an enormous line for the D.C. train—I'd never seen a line that long for any train at Penn Station—and it took forever for me to work my way to the platform. When I reached the platform, it was chaos: crowds, shouting. It turned out that two previous trains had been canceled due to ice on the tracks or something so there were all of these people desperate to get on this one, the last train out. They had even added extra cars—I could see them and they looked archaic, like decommissioned cars from the nineteenth century—to try to accommodate the overflow of passengers. I could picture all of this as we drove to Topeka, I said to Alex, with unusual vividness, maybe because the windows were fogged up and so little of the landscape was visible to distract me. And maybe I could picture it so vividly across from Alex because of the bar's anachronistic décor. I imagined the clock at Penn Station as my dad tried to get home, probably inserting an image from Marclay's video. But even so, my dad said to me, by the time I reached one of the car doors where there was both a man collecting tickets and a police officer trying to keep everybody calm, I was told that the train was full, that there were simply no more seats, that I'd have to stay the night in New York and catch the first morning train.

At first, my dad said to me, his eyes fixed on that part of the highway illuminated by his high beams, the sleet turning to snow in the headlights, I felt relieved. I didn't want to go home to the house without my mother and face the bizarre denial of my dad and my confused younger brothers around whom I kept trying to act like everything that was happening was normal. But then I started getting—I remember this surprised me—really angry, and I said to the ticket collector with such intensity that he turned and looked at me, as did a couple of the other people around us: *I am getting on this train*. I think I sounded like a lunatic. I'm afraid that's not possible, son, the ticket collector said after looking me over, my dad said to me, I said to Alex, and maybe it was the fact that he said it kindly, and that he said "son," but the next thing I knew, I burst into tears there on the platform. I mean, I really lost it, tears and snot and everything, standing there freezing in my suit, maybe still with smelling salts in my breast pocket, all the repressed emotion, all the emotion I'd been planning to share with Rachel when I'd called her the day our parents died and held in during her father's funeral, all of it started to surface. And then I said to the conductor: Please, I said, please: my mother is dying. I have to get back. I have to get back in time, please, I kept repeating. My mother is dying. And I felt as if it were true: as if she were dying and not dead, or as if the train could take me back in time.

I drank my drink and Alex drank her water in silence for a minute and I placed my hand on the table so it was touching hers in order to communicate that I was also thinking about her mom. Then my dad was quiet in the car, nothing but the sound of the windshield wipers, as if that were the end of the story, so finally I said: And then? And then, he said, as if it were an afterthought, they let me on the train, one of the decommissioned cars, and an older woman who had overheard my outburst on the platform ended up sitting beside me. And I remember she bought me tea and cookies from the food car and I slept a big part of the ride back on her shoulder. I remember her saying every once in a while: Your mom is going to be just fine.

I finished my drink, accidentally swallowing some mint. "We were going the wrong direction, by the way."

"What?"

"My dad drove us an hour into Missouri; he was so caught up in the story, he missed the exit for Topeka."

"Maybe he was driving toward D.C."

Then, voluble from the alcohol, I told her about Noor and Mrs. Meacham and she told me a story about her mother she made me swear I'd never include in anything, no matter how disguised, no matter how thoroughly I failed to describe faces or changed names.

o

A circuitous path leading through several museum buildings allows the visitor to trace the evolution of vertebrates, a walkable cladogram with alcoves on either side of the path displaying fossils of species that shared physical characteristics—e.g., "four limbs with movable joints surrounded by muscle" (tetrapods). I'd paid almost fifty dollars for two tickets to the American Museum of Natural History so that Roberto and I could tour the osseous remains, could track the evolution of new traits, a field trip I'd been promising him for many months and had finally proposed to his mother when I handed him off one afternoon after tutoring; she either forgot about my offer or considered it for several weeks before letting me know through Aaron which Saturdays—Sundays were taken up with church and family—were workable. I'd called her to finalize arrangements: I would meet her and Roberto at the subway stop nearest their apartment, the D on Thirty-sixth in Sunset Park, and he and I would travel together, transferring to the C at West Fourth, to the Museum of Natural History on the Upper West Side. We'd spend several hours at the museum, assuming his attention held, then I'd take him out to lunch, mindful of his allergies, and return him to the family home in the late afternoon. Roberto's older sister, Jasmine, was initially planning to join us—primarily, I assumed, to make Anita feel more comfortable—but, Anita explained to me when we exchanged *holas* at the Thirty-sixth Street stop,

Jasmine had had to work an unexpected shift at the Applebee's in Flatbush. Anita seemed a little nervous as she transferred Roberto, tremulous with excitement, to my care.

It was not until we were standing on the platform and Roberto approached its edge to point out two soot-colored rats moving among the garbage on the tracks that I consciously registered the fact that I had never been so responsible for another person, at least not a young person. I'd babysat my nephews when visiting Seattle, but always in their home, never abroad in a crumbling metropolis; I'd carried a passed-out Alex back to her dorm from a party after we'd split a horse tranquilizer in college; I'd taken Jon to the emergency room three times for injuries he'd sustained through drunken athletic idiocy or defending his or Sharon's honor in brief and clumsy fights, etc.; but none of my peers was a flight risk or a possible kidnapping victim. With a sinking feeling I realized that, if I were Anita, I might well have declined to entrust my child to my care. But then, Aaron had vouched for me: I was a published author.

I told Roberto to step back from the platform as the train approached and as soon as we sat down I showed him the notebooks I'd brought for jotting down our observations—the notebooks had been Alex's suggestion—and explained our goals for the day in a tone that implied we were embarking on a solemn paleontological mission that would admit of no spontaneity, let alone insubordination. Roberto was particularly excited to see the display of an allosaurus skeleton positioned over an apatosaurus's corpse as though it were scavenging and he kept leaping up from the seat to mimic the bipedal predator's posture—he'd seen it on the Internet—and I kept telling him to sit down.

At West Fourth we caught the C and it was crowded. At Fourteenth a crush of new passengers entered the train and bodies imposed themselves between Roberto and me. I wondered if people would have stepped between us if we were racially indistinguishable; I pushed my way back to him and took his hand. This was the first time our bodies had come into willed contact in the many months of our relationship and he looked up at me, maybe with curiosity, maybe reacting to the sweatiness of my palm; we are going to stick together at all times, I said to him, noting the desperation in my own voice. To dispel it I smiled and complimented his red *Jurassic Park* T-shirt and asked him to remind me what giant sauropods most likely ate. While he enumerated prehistoric flora, I was thinking: holding his hand is the only permissible physical contact; if he were to run away from me, I couldn't grab or otherwise discipline him; if he reported any form of restraint beyond hand-holding during transit, who knows what would happen; an undocumented family wasn't going to call the cops, but his dad might run me over in the truck Roberto was always bragging about; they might report Aaron, who had let me enter the school without observing protocol. "You're not my teacher," Roberto had said on more than one occasion when I'd tried to force him to focus on our book; I imagined him exclaiming it in the museum and then disappearing into the depths of the bioluminescence exhibit, never to be seen again.

By the time we reached the Eighty-first Street entrance, I was debating two strategies: either establish a draconian presence at the outset of our visit that would deter all forms of noncompliance, promising to cut short the trip at the first infraction—that there would be trouble I now considered inevitable, although it had never worried me before—and threatening to call his mom, whose cell phone number I had, maybe even evoking Joseph Kony, but then, at the end of the visit, buying him whatever he desired from the gift shop, my largesse making me appear to him retrospectively benevolent; or I'd just skip the disciplinarian stuff and bribe him at every opportunity until the time I returned him, loaded with presents and full of artificial dyes, to his family, who now seemed a country away. As Roberto and I stood in line for tickets in the packed lobby, I devoted some small portion of my brain to chatting with the boy about museum highlights, some portion to objecting to the admission price, but most of my consciousness was working its way toward the horrible realization that I simply was not competent to take a prepubescent on an educational day trip. I could feel the urea and salts emerging from my underarms as I longed for Jasmine, whom I'd never met, or for Alex, whom all kids seemed instinctively eager to obey.

We bought our tickets and walked quickly through the Space and Earth displays, past the giant Ecosphere, which interested the child not at all—"No running, Roberto"—until we reached the steps and ascended to the fourth floor, where a guard directed us to the Orientation Center, starting point of the evolutionary path. How did this happen, I wondered, still catching my breath from the stairs, how is it that a thirty-three-year-old man who appears to meet most societal norms of functionality—employed (however lightly), sexually active (however irresponsibly), socially embedded (if unmarried and childless)—is in the grip of a fear so intense as to overwhelm reason as a result of taking a sweet kid to a museum? But as we began our journey along the circuitous path and through the Hall of Vertebrate Origins, Roberto pulling me by the arm as quickly as possible through the cases of jawless fish and placoderms toward the Hall of Ornithischian Dinosaurs, I had to question any account of myself as normative, mature. Thus began my second-order panic: not only was I horrified of something going wrong with

Roberto, but I was horrified of being horrified, as it indicated my manifold inadequacy. I recalled the initial consultation with the fertility specialist when she'd asked about our mental health histories: while I'd had three protracted bouts of serious depression and plenty of anxiety, and while I'd had a long-term if intermittent relationship with SSRIs and benzodiazepines, there was no major mental illness in my family, and I thought of myself more as darkly ruminative and inclined to complain than as sufficiently disturbed to have implications for reproduction or parenting; Alex, who knew me as well as anyone, had obviously agreed. But now, as I heard myself command Roberto to write down every evolutionary advance the museum placards noted ("development of braincase"; "the palatal opening"; etc.), a highlight reel of my lower moments played before me.

I remembered the *pavor nocturnus* of my eighth year, my baffled brother trying to comfort me by offering his semi-precious baseball cards, although I was, with the exception of one frightening summer, a happy enough child. The more serious trouble started, as it often does, in college: tremors and numbness in my hands, the feeling that they belonged to someone else or were autonomous; the sense that if I did not will every breath, did not breathe manually, I would cease to breathe entirely; there among the primitive vertebrates, I experienced the echo of each symptom I recalled. Then there was splashing water on a face with which I failed to identify in the dorm, its blown pupils, or slowly coming to realize during an evening seminar on Thomas Hobbes that the irruption of hysterical laughter was my own; there was the episode of sleep paralysis and an attendant incubus hallucination so severe that I couldn't shut my eyes without Alex's company for several days ("Write 'antorbital opening,'" I instructed Roberto; "write 'three-fingered hand' "); I remembered weeping, although it never happened, as quietly as possible in a bathroom stall at a fancy restaurant in Madrid, my blood a patchwork of sertraline, tetrahydrocannabinol, clonazepam, and Rioja. All these lacrimal events and bouts of depersonalization were no doubt leading, I was then convinced, to the onset of schizophrenia. Indeed, the irony of my recent cardiac diagnosis was that it gave me an objective reason for my emotional turbulences and so was, in that sense, stabilizing: now I was reckoning with a specific existential threat, not just the vacuum of existence. But as a dozen proprioceptive breakdowns flashed before me in the museum, there was a reversal of figure and ground: I wasn't a balanced person who had his difficult periods; I was an erratic blind to his own psychological precariousness; I was no more a functional adult than Pluto was a planet.

We stopped before a display explaining the development of the vertebrate jaw and, as I instructed Roberto to sketch the remains of a pterosaur in his notebook, I felt despair spread through me like contrast dye. The eight-year-old is having a fine time learning about evolution while his guide is freaking out because of all the strangers and stimulation; I was the nervous kid far from home longing for my parents, not Roberto; I was the one who kept clinging to his hand; I'd become the unreliable narrator of my first novel. Roberto tried to bolt with excitement toward the next alcove and I instinctually grabbed his arm to stop him, jerking it a little. "Ow," he said, not hurt, but understandably disconcerted. I said I was sorry and knelt down and looked him in the eye and explained to him in Spanish, no doubt visibly pale and perspiring, that we must avoid getting separated. Then I told him, probably sounding as if I were giving orders for a suicide mission, that if we somehow did lose each other, we should meet at the *Tyrannosaurus rex* skeleton. He smiled, but didn't say anything; I wondered if he was embarrassed for me.

We entered the Hall of Saurischian Dinosaurs—a room containing some of the museum's most impressive fossil displays—and found the apatosaurus skeleton, recently remounted to reflect new research, a placard explained, about how the dinosaur was likely to have carried itself; the tail was now aloft, no longer dragging on the ground. There was a large group of Asian children, Korean I guessed, standing around the skeleton in matching blue T-shirts, listening to their guide; Roberto couldn't get as close as he wanted to the bones. By the time I finished asking him to sketch the tail, he had rushed off with excitement toward the allosaurus depicted feeding on a carcass. I followed him with enforced calm, stood beside him and uttered some vaguely educational instruction, and then he ran to the next arrangement of mineralized tissues and I followed. This was how we proceeded through the hall, Roberto occasionally reversing the evolutionary course by sprinting back to see a highlight—I at least had the presence of mind to take his picture on my cell phone before the giant *Tyrannosaurus rex*, mounted as if stalking prey—and then running back to the future to admire, say, some protoceratops skulls arranged in a growth series. As long as I keep him within sight, I told myself, everything will be fine; it's not as though there are kidnappers lurking among the relatives of extinct mammals; most crazy people can't afford the exorbitant admission price.

Around the time the synapsid opening evolved, I realized I had to pee. I asked Roberto if he had to go to the bathroom and he said no and darted off again. I would have to hold it; there was no way I was going to leave him unsupervised while I went, and I couldn't imagine dragging him into the men's room so I could piss. All over the world people were tending their children ingeniously in the midst of surpassing extremities, seeing them through tsunamis and civil wars, shielding them from American drones, but I was at a total loss as to how one could both be responsible for a child at a museum and empty one's bladder. I followed Roberto through the Hall of Mammals and their extinct relatives, taking another picture of the boy before the brontops, who most likely subsisted on a diet of soft leaves. I caught myself shifting my weight a little from foot to foot as the cell phone made its simulated click, something I did as a child when I had to go to the bathroom, and I had an involuntary memory of wetting myself at the Topeka Zoo at four, having refused to go when I had the chance, the humiliating warmth spreading down my leg, darkening my corduroys.

By the time we stood together before the great mammoth skeleton at the end of the vertebrate cladogram—the mummified remains of a baby woolly mammoth displayed in a case beside the pedestal—I had regressed so severely that it felt like a form of devolution. Roberto calmly if clumsily sketched the great curving tusks while I tried not to wet myself and longed for a guardian. Half the men walking around the fossils seemed to have a baby strapped to their chests and I tried to reassure myself by remembering that Alex, the sanest person I knew, believed I was genetically and practically competent to be a father, to perpetuate the species. But why, exactly, had she selected me? Because we were best friends, of course—because our relationship was more durable than any marriage we could imagine, because she thought I was smart and good. I had never really doubted myself enough to doubt her reasons, but now it occurred to me with the force of revelation: She wants you to donate the sperm precisely because she doesn't think you'd ever get it together enough to be an active father; she's much more afraid of raising a child with an onerous father than without a father at all; she comes from a line of self-sufficient women whose partners disappear. You appeal because you'll be sweet and avuncular and financially supportive and someone she can talk to for emotional advice, but she assumes you're too scattered and scared to intervene dramatically in the child's early development and daily life. She doesn't want to do it entirely alone, but she doesn't want to do it with a full partner; you come from great stock—Alex loved my parents—and will never go totally AWOL, but you're also sufficiently infantile and self-involved to cede all the substantial parenting to her. She chose you *for* your deficiencies, not in spite of them, a new kind of mating strategy for millennial women whose priority is keeping the more disastrous fathers away, not establishing a nuclear family.

"I have to go to the bathroom, Roberto. Why don't you come with me?"

"I don't have to go."

"Come with me and wait for me." I was shifting my weight back and forth again.

"I'll wait for you here."

"You are coming with me. Now."

"But—"

"Do you want something from the gift shop or not?"

As we approached the restrooms I repeated to Roberto that if he was in the exact spot I left him in when I came back out he could have a gift of his choice. I tried to joke away my worry and enlist his compliance by making it a game: see if you can stand as still as a fossil. I parked him beside the drinking fountain and went into the restroom while he positioned himself in a dinosaur pose, and when I emerged tremendously relieved two and a half minutes later I found that he was gone. Terror seized me and I had to keep myself from running back toward the galleries. As soon as I turned the corner, he leapt out at me, shrieking like a velociraptor. Before it dissipated, the fear turned to fury, and I knelt down and gripped his shoulders and all my accumulated anxiety and self-loathing issued forth in a hiss: I am going to tell your mom you've misbehaved; you're not getting anything from the gift shop.

Roberto, eyes lowered, said he was just joking and hadn't gone far and hadn't done anything wrong. As my fury dissolved into remorse, he turned and walked away from me. For a second I feared he'd accelerate and try to lose me—he didn't respond when I called his name—but instead he walked slowly and dejectedly to the stairs and descended to the third floor and I followed a few feet behind as he moped through the dioramas of Pacific Peoples and Plains Indians. The surrounding nineteenth-century taxidermy and painted backgrounds felt at once dated and futuristic: dated because low-tech and methodologically presumptuous and insensitive; futuristic because postapocalyptic: it was as if an alien race had tried to reconstruct the past of the wasteland upon which they'd stumbled. It reminded me of *Planet of the Apes* or other movies from the sixties and seventies that I'd seen as a child in the eighties—movies whose distance from the present was most acutely felt in the quaintness of the futures they projected; nothing in the world, I thought to myself, is as old as what was futuristic in the past.

On the second floor, in the strangely empty Hall of African Peoples, I stopped him and apologized, explained that I'd been worried and overreacted, pledged to give his mom a glowing report, and asked him to pick out whatever he wanted from the gift shop, where we proceeded together hand in hand; Roberto forgave me, but his excitement now was muted.

I bought him a sixty-dollar *T-rex* puzzle because I would make strong six figures and the city would soon be underwater. I made sure the cashier removed the price tag, and I also purchased a couple of packets of astronaut ice cream, which Roberto had never tried.

We ate the freeze-dried Neapolitan stuff—a food from the future of the past, taken to space only once on *Apollo 7*, 1968—on a bench in front of the museum. It was an unseasonably warm day and the bizarreness and novelty of the food cracked Roberto up, restored his spirits; I broke off my chocolate and traded it for a fragment of his strawberry, which he found gross. He showed me his various drawings, which I praised, we discussed some additions to our diorama, and I told him how he'd one day be a famous paleontologist. His energy was back and it was as if I'd never caused a scene. We had a nice lunch at Shake Shack near the museum—a fast-food restaurant where the meat is carefully sourced, all the garbage compostable—and I returned him smiling and full of dinosaur factoids to Anita by four.

o

The baby octopuses are delivered alive from Portugal each morning and then massaged gently but relentlessly with unrefined salt until their biological functions cease; according to the menu, they are massaged "five hundred times." The beak is removed and the small eyes are pushed out from behind. The corpses are slowly poached and then served with a sauce composed of sake and yuzu juice. It is the restaurant's signature dish and so plate after plate of the world's most intelligent invertebrate infants were being conducted from kitchen to table by the handsome, agile waitstaff. There were three on the plate finally placed before us, and my agent and I, after a moment of admiration and guilty hesitation, simultaneously dipped and ingested the impossibly tender things entire.

I had arrived for what would be an outrageously expensive celebratory meal still incredulous about the amount of money a publisher was willing to pay me to dilate my story, but, after we ordered and before the octopus and flights of bluefin arrived, I had quickly signed two copies of a contract. I asked my agent to explain to me once more why anybody would pay such a sum for a book of mine, especially an unwritten one, given that my previous novel, despite an alarming level of critical acclaim, had only sold around ten thousand copies. Since my first book was published by a small press, my agent said, the larger houses were optimistic that their superior distribution and promotion could help a second book do much better than the first. Moreover, she explained, publishers pay for prestige. Even if I wrote a book that didn't sell, these presses wanted a potential darling of the critics or someone who might win prizes; it was symbolic capital that helped maintain the reputation of the house even if most of their money was being made by teen vampire sagas or one of the handful of mainstream "literary novelists" who actually sold a ton of books. This would have made sense to me in the eighties or nineties, when the novel was more or less still a viable commodity form, but why would publishers, all of whom seemed to be perpetually reorganizing, downsizing, scrambling to survive in the postcodex world, be willing to convert real capital into the merely symbolic? "Keep in mind that your book proposal . . ." my agent said, and then paused thoughtfully, indicating that she was preparing to put something delicately, "your book proposal might generate more excitement among the houses than the book itself."

"What do you mean?"

"Well, your first book was unconventional but really well received. What they're buying when they buy the proposal is in part the idea that your next book is going to be a little more . . . mainstream. I'm not saying they'll reject what you submit, although that's always possible; I'm saying it may have been easier to auction the idea of your next book than whatever you actually draft."

I loved this idea: my virtual novel was worth more than my actual novel. But if they rejected it, I'd have to give the money back. And yet I planned to spend my advance in advance.

"Also, you have to remember an auction has its own momentum."

This I understood, or at least recognized, from experience: most desire was imitative desire. If one university wanted to buy your papers, another university would want to buy them, too—consensus emerges regarding your importance. Competition produces its own object of desire; that's why it makes sense to speak of a "competitive spirit," a creative deity.

With my chopsticks I lifted and dipped the third and final baby octopus and tried to think as I chewed of a synonym for "tender." Imitative desire for my virtual novel was going to fund artificial insemination and its associated costs. My actual novel everyone would thrash. After my agent's percentage and taxes (including New York City taxes, she had reminded me), I would clear something like two hundred and seventy thousand dollars. Or Fifty-four IUIs. Or around four Hummer H2 SUVs. Or the two first editions on the market of *Leaves of Grass*. Or about twenty-five years of a Mexican migrant's labor, seven of Alex's in her current job. Or my rent, if I had rent control, for eleven years. Or thirty-six hundred flights of bluefin, assuming the species held. I swallowed and the majesty and murderous stupidity of it was all about me, coursing through me: the rhythm of artisanal Portuguese octopus fisheries coordinated with the rhythm of laborers' migration and the rise and fall of art commodities and tradable futures in the dark galleries outside the restaurant and the mercury and radiation levels of the sashimi and the chests of the beautiful people in the restaurant—coordinated, or so it appeared, by money. One big joke cycle. One big totaled prosody.

"Of course, as we talked about, there are risks to taking a big advance—because if the book doesn't sell at all, nobody's going to want to work with you again."

A quiet set of couples left the table beside us and almost instantly a loud set of couples took their place; the men, both around my age, both dressed in dark suits, both in great shape, were talking about a friend or colleague in common, mocking him for drunkenly spilling red wine on a priceless couch or rug; the women, eyes lined with shadow, were passing a cell phone back and forth, admiring a picture of something. I was confident my book wouldn't sell.

"Just remember this is your opportunity to reach a much wider audience. You have to decide who you want your audience to be, who you think it is," my agent said, and what I heard was: "Develop a clear, geometrical plot; describe faces, even those at the next table; make sure the protagonist undergoes a dramatic transformation." What if only his aorta undergoes change, I wondered. Or his neoplasm. What if everything at the end of the book is the same, only a little different?

The sake-based cocktails were making the adjacent quartet increasingly garrulous. Investment bankers or market analysts in their twenties, whose proximity was particularly unwelcome since I was crossing my art with money more explicitly than ever, trading on my future. The first draft was due in a year.

"I think of my audience as a second person plural on the perennial verge of existence," I wanted to say. A waiter shook the bottle to mix the sediment and turn the sake white.

"They need a highly liquid strategy," someone at the adjacent table said.

"What happens if I give them a totally different book than the one described in the proposal?" I asked. Small plates of miso-glazed black cod were put before us. Someone refilled my glass.

"Depends. If they like it, fine. But you need to keep the *New Yorker* story in there, I think."

"I can't see my audience because of the tungsten lights." I emptied my glass.

"Do you have other ideas?"

"They got married on Turtle Island. Fiji. Karen said she saw Jay-Z on the beach."

"A beautiful young half-Lebanese conceptual artist and sexual athlete committed to radical Arab politics is told by her mother, who is dying of breast cancer, that she's been lied to about her paternity: her real father turns out to be a conservative professor of Jewish studies at Harvard. Or New Paltz. Wanting her own child, she selects a Lebanese sperm donor in an effort to project into the future the past she never had." I shook my head no. Swift, Spanish-speaking laborers took away the plates. "Or maybe something more sci-fi: an author changes into an octopus. He travels back and forth in time. On a decommissioned train."

She excused herself to go to the bathroom and the next small blue bottle was on the table so quickly it seemed to precede my signaling to the waitress, my ordering it. I shut my eyes for a long moment. "Perfume and youth course through me, and I am their wake." The noise was deafening now that I wasn't talking or listening to anyone in particular. I tasted hints of pear, then peach. For a second all I heard was the desperation, the hysterical energy of passengers on a doomed liner. The rise and fall. The laughter of Mrs. Meacham's class. My parents were dead, but I could get back to them in time. Seventy-three seconds into takeoff, my aorta dissected, producing high cirrus clouds, sign of an imminent tropical depression.

"That market's completely underwater. Probably forever."

I looked at my phone. "Your presence is requested at the Institute for Totaled Art," Alena had texted.

Dessert was a yuzu frozen soufflé with poached plums. Money was a kind of poetry. The glasses of sweet wine were on the house. I was drunk enough now to down the remaining sake instead of setting it aside. The ink contains a substance that dulls the sense of smell, making the octopus more difficult to track.

"How exactly will you expand the story?" she asked, far look in her eyes because she was calculating tip.

"Like the princess in *Sans Soleil*, I'll make a long list of things that quicken the heart." We emerged from the restaurant into moving air. "And you can be on it." The streets were wet, but it wasn't raining now. We walked to the High Line entrance on Twenty-sixth and climbed the steps. The smell of viburnum, which either flowers in winter or had flowered prematurely, mixed with the smell of car exhaust.

"I'm going to write a novel that dissolves into a poem about how the small-scale transformations of the erotic must be harnessed by the political." Three-fifths of my neurons were in my arms as I touched each stand of sumac carefully placed among the disused rails. Never again would I eat octopus.

"My advice, having sold some other proposals, is not to wait too long." Now we were sitting on the wooden steps that overlook Tenth Avenue, liquid ruby and sapphire of traffic. "I mean, to get to work. The more you wait, the more the deadline looms. It can drive people crazy." She lit a cigarette. "The residency is perfect timing. Don't underestimate how much you can get done in those five weeks."

I was leaving in two days. A foundation in Marfa, Texas, gives you a house, a stipend, a car. I'd accepted the offer almost a year ago, when I knew I'd be on leave from teaching, but not that I had a dilated aortic root or that there was acute demand for my abnormal sperm. I'd never done a residency or been to Texas. It was where Creeley died in the spring of 2005—they had rushed him to the nearest hospital three hours away in Odessa. My little house would be across the street from his. "I hope there will be another occasion soon to be in each other's company," I'd written in his voice to a version of myself.

FOUR

I felt like a ghost in the green hybrid, driving slowly around Marfa in the dark. It was my first night there: Michael, the caretaker of the residency houses, who was also a painter, had picked me up at the El Paso airport that afternoon and driven me in amicable silence for three hours through the high desert until we reached the little house at 308 North Plateau Street; I remember the address (you can drag the "pegman" icon onto the Google map and walk around the neighborhood on Street View, floating above yourself like a ghost; I'm doing that in a separate window now) because I had to have my beta-blockers mailed there twice during the residency, pills I take to reduce the vigor of my heart's contractions, and which have the paradoxical effect of causing a minor tremor in my hand. When I arrived at the house—one floor, two bedrooms, with one room converted to a writer's studio, no internal doors—I had set down my bags and, although it was only late afternoon, gone immediately to bed, not waking until a little before midnight. I lay in the alien sheets slowly remembering where I was: having slept through most of the ride, and then what was left of the daylight, I felt as though I'd moved from Brooklyn to the Chihuahuan Desert without transition. I tried to remember the light snow that morning in New York, beads of precipitation on the oval window streaking as the plane took off. It was Thursday; had I been at home, I would have heard the sound of the poor picking glass out of the recycling set along the street for Friday morning. Here it was quiet enough that I should have heard my heart beating; I imagined it was inaudible because of the drug.

I'd planned to walk around, not drive, but the dark outside was total. I was stunned by the panoramic sky, the impossible number of stars—any remaining jet lag dissipated at the sight. The thin winter air was cool but unseasonably warm; it was probably in the forties. The sound of the garage door opening tore a hole in the night and I sensed, whether or not they were there, small animals fleeing all around me at the noise. I backed out of the garage, remotely closed it, and began to whisper through the streets, as nervous and alive as a teenager sneaking out on some kind of furtive mission in his parents' car. I found my way downtown and circled the nineteenth-century courthouse and turned onto the town's main commercial street; no one was out. I parked under a streetlight and walked past the dark storefronts, a mixture of small-town municipal offices, abandoned spaces, and upscale boutiques. Marfa had been an "art tourism" destination ever since Donald Judd established the Chinati Foundation in the eighties, a museum just outside of town that presents Judd's large-scale works in permanent installation, along with work by his contemporaries. I'd heard New York artists speak of making pilgrimages, that collectors fly down for visits in their private jets, but it was difficult to picture encountering them here. An interesting building across the street attracted my attention and I crossed to take a closer look; later I would learn it was the old Marfa Wool and Mohair Building. I walked around the side of the building, along the railroad tracks, and, stepping over various desert shrubs, approached one of the side windows to look in.

At first I saw nothing through the glass, then slowly made out hulking shapes, shapes that further resolved into what looked like giant flowers of crushed metal or perpetual explosions. I cupped my hands around my eyes and held my forehead to the cool window and slowly recognized what I was seeing as a series of John Chamberlain sculptures, which are largely hewn from chrome-plated and painted steel, often the mangled bodies of cars, an art of the totaled. I'd seen a few of his sculptures in New York, had been indifferent, but they were powerful now, their colors becoming more discernible in the faint glow of some kind of security light. Maybe I liked his sculpture more when I couldn't get close to it, had to see it from a fixed position through a pane of glass, so that I had to project myself into the encounter with its three-dimensionality. I stepped back a little and regarded his work through my own faint reflection in the window. Or maybe I like his sculpture more when I'm lurking at night among creosote bushes in the desert, nerves singing, my life in Brooklyn eighteen hours in the past, receding.

I heard the *norteño* music, accordion and *bajo sexto*, before I saw the beams of the approaching truck. Instinctively, stupidly, I dropped to one knee on the gravelly soil so as not to be seen doing whatever it was that I was doing beside the dark building. A woman in the passenger side was singing along to the radio, maybe drunkenly, her window down: "*Lo diera por ti, lo diera por ti, lo diera por ti.*" When the truck passed, I stood up, brushed the dust off my pants, and walked back to the car. I drove across the railroad tracks and turned right onto a larger road; there was a gas station open. I stopped, bought a four-pack of butter, tortillas, eggs, and a large can of Bustelo espresso, and then drove silently back to the house on North Plateau. Right before I turned into the garage, my headlights reflected green off the eyes of a small animal, probably a neighbor's cat or dog, but maybe a raccoon, if they had those in Marfa. The *tapetum lucidum*, the "bright tapestry" behind the eyes, bounces visible light back through the retina, making the pupils glow. I remembered the red-eye effect in the photographs of my youth, the camera recording the light of its own flash, the camera inscribing itself in the image it captured. Once inside the house I heated and ate several tortillas while I waited for the coffee to percolate in the rusty stovetop espresso machine, then took the pitch-black coffee to the desk in the studio, set up my computer, and began to write.

Thus, instead of beginning my residency by rising at 6:00 a.m. and walking several miles in the early morning dark, then working until lunch, walking again, then working again until dinner, at which point I'd take a third walk—I'd outlined this strict schedule to Alex, who had nodded politely, before I left New York—I went to sleep at sunup, having finished the tortillas as the first light filtered into the kitchen. It was 5:00 p.m. when I woke and, because I'd already woken in the bed once the previous day, it felt like the morning of my second full day, not the late afternoon of the first; I was already falling out of time. I walked into the bathroom and got out my razor and looked at myself in the mirror to find much of my face was covered in dark, dried blood; for a moment I was dizzy with fear and confusion, then realized I'd had a nosebleed. My first thought was of a brain tumor, but, after calming down and consulting Google, I realized it was no doubt altitude-induced; I'd had nosebleeds as a child when we vacationed in Colorado. I washed the blood off my face with a rag but couldn't bear, after the shock, to draw a razor across my neck.

The sun was setting by the time I sat down at the desk to start my day. I had my lunch of scrambled eggs around 1:00 a.m. on the little porch, looking carefully for the first time at the house where Creeley began to die; I kept my porch light off. The house looked identical in layout to mine and it was occupied: the resident, Michael had told me on the way in from the airport, was a Polish translator and poet of whom I'd never heard. (There was a lunch planned for the next day so all the residents could meet one another if they wished, but I'd already sent an e-mail to Michael with my regrets, explaining that I was focused on work and keeping strange hours.) There was a light on somewhere in the house, probably the studio; the rest of the windows on the street were dark.

When I was about to go back in, having stood and opened the screen door, I heard the creak and bang of the screen door on the porch across from mine, the noise setting off a chain reaction of barking dogs. I hesitated; having hesitated, and knowing I'd been seen, even in the dark, I felt a pressure to turn around and signal some kind of greeting to the other nocturnal resident, who hadn't put his porch light on. I did turn, plate and silverware in one hand, and saw the cupped flame as he lit his cigarette, thought I could make out a beard and glasses. I stood there awkwardly for a moment and then he raised his arm and I raised mine, feeling as I went back in, and feeling ridiculous for feeling it, that I'd just waved to Creeley.

The only book I'd brought with me to the residency, knowing that the house was full of books, was the Library of America edition of Whitman, its paper so thin you could use it to roll cigarettes. I'd brought that particular volume because I was teaching a course on Whitman next fall, assuming I wasn't on medical leave, and hadn't read him carefully in years—and hadn't read much of his prose at all.

Those first days of the residency, days that were nights, I would sit at my desk and read *Specimen Days*, his bizarre memoir, for hours. Part of what makes the book bizarre is that Whitman, because he wants to stand for everyone, because he wants to be less a historical person than a marker for democratic personhood, can't really write a memoir full of a life's particularities. If he were to reveal the specific genesis and texture of his personality, if he presented a picture of irreducible individuality, he would lose his ability to be "Walt Whitman, a cosmos"—his "I" would belong to an empirical person rather than constituting a pronoun in which the readers of the future could participate. As a result, while he recounts a few basic facts about his life, most of the book consists of him describing natural and national histories as if they were details of his intimate biography. And many of his memories are general enough to be anyone's memory: how he took his ease under a flowering tree or whatever. (Whitman is always "loafing," always taking his ease, as if leisure were a condition of poetic receptivity.) As a memoir, it's an interesting failure. Just as in the poems, he has to be nobody in particular in order to be a democratic everyman, has to empty himself out so that his poetry can be a textual commons for the future into which he projects himself. And he is always projecting himself: "I am with you, you men and women of a generation, or ever so many generations hence; / I project myself—also I return—I am with you, and know how it is."

The most riveting and disturbing and particular passages of *Specimen Days* are about the Civil War. What disturbed me as I read was what I perceived, rightly or wrongly, as the delight he took in the willingness of young men to die for the union whose epic bard he felt he was destined to be, and his almost sensual pleasure in the material richness of the surrounding carnage. Maybe I was projecting, but when Whitman walks the makeshift hospitals delivering to the wounded gifts of money that the rich have asked him to distribute, when he gives tobacco to those who haven't suffered damage to the lungs or face, I thought he was in a kind of ecstasy. From the distance of my residency late in the empire of drones, his love for the young boys on both sides whose blood was to refresh the tree of liberty was hard to take. When I could no longer focus my eyes on the page, I would lie down on the hardwood floor and listen to recordings of Creeley, scores of which were available online; again and again, I played him reading "The Door" in the early sixties, static like rain on the recording, New York traffic sometimes audible in the background. And then I would listen at intervals to the one extant recording of Whitman, made by Edison: he recites four lines from "America," a digital transfer from wax cylinder.

Days passed like this: turning in around sunrise, waking a couple of hours before sunset, my only contact with other humans the few words I exchanged with the attendant at the gas station where I continued to buy groceries, although there was an organic market in town, or with the elderly Mexican woman, Rita, whom Michael had recommended, who sold burritos out of her house. (I would drive to her house and buy a burrito soon after I woke, then reheat it for my midday meal at midnight; soon this meal was the only one I reliably took.) With the exception of one other wave on the porch when Creeley came out to smoke, I didn't see the resident in the reflection of my house across the street, nor did I see anybody else. I had poor cell phone service and largely kept it off, exchanging some e-mails with Alex, none with Alena, and I talked to nobody from home. Before bed in the hour before sunrise I would walk the perimeter of the town, ranchland spreading out beyond it, hawks or maybe buzzards starting from the trees at the sound of my footfall on gravel. As the sun came up, I could see the white dirigible in the distance, a tethered aerostat surveillance blimp containing some kind of radar, searching for *narcotraficantes* passing over from northern Mexico, maybe also for immigrants, a strange helium-filled thing on the horizon that began to enter my dreams, as a version of it had long since entered Roberto's.

Eventually a few people in town wrote me: a friend of a friend who wintered in Marfa asked if I wanted to get a drink; another resident, a novelist I'd met briefly before, asked if I wanted to go and see the Judd; I was invited, through Michael, to a party for an artist who was passing through town. I was keeping strange hours; I was working furiously; I was under the weather, having trouble adjusting to the altitude; I'd love to see you sometime in the coming weeks—I paid little attention to what excuses I deployed as I declined. Again I would find myself standing razor in hand as the sun set, and again I would decide not to shave, wondering how long it would take me to grow my neighbor's beard, obscure my face. Again I would see a woman watering an ocotillo in her yard at dawn despite the desert cold as I took my last walk of the night, and again she'd fail to see me wave.

And I *was* at work, but on the wrong thing. Instead of fabricating the author's epistolary archive, earning my advance, I was writing a poem, a weird meditative lyric in which I was sometimes Whitman, and in which the strangeness of the residency itself was the theme. Having monetized the future of my fiction, I turned my back on it, albeit to compose verse underwritten by a millionaire's foundation. The poem, like most of my poems, and like the story I'd promised to expand, conflated fact and fiction, and it occurred to me—

not for the first time, but with a new force—that part of what I loved about poetry was how the distinction between fiction and nonfiction didn't obtain, how the correspondence between text and world was less important than the intensities of the poem itself, what possibilities of feeling were opened up in the present tense of reading. I set it in Marfa, but in the extreme heat of the summer: "I am an alien here with a residency, light / alien to me, true hawks starting from the trees / at my footfall on gravel, sun-burnt from reading / *Specimen Days* on the small porch across / the street from where another poet died / or began dying . . ."

> . . . They are dead in different ways,
> these poets, but I visit them both because
> a residency affords me time, not sure where
> the money comes from, or what money is,
> how you could set it beside a soldier's bed
> then walk out across the moonlit mall in love
> with the federal, wake up refreshed and bring
> tobacco to those who haven't received
> wounds in the lung or the face. Tonight
> I listen to their recordings at once
> in separate windows, four lines from "America"
> might be recited by an actor, but the noise
> of the wax cylinder is real, sounds how I
> imagine engines of old boats would, while
> "The Door" incorporates distress into the voice,
> could be in the room. The former says
> he waits for me ahead, but I doubt I'll arrive
> in time . . .

One morning, which was for me late at night, I'd fallen asleep with the Whitman in my lap when I was awoken by the sound of hammering on the roof above me, the first real interruption of my ghostly rhythm. Then I heard tinny music on a portable radio, voices in Spanish: men were working on the roof. There was no way I could sleep with the noise, so I decided to make coffee and walk a little—for the first time in broad daylight since I'd arrived. I left through the house's back door and only glanced once behind me at the roof, but I made eye contact with one of the young Mexican men laboring there. I turned and waved and said—my own voice strange to me from disuse—good morning. He called another Mexican man over who said to me in English that they had to do some repairs on the houses over the next couple of days and that he hoped they weren't making too much noise. I said they weren't, and to let me know if they needed anything from inside, coffee or water or whatever, and then I somnambulated on—unshowered, unshaven—in the dazzling light, trying to imagine how they imagined me or the other residents in the houses they maintained, residents whose labor could be hard to tell apart from leisure, from loafing, people who kept strange hours if they kept them at all. Did the workers themselves have legal residency here, in what was for them the north, for me the extreme south?

When I returned to the house a couple of hours later the men were still at work, so I put them in the fictional summer of the poem as they hammered above me, turning the day into night:

> There are men at work on the roof
> when I return, too hot to do by day, wave
> and am seen, an awkward exchange
> in Spanish, who knows what I said, having
> confused the conditional with the imperfect.

Norteño from their radio fills the house
I hope they know isn't mine: I just write here.
Soon they move on to the house I call his
because Michael, who manages the compound,
rushed him from there to hospital in Midland
or Odessa . . .

When the workers had moved on to Creeley's house and I could read—I can only read if it's quiet, but I can write against noise—I returned, as I did almost every day, to the Civil War passages:

. . . he feels no need to contain his love
for the material richness of their dying, federal
body from which extremities secede, a pail
beside the bed for that purpose, almost never
mentions race, save to note there are plenty
of black soldiers, clean black women would
make wonderful nurses, while again and again
delivering money to boys with perforated organs:
"unionism," to die with shining hair
beside fractional currency, part of writing
the greatest poem. Or is the utopian moment
loving the smell of shit and blood, brandy
as it trickles through the wound, politics of pure
sensation? When you die in the patent-office
there's a pun on expiration, you must enter one
of the immense glass cases filled with scale
models of machines, utensils, curios. Look,
your president will be shot in a theater,
actors will be presidents, the small sums
will grow monstrous as they circulate, measure:
I have come from the future to warn you.

Awake during the day for the first time since I had arrived, I resolved to stay up and reclaim some semblance of my ordinary rhythm. When I felt too tired to write, I streamed Dreyer's *The Passion of Joan of Arc* on my computer, Alena's favorite film; it was like I was Skyping with Falconetti, whom Dreyer had kneel on stone floors in order to make the expressions of pain look real. I resolved to make plans for the next day, to visit Chinati; I looked through the various books about Judd in the house. I was going to shave and reenter time from the heat wave of the poem. Tomorrow I'd begin work on my novel.

Tomorrow I'll see the Donald Judd
permanent installations in old hangars, but
now it's tomorrow and I didn't go, set out hatless
in the early afternoon, got lost and was soon
seeing floaters and spots, so returned to the house,
the interior sea green until my eyes adjusted,
I lay down for a while and dreamt I saw it.
Tonight I'll shave, have two drinks with a friend
of a friend, but that was last week and I canceled,
claimed altitude had sickened me a little, can
we get back in touch when I've adjusted?
Yesterday I saw the Donald Judd in a book
they keep in the house, decided not to go until
I finished a poem I've since abandoned
but will eventually pick back up. What I need
is a residency within the residency, then
I could return refreshed to this one, take in Judd
with friends of friends, watch the little spots
of blood bloom on the neck, so I'll know
I've shaved in time, whereas now I'm as close
to a beard as I've been, but not very close.

Shaving is a way to start the workday by ritually
not cutting your throat when you've the chance,
"Washes and razors for foofoos—
for me freckles and a bristling beard,"
a big part of reading him is embarrassment.
Woke up today having been shaved in a dream
by a nurse who looked like Falconetti,
my cot among the giant aluminum boxes
I still plan to see, then actually shaved and felt
that was work enough for one day, my back
to the future. The foundation is closed
Sundays and nights, of which the residency
is exclusively composed, so plan your visit
well in advance, or just circle the building
where the Chamberlain sculptures are housed,
painted and chromium plated-steel, best
viewed through your reflection in the window:
In Bastien-Lepage's *Joan of Arc* (1879)
Joan reaches her left arm out, maybe for support
in the swoon of being called, but instead
of grasping branches or leaves, her hand,
in what is for me the crucial passage, partially
dissolves. It's carefully positioned
on the diagonal sight line of one of three
hovering, translucent angels he was attacked
for failing to reconcile with the future saint's
realism, a "failure" the hand presents
as a breakdown of space, background
beginning to swallow her fingers, reminding me
of the photograph people fade from, the one
"Marty" uses to measure the time remaining
for the future in which we watched the movie,
only here it's the future's presence, not

absence that eats away at her hand: you can't
rise from the loom so quickly that you
overturn the stool and rush toward the plane
of the picture without startling the painter, hear
voices the medium is powerless to depict
without that registering somewhere on the body.
But from our perspective, it's precisely
where the hand ceases to signify a hand
and is paint, no longer appears to be warm
or capable, that it reaches the material
present, becomes realer than sculpture because
tentative: she is surfacing too quickly.

Now I believe I might have surfaced too quickly. I had gone more than two weeks without really speaking to anyone, a period of silence with no precedent in my life. It might also have been the longest I'd ever gone without speaking to Alex, who was, as she put it in an e-mail, respecting my distance. Finally I shaved, showered, did laundry (there were machines in the garage), and, feeling at least semihuman and diurnal, I went to look around at the Marfa Book Company, a well-regarded bookstore downtown. On the way I happened upon a coffee shop I'd never seen before. I asked for their largest iced coffee, and it was delicious; there were a few young people in the shop typing on their laptops. A basic, acute physical desire for one of the women passed through me, and was gone, as if the desire were en route to someone else.

I was sipping my coffee in the surprisingly good poetry section, full of small-press books, when a man approached me, casually said my name:

"I heard you were here—Diane and I have been waiting to run into you." Who was Diane? He was vaguely familiar to me. Shaved head, those transparent glasses frames, in his midforties—I had seen him at art openings in New York. He might have been a friend of Alena's. I couldn't remember if I knew him too well to ask him to remind me of his name, and then it was too late.

"What are you doing here?"

"Chinati. And Diane has an old friend here." He said the name of the friend as if she were famous. "We're going to get a private look at the Judd boxes in a couple of hours and then dinner and drinks, if you're interested."

"I'm not a big Judd fan."

He laughed at this. Nobody saying that in Marfa could be serious.

"I'm really exhausted," I lied, the iced coffee having burnt off all fatigue. "I haven't slept and think I'll be dead tonight."

"It's not like you have to work in the morning," he joked.

After all the silence, I was socially disoriented, more so for having first encountered somebody from New York out of context. Trying to figure out how to politely persist in refusing his invitation seemed to require a series of operations I could no longer recall how to perform; it was like trying to solve one of those word problems on a high school math test. "I guess I can go," I said, not up to the challenge.

I gave him my address and they picked me up about an hour before sunset. I recognized Diane immediately (she had been introduced to me as Di), a painter who also ran a gallery whose shows I had reviewed, probably in her midfifties, but the man's name still wouldn't come to me; I hoped Diane would use it.

The Chinati Foundation was on a few hundred acres of land where there had once been a military fort. A young woman and a younger man met us in front of the office—it was Sunday, and the foundation was closed to the public. Diane introduced me to the woman, Monika, who she explained was a sculptor from Berlin, here for a few months as the Chinati artist in residence. She was tall and about as heavy as I, but stronger-looking, probably twenty-five; she had close-cropped blond hair, and I could see tattooed flames or maybe flower petals peeking above the neck of her denim jacket. The man, who looked barely twenty, was a Chinati intern in skinny jeans, his black hair arrested by some product in stylized disarray; he had the keys to the sheds where Judd's aluminum boxes were housed.

I had never had a strong response to Judd's work, not that I was any kind of expert. I believed in the things he wanted to get rid of—the internal compositional relations of a painting, nuances of form. His interest in modularity and industrial fabrication and his desire to overcome the distinction between art and life, an insistence on literal objects in real space—I felt I could get all those things by walking through a Costco or a Home Depot or IKEA; I'd never cared more for Judd's "specific objects" than any of the other objects I encountered in the world, objects that were merely real. The work of his I'd seen—always in museums or small gallery installations—had left me cold, and so many of his followers celebrated his cool that I'd never questioned my initial response.

But things were different when I was an alien with a residency in the high desert entering a refashioned artillery shed that had once held German prisoners of war. German-language messages were still painted on the brick: DEN KOPF BENUTZEN IST BESSER ALS IHN VERLIEREN, read one. I asked Monika to translate: "Better to use your head than lose it," she said. The sheds had been ruins when Judd took them over. He replaced what had been garage doors with walls of continuous squared and quartered windows, and he placed a galvanized-iron vaulted roof on top of the original flat roof, doubling the building's height. The space was so flooded with light, and the milled aluminum so reflective—you could see the colors of the grass and sky outside the shed—that it took me a minute to see what I was seeing: three long rows of evenly spaced silver, shimmering boxes, positioned carefully in relation to the rhythm of the windows. Although all the boxes have the same exterior dimensions (41"×51"×72"), each interior is unique; some are internally divided in a variety of ways, some sides or tops are left open, etc., which means that, as you walk along the boxes, you might see dark volumes, or a band of dark between light-filled volumes, or, depending on your angle, no volume at all; one box is a mirror, another an abyss; all surface one moment, all depth the next. Although the material facts of the work were easy to enumerate—the intern was reciting them a little didactically, his voice echoing throughout the shed—they were obliterated by the effect. The work was set in time, changing quickly because the light was changing, the dry grasses going gold in it, and soon the sky was beginning to turn orange, tingeing the aluminum. All those windows opening onto open land, the reflective surfaces, the differently articulated interiors, some of which seemed to contain a blurry image of the landscape within them—all combined to collapse my sense of inside and outside, a power the work had never had for me in the white-cube galleries of New York. At one point I detected a moving blur on the surface of a box and I turned to the windows to see two pronghorn antelope rushing across the desert plain.

I had read or half listened to people praise these boxes before, but nobody had ever mentioned the German stenciled on the wall, or talked about how their being set in a refurbished artillery shed influenced his or her experience of the work. For me, surfacing from my silence and my Whitman, a privileged resident in the region of a militarized border, the works felt first and foremost like a memorial: a line of boxes in a military structure that once had housed prisoners from Rommel's Afrika Korps recalled a line of coffins (I thought of Whitman visiting makeshift hospitals); the changing rhythm of the boxes' interiors felt like a gesture toward a tragedy that was literally uncontainable, or a tragedy that, since some of the "coffins" internally reflected the landscape outside the shed, had itself come to contain the world. And yet *memorial* wasn't really the right word: they didn't seem intended to focus my memory, they didn't feel addressed to me or any other individual. It was more like visiting Stonehenge, something I've never done, and encountering a structure that was clearly built by humans but inscrutable in human terms, as if the installation were waiting to be visited by an alien or god. The work was located in the immediate, physical present, registering fluctuations of presence and light, and located in the surpassing disasters of modern times, *Den Kopf benutzen ist besser als ihn verlieren*, but it was also tuned to an inhuman, geological duration, lava flows and sills, aluminum expanding as the planet warms. As the boxes crimsoned and darkened with the sunset, I felt all those orders of temporality—the biological, the historical, the geological—combine and interfere and then dissolve. I thought of the "impossible mirror" of Bronk's poem.

When we left Chinati, we drove to Cochineal, a restaurant downtown that Diane preferred; she'd invited both Monika and the intern along, but they rode their bikes. We only beat them by a minute or two. I'd said next to nothing at Chinati, and, trying to make normal conversation as we waited for our drinks, I felt like a character actor trying to return to an old role. All of that vanished with the first sip of gin; I realized that the weeks I'd gone without speech or alcohol was as long a period of abstinence as I could remember having undertaken since my early teens; the second martini transformed all my accumulated circadian arrhythmia into manic energy. Without ceremony I dispatched the giant steak I had ordered, inhaled it, basically, eating most of the fat off the bone, finishing it while the others were only a bite or two into their barramundi, which left me free to focus on the wine. Here, I noticed, none of the waitstaff spoke Spanish.

The drink seemed to have a similar effect on Monika, and we talked a little frantically about the Judd, although I was embarrassed to concede how much I had been moved, and wasn't sure about turning the conversation toward the German inscription and World War II. Her English was very good, but she seemed to deploy a limited number of words, rearranging them like modular boxes. She liked to call things "trivial" ("Flavin is a trivial artist," a bold claim for Marfa) or "nontrivial" ("I am trying to figure out what nontrivial things sculpture can do"), and when, making fun of her own repetitiveness, she described the gorgeous sunset we'd witnessed as "nontrivial," I found it both funny and beautiful. Whenever the intern tried to contribute to the conversation, the man whose name nobody had used talked over him, cut him off.

I don't know what part of my largesse was due to alcohol, or to the disorienting power of the Judd, or to my sudden return to human company, but I insisted on using my "stipend" to pay for everybody's food, even though Diane and the nameless man were almost certainly very rich. We said goodbye to the intern, who biked away, and Diane said we should all go to a gathering at her friend's. I said I should probably go home and work on my novel, but never intended to, and soon the four of us were driving through the dark to the party. There were a few flakes of snow in the high beams, melting against the windshield, but I saw them as moths, or saw them first as one and then as the other, as if it were winter and then the midsummer of my poem.

We arrived at the same time as the intern, who must not have known if he had the authority to invite us, and when we confronted each other in the gravel driveway, he smiled with embarrassment. Before he could try to account for himself, I hugged him as if he were an old friend I was thrilled to see after an interval of years—a kind of humor totally out of character for me—and everyone laughed and was at ease. How many out-of-character things did I need to do, I wondered, before the world rearranged itself around me?

Because the house had only two low stories, I was not prepared for the vastness when Diane, without knocking, opened the door and let us in. It seemed like the giant living room we entered was an acre wide; the floor was an orange Spanish tile, with carpets and animal skins thrown here and there. All over the room were clusters of furniture, most of it black and red leather, organized around little tables; some of the furniture was art deco and some of it, for lack of a better word, southwestern. There were people, most of them younger than I, sitting and smoking and laughing in these various groupings, and some kind of country music emanating from a stereo I couldn't locate—country music, but the singing was in French. There was a sense of incoherent opulence: a giant retablo shared space on a beige wall with a Lichtenstein painting or print. Near a vaguely familiar abstract canvas there was a large, silvery photograph of a half-naked, androgynous child facing the camera with a dead bird in its hand.

The intern broke off from us to join one of the groups

and Diane led us out of the room and into the adjacent kitchen, also giant, a thousand copper pots and pans hanging from a rack above an island the size of my apartment. I was introduced to Diane's friend, a handsome woman with silver hair, silver jewelry, and green eyes, who then introduced me to the other people drinking wine and beer around a table that had once been a door; Monika knew everyone. The people in the kitchen were considerably older than those in the living room, as if the parents had retreated to let the kids have their fun at the party—except, disrupting that image, a heavy man with long hair and a beard was dividing a small pile of cocaine with a straight razor on a silver tray. His T-shirt read: JESUS HATES YOU. Diane's friend pointed us to the drinks.

The man asked politely if anybody would like to join him, and only one of the women at the table said in her British accent that she'd have a little for old times' sake. The man then proceeded to separate two thin lines from the small mass of cocaine, rolled a crisp bill into a straw, and handed it to his friend. She snorted one of the lines off the tray, inhaling harder than she needed to, and tipped her head back, laughing, saying she was out of practice. The man then took the bill and, after hesitating theatrically over the small line, proceeded to inhale the entire mass of cocaine he had not divided. I stared at him wide-eyed, waiting for him to die or dissect, while everybody else at the table laughed. At this point a young woman in a cowboy hat entered from the living room, her hair down her back in a long blond braid, and asked what was so funny. "Jimmy did the pile," Diane's friend said. The young woman smiled in a way that made it clear that this was a thing that Jimmy did. He offered the bill around for whoever wanted the remaining small line; Monika took it.

I carried my beer back to the living room and roamed around looking at the walls. The place was bizarre. A young man and a woman were intertwined on a long burgundy leather couch talking about the pros and cons of raising chickens in their yard. Beside them on the floor a young woman in a swimsuit with a towel draped around her shoulders was texting, saying to nobody in particular, "This is why I left Austin." The intern appeared with a bottle of white wine and glasses for the group and, seeing me milling around, introduced me to the others as one of the residents, a novelist. More of a poet, I said. They were going to go outside and smoke a joint—although it seemed they had permission to smoke indoors—and wanted to know if I wanted to join them; I said I'd tag along, which wasn't an expression I ever used.

We exited the house into a courtyard that had a raised pool and joined some other smokers around a table next to one of those tall portable patio heaters I associated with touristy restaurants. Some of the partygoers—although this felt less like a party than a place where people were always hanging out—seemed related to Chinati, others were people who lived in town, and some were visiting, friends of Diane's friend, whose husband, I started to infer, was a director; all of the people in the courtyard were younger than I. A woman whose curly hair I could just tell was red in the dim light handed me the joint and said, "Did you know we're under one of the darkest skies in North America?"

It was as if, by the time I exhaled, I was already a little too high, my breathing labored, and the speed and cadence of the speech around me hard to follow. I stood up suddenly, but then decided I didn't want to go back into the light and face the grown-ups, so I sat down again without explanation; I thought the kids were laughing at me. Monika appeared and pulled up a chair beside us; she offered me a cigarette, which I took but didn't smoke, just rotated in my fingers. Soon more cocaine was being emptied from a plastic bag onto the table, and the woman in the towel and swimsuit was chopping it up with a credit card she'd magically produced; more than the heaters, I suspected drugs were keeping her warm. Part of me said: Do a tiny bump of cocaine and you'll feel sober, centered, back in control, and probably a little euphoric; the better part of me said, You have a cardiac condition, don't be an idiot, come down a little and go home. The better part of me easily won the debate: I decided not to do it, but I decided not to do it after I was already looking up from the glass top of the table, having insufflated a small line.

I passed the straw to the intern and waited for the crystalline alkaloid to sober me, and then raise me into a state of preternatural attention, obliterating whatever anxiety I had about having done it. While I waited, I watched the intern whose dinner I'd purchased do three substantial lines in quick succession; I had the vague sense he wanted to impress me. Monika told him, "Hold your horses," by which she meant something like "take it easy"; everybody laughed at her apt misuse of the proverbial phrase.

I was laughing too—in fact I saw myself from the outside, in the third person, in a separate window, laughing in slow motion—but then, having done such a stimulant, why was I outside of myself; why was time slowing? Before I knew it, I was trying hard to hold on to that question, felt it was the last link between me and my body, but soon the question didn't belong to me, was just another thing there in the courtyard from which my consciousness was turning away. Then I was a relation between the heaters, the sky, and the blue gleam of the pool, and then I was gone, wasn't anything at all, the darkest sky in North America. The last vestige of my personality was my terror at my personality's dissolution, so I clung to it desperately, climbed it like a rope ladder back into my body. Once there, I told my arm to move the cigarette to my lips, watched it do so, but had no sense of the arm or lips as mine, had no proprioception. But when I inhaled the smoke—I didn't know how the cigarette came to be lit—I could recognize it as traveling down into my chest, which was comforting, anchoring; it was the first cigarette I'd had since they'd discovered the dilation. Only after the young woman in the bathing suit said, "K—ketamine—mainly, I thought you knew," did I hear myself ask: "What the fuck was that?"

I had done very little, and soon I was basically back in my body and in time, although my vision, if I moved my head too quickly, would break down into frames; everybody but Monika and the intern had gone back inside. But the intern, who I believe was also confused about which drug he had ingested, was not doing so well: as I watched him he raised his arms in front of his chest as if he were bench-pressing something; his eyes were open but unseeing, his eyelids fluttering; drool was trickling out of the corner of his mouth. Monika said his name, and he managed a groan. To my surprise, she just laughed, said he'd be okay, and left the two of us alone at the table. My mouth felt rubbery, but I managed to say, "You're going to be fine, it will pass soon," but he didn't seem to hear me.

We sat there for I don't know how long. My plan was to wait for someone to come out and, when I knew the intern wasn't alone, to say I had to go and wander home, although I wasn't sure how far my legs could take me. I was practicing my lines in my head—"I have to leave, I have to get up early tomorrow"—when the intern vomited all over himself, not really seeming to notice that he'd done so; he'd probably had a lot to drink. Not sure what to do, I asked him if he was okay, and he mumbled something in which I heard the words *Sacramento* and *death*, or maybe *debt*. I managed to stand up and walked awkwardly back into the house—my coordination hadn't fully returned—with the idea of getting one of his friends to help him.

The living room, which seemed to have doubled in size, was empty, the music off. How long had we been outside? The kitchen, where I assumed people were, was a mile away, but eventually I got there; only Monika and Diane's nameless partner were at the table. I had the vague sense I'd surprised them in a moment of intimacy.

"Where is everybody?" I asked.

"Some people went on a moonlit bike ride," the man said. "Most went to bed."

"The intern is sick. And I have to go home. Can somebody help him?"

"He'll be fine," the man said.

"He threw up," I said.

"Good for him," Monika said. "It will help." A sadist.

"I have to go home," I repeated.

"Okay," said the man, clearly impatient for me to leave the kitchen.

"Can you help me put the intern to bed somewhere and drive me home?" It felt as if I were speaking underwater.

"It's a short walk." Now I hated him.

"What is your name?"

"What?"

"What is your name? I don't know your name. I've never known it." Monika laughed awkwardly. I believe I sounded crazy.

"Paul," he said, his confusion making it sound like a question.

"Paul," I repeated, as if confirming it, as if fixing him to his trivial self with a pin.

"You knew that," he said.

"I swear to you," I said, lifting a hand to my heart, "I didn't." I went to the giant silver refrigerator and opened it and found two cans of lime soda. I took the dish towel that was hanging from its handle and wet it in the faucet. I stopped before I left the room. "Paul," I said again, basically spitting it, as if the absurdity of the name were readily apparent.

The intern could move his head to look at me when I approached, a good sign. But he was near tears. "I'm freaking out, man. I saw all these things. Horrible."

"You're going to be okay," I said, and opened the cans of soda and put them on the table and then wiped the intern's face and shirt. "The worst is over. I am with you," I quoted, "and I know how it is." He started to cry. He was probably twenty-two years old and far from home. The whole scene was ridiculous, but his fear, and so my sympathy, were genuine.

"Do you think you can walk inside?" I asked, after drinking some of the soda, which was delicious; the intern wasn't able to muster interest in his. He shook his head no, but I saw he was willing to try. The smell of his button-down shirt was repulsive, and I helped him get out of it, and then threw the sodden thing in the pool. With his arm around my shoulder and mine around his waist, I walked him slowly inside, a parody of Whitman, the poet-nurse, and his wounded charge.

Jimmy was in one of the chairs, looking through an art book. "What's wrong with the kid?" he asked. In the light, the intern was horribly pale.

"He did the pile," I said. "Is there a bedroom I can put him in?"

"Right through that door and down the stairs."

We managed to find the door and descended some white-carpeted stairs. I turned on the light and saw a large four-poster bed; no curtains hung from the posts, it was a kind of cube, a work of modern art. I got him to the bed and lowered him into it gently and helped him get under the covers. "Now go to sleep," I said.

"Don't leave me."

"You'll fall right asleep. I have to go home," I said.

"I saw all these things. I'm fucked up. I feel like if I shut my eyes I'm going to die."

"You're fine, I promise."

"Please," he basically sobbed. He was desperate. I lay down on my back on the soft carpet and asked him what he'd seen. We were both staring at the white ceiling.

"I was sitting there in the chair. I could feel the chair. But it wasn't pressing against my back, it was pressing against the front of my chest. Pressing hard. But I knew it was behind me. I can't explain. My back and chest had become the same thing. No front or back. One thing. I couldn't breathe in, wasn't any space. No in to breathe into. And you and everybody else started flattening too. It was like Silly Putty."

"Silly Putty?"

"Yeah, when we would flatten it and press it against newspapers and pull it off and it would have the image. I thought of it and then that's what you were, everybody out back, just these images of yourselves against this flattened stuff. You were putty. Worse: meat. With your image on it, talking. Distorted. And I knew I'd made that happen because I thought it. I thought it was like Silly Putty and then it was Silly Putty and then I knew that if I thought something was like something else it would become that thing.

I was trying to move and I felt like I was moving but the view wouldn't change. My vision was locked. I remember I thought, 'Locked like a jaw.' Lockjaw. And then my jaw was locked. And then I thought like with rabies, like rabid dogs get. Like the Guzeks' dog they had to put down when I was a kid, and then I could feel it, the foam at my mouth. Or I couldn't feel it, that's wrong, I could see it. Foam pouring out of my mouth, doglike. Pink for some reason. So where was I seeing it from? And I knew before I thought it that I was going to think: It's like I'm dead, like I'm a ghost looking at my corpse, and I was trying not to think that because I would die if I did. But then I realized that trying not to think about something is like thinking about something, know what I mean? It has the same shape. The shape of the thought fills up with the thing if you think it, or it empties if you try not to think it, but either way it's the same shape. And when I thought that I just felt like there was no difference between anything. And then there was no difference. Because nothing is like nothing. And there wasn't any space."

"The drug didn't agree with us," I said, to say something.

"I still don't feel like I'm here." Another sob. "Will you just talk to me?"

"You're right here," I said, and reached up from the floor and touched his shoulder, forehead, and then, a little surprised at myself, I sat up and smoothed back his hair, remembering how my father would do that to me when I had a fever as a child. Whitman would have kissed him. Whitman would have taken the intern's fear of the loss of identity as seriously as a dying soldier's.

"Keep talking," he said, so I lay back down and did. I began by describing my response to the Judd, but he groaned, so I fished around for a subject, and decided on the construction of the Brooklyn Bridge, having watched a documentary about it on my computer a few nights before. I talked about how Hart Crane had written *The Bridge* in a Brooklyn Heights apartment he only learned after the fact had been occupied by the bridge's engineer, Washington Roebling, where he'd retreated after getting decompression sickness. (I wanted to describe the men laboring in poorly lit caissons, in danger, if they surfaced too quickly, of developing nitrogen bubbles in the blood, but I thought it might disturb the intern.) When the bridge was finished, the celebration surpassed that marking the end of the Civil War, I remembered the narrator saying over still images of crowds and fireworks. That was 1883, the year that Marx died at his desk. The year that Kafka was born. I talked about Kafka for a while, about how I had only recently learned how successful the author had been as an insurance lawyer, betting on the future. I repeated the phrase "pooled risk" a few times, said how lovely it was. Then I moved on to 1986.

When the intern was asleep, breathing regularly, I kissed him on the forehead and walked back upstairs to the living room to find that various young people were lounging there again, having presumably returned from their bike ride, no sign of Monika or Paul. I asked the redhead, whose eyes I now saw were the same green as Diane's friend's, and whom I was not ashamed to desire, how to get to 308 North Plateau, and she told me to turn right out of the driveway, then left when I couldn't go any farther.

Relieved to be in the cold air and increasingly sober, I felt stupid about the drugs and drama, but I was happy I'd helped the intern, felt a tenderness for him. As I walked I heard the whistle of a train and imagined my dad was on one of its decommissioned cars. I thought of the dimly gleaming boxes in the artillery sheds, and then I imagined a long train of them, each car a work of shimmering aluminum, reflecting the moonlit desert it was moving across.

When I turned onto what I hoped was North Plateau—I couldn't see any signs—an electric car quietly passed me going the other direction. It doubled back at the corner, the headlights now illuminating the street in front of me as I walked, and pulled up slowly beside me. Creeley was driving, his posture awkward because the seat was too far forward. He stopped and rolled down the window and said hello, that he was going to see the Marfa Lights, and he asked, in touchingly formal, accented English, if I would care to honor him with my company.

Thus the author found himself, his body still a little heavy with the traces of a veterinary dissociative anesthetic, driving nine miles out on Route 67 so as to catch a glimpse of the famous "ghost lights" with a man on whom he'd overlaid the image of a phantom. After about twenty minutes in the dark, we arrived at the viewing center, a platform faintly illuminated by red lights next to a little structure with restrooms. We shivered on the platform and looked into the westward distance.

What people report, have reported for at least a hundred years, are brightly glowing spheres, the size of a basketball, that float above the ground, or sometimes high in the air. They are usually white, yellow, orange, or red, but some people have seen green and blue. They hover around shoulder-height, or move laterally at low speeds, or sometimes break suddenly in unpredictable directions. People have ascribed the Marfa Lights to ghosts, UFOs, or ignis fatuus, but researchers have suggested they are most likely the result of atmospheric reflections of automobile headlights and campfires; apparently sharp temperature gradients between cold and warm layers of air can produce those effects.

Finally, I did see something—but it was in the other direction, and there weren't any spheres. Far in the distance to the east I saw an orange glow on the horizon and, here and there, patches of red. At first I thought it was the light of a town, but then I realized they were wildfires or preventative controlled burns. I drew the poet's attention to them and he nodded.

The poet lit one cigarette from another. Who was I to him? I wondered. I liked to think he also saw me as a ghost, a departed Polish poet. I saw no spheres, but I loved the idea of them—the idea that our worldly light could be reflected back to us and mistaken as supernatural. I fantasized that a couple of aluminum boxes were positioned in the distance to facilitate the mysterious radiance.

Some say the glowing spheres near Route 67
are paranormal, others dismiss them as
atmospheric tricks: static, swamp gas, reflections
of headlights and small fires, but why dismiss
what misapprehension can establish, our own
illumination returned to us as alien, as sign?
They've built a concrete viewing platform
lit by low red lights which must appear
mysterious when seen from what it overlooks.
Tonight I see no spheres, but project myself
and then gaze back, an important trick because
the goal is to be on both sides of the poem,
shuttling between the you and I.

I thought of Whitman looking across the East River late at night before the construction of the bridge, before the city was electrified, believing he was looking across time, emptying himself out so he could be filled by readers in the future;

I took him up on his repeated invitations to correspond, however trivial a correspondent I might be. I imagined the lights I did not see weren't only the reflections of fires and headlights in the desert but also headlights from Tenth Avenue and the brilliant white magnesium of the children's sparklers in the community garden of Boerum Hill and a little shower of embers on a fire escape in the East Village, or the gaslights of Brooklyn Heights in 1912 or 1883 or the eyeshine of an animal approaching in the dark, ruby taillights disappearing on the curve of a mountain road in a novel set in Spain. I'd been hard on Whitman during my residency, hard on his impossible dream, but standing there with Creeley after my long day and ridiculous night, looking at the ghost of ghost lights, we made, if not a pact, a kind of peace. Say that it was standing there that I decided to replace the book I'd proposed with the book you're reading now, a work that, like a poem, is neither fiction nor nonfiction, but a flickering between them; I resolved to dilate my story not into a novel about literary fraudulence, about fabricating the past, but into an actual present alive with multiple futures. In a few weeks, just before this book began, the poem would end:

> I've been worse than unfair, although he was
> asking for it, is still asking for it, I can hear
> him asking for it through me when I speak,
> despite myself, to a people that isn't there,
> or think of art as leisure that is work
> in houses the undocumented build, repair.
> It's among the greatest poems and fails
> because it wants to become real and can
> only become prose, founding mistake
> of the book from which we've been expelled.

And yet: look out from the platform, see
mysterious red lights move across the bridge
in a Brooklyn I may or may not return to,
phenomena no science can explain,
wheeled vehicles rushing through the dark
with their windows down, streaming music.

Permanent installation

FIVE

"The quality of the photographs is implausibly high," I said, "and there aren't any stars."

"The angle and shadows are inconsistent, suggesting the use of artificial light," she quoted, eyes beginning to shine.

In college, Alex had dated a humorless astrophysics major, now the youngest full professor of something at MIT; after a few months of growing intimacy, she'd felt obliged to introduce us. The three of us met for dinner at a Cambodian restaurant not far from campus where, slamming can after can of Angkor, I insisted the Apollo moon landing had been faked. I was so persistent, he believed I was at least half serious and it drove him insane. Long after it had ceased to be funny, and after Alex had repeatedly tried to change the subject, I was still passionately identifying supposed inconsistencies in the images and astronauts' reports. (I was familiar with the arguments of disbelievers from a paper I'd written about conspiracy theories for a psychology course.) The scientist couldn't stand me, was clearly baffled by how Alex could consider me her best friend; she was furious, dodged calls from me for days.

Now we were sitting side by side on a lawn swing in the middle of an expansive, unkempt backyard in New Paltz, and, having indicated the gibbous moon visible in the daytime sky above us, I was again listing the reasons why I "believed" the landing was a hoax. Over the years this had become one of our ritual ways of affirming the priority of our relationship over other modes of coupling—half inside joke, half catechism. My arm was around her, and the cancer had spread to her mother's spine.

"There appear to be 'hot spots' in some photos indicating that a large spotlight was used."

"You can see the spotlight when Aldrin emerges from the lander."

"And why would they fake it?" her emaciated mother asked, laughing. Now it was night and we were sitting in the screened-in porch, Alex's stepfather in the kitchen preparing a bland meal rich in bioflavonoids while the three of us smoked some of the marijuana I'd brought at her mom's request, her doctor's off-the-record suggestion. With what I thought of as my advance, I'd purchased from a head shop on Saint Mark's what Jon described as the "Rolls-Royce of vaporizers"; there would be no carcinogenic particulates to irritate her throat. We passed a small balloon filled with the vapor back and forth between our wicker chairs. The head scarf she wore was gold; the otherwise tasteless vapor had a note of mint.

"Are you kidding, Emma?" I asked with mock incredulity, intensity. "Cold War space race? Kennedy talking about the 'final frontier'?"

"The 'final frontier' is a phrase from *Star Trek*," Alex corrected me.

"Whatever," I said. "The moon landings stop suddenly in 1972. The same year the Soviets develop the capacity to track deep spacecraft. Or to discover we had no spacecraft deep in space."

“That’s around the end of official military involvement in Vietnam,” Alex’s stepdad said, as he brought in a tray of sliced vegetables and hummus. “Televised landings could have been an attempt to distract Americans from the war.”

“That’s good thinking, Rick,” Emma and Alex both laughing at my mock professorial tone. Rick sat, opened a beer, ate a slice of yellow pepper, then stood up and returned to the kitchen, forgetting the beer; he couldn’t sit still for half a minute. Soon Alex followed him in.

“Not to mention NASA having an interest in securing funding,” I said, but knew the joking was over. Emma chuckled politely in the changed air. I had to fight back my tendency to fill the ensuing silence. A minute or so later:

“So we don’t know how long this is going to take,” she said, and by “this” she meant dying. I swallowed the cliché about none of us knowing how much time we had, and said:

“We’ll be with you. Every step of the way.” She looked at me steadily; I felt thanked.

“It’s not any of my business,” she said after a while, “but I don’t want you two to—how should I put this. I’m a little worried—I’m worried you and Alex might be rushing into all of that because of this,” where “that” meant procreation.

“She’s wanted a kid for a long time,” I said, but thought of my dad’s brief and ill-conceived marriage to Rachel.

“She’s wanted it and not wanted it. She’s had plenty of opportunities, men who would have settled down. Or at least wanted kids. There was Joseph—”

I made a noise that belittled Joseph.

“They were a good match in a lot of ways. I think it’s stuff around her own dad, as I’ve told her. She can’t decide if she wants her kid to have a father.” I felt my presence flicker. “I just want to make sure you guys know what you’re doing.” We didn’t, but we’d scheduled new IUIs, the next one in a few days. They believed that they could effectively wash and scrub my sperm. If they can put a man on the moon, I joked to myself, and said:

"Maybe this"—a pause—"is a fine reason." I had thoughts about why, but just let the statement sit there. She considered it for a while.

"Maybe it is."

Maybe it was. The hot tub had been installed in the basement where we were staying as part of a regime of hydrotherapy intended to help with the pain, but her mom never used it. Perhaps we erroneously assumed water would aid lubrication; maybe we thought it described the future we were inheriting or would obscure the boundaries of our bodies in a way that would diminish the bizarreness; but water, as we should have known, washes away natural lubricants, and silicone substitutes, even if we'd had one on hand, aren't recommended for couples trying to conceive.

It was probably all shot on a soundstage in L.A. Or the desert, slow-motion photography simulating zero gravity.

Not that we were a couple. We withdrew from the tub into the next room, where earlier that day Rick had made up the foldout sofa bed. By the time we reached it, however, I was no longer physiologically prepared. For whatever complex of reasons, I stopped her from initiating oral stimulation and kissed her with a passion I did not feel, but which rose within me as I faked it; soon, to my relief and frankly my surprise, I was capable of going on.

Lubrication, however, still posed a problem, a problem compounded by our being under the impression, possibly erroneous, that cunnilingus can imperil conception, saliva interfering with sperm transport. Thus we relied on manual stimulation in which she assisted and, aided by whatever she was imagining behind closed eyes, eventually we were able to proceed. When I was on top of her, she opened them, dark epithelium and clear stroma, and said, no doubt trying to encourage us both, "Fuck me." But the unmistakable affectation in the voice of the least affected person I knew caused me to smile: then we both started laughing, producing what felt like instant flaccidity. I rolled off her and we lay there together on our backs. There are identical soil formations in photos that, according to their captions, were taken miles apart.

We inhaled some more weed from the vaporizer I'd left plugged in by the wall—although who knew what that was doing to my sperm—and eventually she attempted to restart things; this time I didn't stop her. I stared at the ceiling and tried not to think of her mother two stories above me; wasn't this also detrimental to conception? Abetted by the image of the redheaded Marfan from the party, we were soon able to resume. She climbed on top of me. Before I could take in the view of her strong body, she pressed the heel of her palm hard into my chin and, perhaps wanting to avoid my face or gaze, pushed my head back so that my eyes were directed toward the wall behind me; I bit my tongue, mint aftertaste of vapor mixing with the ferric taste of blood.

Experts, however, discourage positions in which sperm has to compete with gravity, and so now we were lying on our sides. I was behind her, trying to figure out what to do with my hands, which felt a little numb. I was somehow too shy to reach for her breasts or genitalia as my instincts bade me, even though we were conjoined. Finally I asked her where she'd like me to place them with a polite formality so incongruous with our situation that it again caused us to laugh. But we were determined not to let hilarity derail us a second time. She turned around and faced me frankly, scissoring her legs through mine. I pulled her hair back so that her neck was exposed, pressed my face into it, and, after many months of trying, came.

Her mom's cells were dividing uncontrollably above us. The oceans, like Judd's boxes, expanded as they warmed. Do you know what I mean if I say that what was most powerful about the experience was how it changed nothing? The flag seems to flutter in the wind, but there's no air on the moon. The child-Alex was sleeping in the room beside her mom's, green plastic stars glowing on the ceiling, her breathing synchronized with the thirty-six-year-old beside me. That our relationship had not been perceptibly deepened by the event was powerful evidence of the relationship's depth. Only that made things a little different.

After I don't know how long I floated up the carpeted stairs to get a bottle of sparkling water from the fridge; I tiptoed even though there was no way I could have woken anyone. I was heading back down with the green glass bottle when I sensed a presence on the screened-in porch, turned my head, and saw the glow of an LED screen; it was Rick. He'd no doubt seen me; I felt I should say hello, and joined him.

"What are you reading?" I asked, sitting in a wicker chair.

"Nothing. I'm addicted to these message boards. Johns Hopkins. Mayo Clinic." He turned it off and we were in the dark. "It's useless. A community of desperate spouses."

"How are you doing," I said, "all things considered?"

"Fine as long as there's some immediate task at hand," he said. "But it's horrible at night."

It might have been too dark to see me nod, but I nodded.

"What I can't stop thinking about—and I know this is crazy—I can't stop thinking about Ashley," he said.

"That makes sense," I said. "It doesn't sound crazy."

"But I keep waiting for Emma to say to me, 'I want to tell you something, but I want you to promise you won't be mad.'"

"To confess that she's faking."

"Yeah. And it's like—sometimes if I haven't been sleeping, if it's like four in the morning, I start to think to myself: she could be faking, I start to suspect. It's hard to explain: I know it's crazy, impossible, I don't really believe it, but it's like this embodied memory of Ashley. Of what it felt like when that reality began to dawn on me."

"Of course you wish it were fake. I understand that."

"But it's more complicated than that, see. I imagine her telling me, my realizing it's all a hoax. But it's not like I imagine relief. What I imagine is trashing the house in a rage, leaving her, never seeing her again. If I were to learn she was faking her death, she'd be dead to me."

I wondered if I could put Rick's story about Ashley in a novel, if he'd feel betrayed.

"And by the way, then I find myself thinking, even though I know it's preposterous: What if Ashley wasn't faking? What if she lied about lying in order to release me?"

Two days later I was in another woman's arms: with one she cradled me and with the other she ran a sonographic wand, its end anointed with a cool, colorless gel, over my chest in search of a clear image. My eyes were shut and hers were focused on the screen where my black-and-white heart was pretending to beat. Every few minutes she'd ask me to change positions, my paper gown crackling against the paper sheet, or to hold my breath, which aids the imaging. The sonographer was around my age, Dominican I guessed, gentler and much more intimate than the last one; behind closed eyes, I kept imagining her as Alex. One moment you are inhaling cannabis vapor in a finished basement in New

Paltz awkwardly attempting to impregnate your best friend, and the next a lubricated transducer is emitting waves of sound into your chest. I felt pregnant: there's no difference between this procedure and fetal echocardiography, save for placement. I pictured my heart as embryonic, except growth at the sinuses could mean death.

In the month or so since my return from Marfa I had presented a range of symptoms Andrews assured me were almost certainly psychosomatic responses to the upcoming test: headaches, disordered speech, weakness, visual disturbances, nausea, numbness in my face and hands. I feared the test more than dissection because I feared the surgery more than death. So clearly could I picture the cardiologist walking in to inform me that the speed of dilation required immediate intervention that it was as though it had already happened; predicting it felt like recalling a traumatic event.

She pressed the wand hard into my ribs; I started. "Sorry, sweetheart, we're almost finished," she said, addressing a child within me. A few minutes later: "Okay, the doctor is going to want to review this," and she left the room. Why was she in such a hurry to fetch him?

Never forget that you can put your clothes back on and leave the institution before the doctor arrives to read your future in your organs, the modern haruspicy that exorbitant insurance barely covers. You can say it's all a hoax and walk out into the unseasonable warmth and take your chances with an asymptomatic idiopathic condition incidentally discovered. Whether cowardly or courageous, that's a choice, and I was tempted on my plastic table. A few millimeters of growth and they'd open me up with what I imagined as a straight razor. I looked at the screen, which had a frozen image of my heart and arteries, and, in the upper right hand corner, saw the flashing numbers: 4.77 cm; 5.2 cm. Cold spread through me; if either were a measure of aortic diameter, I'd be in surgery within days.

I did walk out, but only to get Alex from the waiting room. She followed me back in and I told her I thought it was bad news, had seen these numbers. She hushed me and we waited; a screensaver took over the monitor: WASHING HANDS SAVES LIVES scrolled across the black in red. The real-time lunar communications lacked a sufficient delay; nobody had ever left the earth except to enter it.

He entered smiling. Silver hair, rimless glasses, a purple tie under the white coat. He shook our hands and said, "Let's take a look." An endless minute later: "Everything looks okay. You're showing 4.3."

"But the MRI said 4.2," Alex said before I could, her notebook open on her lap. One millimeter in that period of time could indicate imminent surgery.

"The echo has a wide margin of error. Those are equal values."

"How can 4.2 and 4.3 be equal values?" I asked, relieved he had said there'd been no change, scared because the numbers expressed one.

"What we can see here is that there hasn't been change beyond the margin of error of the echocardiograph and we'll watch you closely as it progresses. If it progresses." I wasn't happy that *if* was an afterthought. "Understand it is most likely not changing that rapidly."

"But what if it's already changed a millimeter?" I asked.

"Then it will continue to change and we'll get it on the next test."

"So 4.3 might mean more than 4.3, might mean 4.3, might mean 4.2," Alex confirmed.

"Yes."

"So we've learned nothing except that it isn't ballooning?" I sounded angry, felt nothing.

"We have demonstrated some minimum of stability," he said. Then, when we didn't say anything: "This is good news."

"This is good news," Alex confirmed. He shook our hands and left to help patients with less virtual conditions.

Two days later at NewYork-Presbyterian I masturbated before *Amateur All Stars 3* into a specimen cup. They washed and placed my suspect sperm in Alex and then the two of us walked across the park to Telepan for her birthday dinner. She was thirty-seven. The author was 4.2 or 4.3. They'd given her mom months. We had Nantucket Bay scallops at market price on the strength of my advance. We would supplement IUIs with coitus during the period of ovulation or vice versa, both to maximize our chances and, although neither of us said it, because we could then narrate conception, if it occurred, as at least potentially independent of the institution.

Two days later I was ending or at least suspending my sexual relationship with Alena because Alex could not for a complex of reasons reconcile our intermittent intercourse with my having another active partner. We were at a basement bar in Chinatown that felt, but was not, candlelit, an effect of paper shades. I explained that I needed to break it off to prioritize my unromantic sexual friendship even though these relationships were not, save for this hopefully brief period of trying to conceive, mutually exclusive. I knew she would be angry.

But she wasn't angry. "Are you sure you're not upset?"

"Not at all."

"Hurt?"

"No."

"Jealous?"

"Jealous of your having scheduled sex with a friend before visits to a clinic?"

"Not even wistful or something?"

"I never really know what wistful means, exactly."

"I mean like melancholy longing. Nostalgic."

"You want me to be nostalgic already?"

"You could anticipate nostalgia."

"I could long to be nostalgic. Yearn for the time when I will yearn for the past."

"I'm glad you're not unhappy." I was unhappy.

"And then in the future I can yearn for the past when I yearned for the future when I would yearn for the past."

"Okay, I'm glad you understand."

"Totally. By the way, I've barely seen you in eight or nine weeks. Our relationship was already on hiatus." Somehow it had never occurred to me that this conversation was perfectly unnecessary. Suddenly, instead of trying to let her go, I felt like I was trying to get her back.

"When she gets pregnant or I quit helping her, maybe we can—check in."

"Let's be sure to check in." She laughed. "But this doesn't get you out of writing the catalogue essay." She had a big show coming up at a Chelsea gallery.

Several sidecars later we were saying something like a real goodbye. We were near the D stop on Grand Street, nobody out except the rats. She was meeting someone uptown and I was going home. It felt like her nails might break the skin on the back of my neck. It was the sexiest kiss in the history of independent film. I felt horrible descending the steps to the downtown platform because I knew I'd hardly ever see her again.

But when I walked onto the platform, there she was,

waiting across the tracks for the uptown train. One or two other people waited far down the platform, a man in a hooded sweatshirt was passed out or had passed away on one of the wooden seats, but otherwise we were alone, having just said our passionate farewell, staring at each other's ghost in the quiet tunnel. You know the embarrassing experience of saying goodbye to someone only to learn they're walking in your direction, meaning the social exchange has to extend beyond its ritual closure, at which point there are no established mores to guide you? I'd ended things aboveground only to resume them below it, electrified rails charging the distance between us. She stared at me calmly and—involuntarily, idiotically, awkwardly—I waved and walked farther down the platform.

But wait: I had supplanted the closure of that kiss with a clumsy half wave that would resonate back through and color her memory of me; that couldn't stand. I walked back toward her but now she was facing the tile wall, scanning a movie poster. I called her name not knowing what I planned to say and, to my surprise and confusion, she wouldn't turn around; no way she couldn't hear me unless there were earbuds I couldn't see. Was she crying and didn't want me to know? Was she angry? Was she expressing indifference or smoldering intensity? I could see the yellow light of a train deep in the tunnel to my left, rails beginning to shine as it approached. I sprinted up the stairs and down the uptown side; as the train roared into the station across the platform, I reached her, which meant it never happened, waking the next morning in the Institute for Totaled Art.

o

Dear Ben, I deleted, *Thank you for your kind invitation to contribute work to the first issue of your journal and for enclosing a poem of your own*. Did Bronk even have e-mail? Probably not. He died in 1999. *There are advantages in being a neglected writer but one doesn't want to enjoy them entirely without relief*, I had paraphrased from a letter he sent to Charles Olson in the early sixties, *and so you were kind to write. I am afraid I do not have any poems to send. Your letter prompted me to look over the notes I do have and trying to read my most recent effort I became aware how much tolerance and prepossession reading me at all requires. Does it please you to know how much I value your description of my poems, your appreciation of "Midsummer" especially, and the fact that they were given to you by Bernard, to whom I hope you will send my warm regards? It is good to know where one's friends are in dark times*. That last line didn't sound like him at all.

Natali had mailed the copy of Bronk's selected poems that I'd brought to the hospital back to me when Bernard was transferred to a rehab facility in Providence. It had a kind of aura now; in the margins were my illegible undergraduate notes and imitations in pencil, in addition to a series of coffee stains, small traces from a previous self in love with the nonexistent daughter of the couple to whom I'd eventually brought the volume as a kind of offering; now all those distances, real and fictive, were reflected in Bronk's poetry, as though in some impossible mirror. I deleted:

I don't know if I know how to read the poem of yours that you enclosed. Understand I am easily baffled. I remember when Cid Corman was printing my work in Origin, *the magazine you mention as a kind of inspiration. Well, every time I saw the magazine I wondered who in the hell these people were and what in the name of God they were talking about. Except maybe Creeley. I would receive books with cordial letters from other contributors but I didn't care anything about their books and I told them so which at the time I thought a coarse necessity. I was reacting to what I saw as the logrolling and mutual back scratching and pretending to like each other that made poetry like any other industry. One should not—no rather cannot as a practical matter—expect one poet often to genuinely like the work of another—not a contemporary's. Even when we think we are writing* to *one another we are not writing* for *one another and so incomprehension is probably a necessity. We poets are not, as Oppen would say, coeval with each other, let alone our readers. It's in this sense the "public" is right to think of poets as anachronisms. It's one reason among others that I could never edit a magazine.*

I looked around the apartment, thinking how, if I weren't abandoning these letters, I might insert some physical particulars into them. I love how in Keats's letters, for instance, he's always describing his bodily position at the time of writing, the conditions of his room: "The fire is at its last click—I am sitting here with my back to it with one foot rather askew upon the rug and the other with the heel a little elevated upon the carpet," for instance. But what I perceived—rain on the skylight, a pigeon cooing beside the idle AC window unit, the smell of cilantro from downstairs, weak yellow of the cactus flower on the sill, beta-blocker beside my glass of water—I couldn't see ascribing to Bronk in his large house in Hudson Falls.

I highlighted the rest of the letter in blue and hit delete. Somehow destroying the fabricated correspondence made it seem real; how many authors have burned their letters? Abandoning the book about forging my archive left me feeling as though I actually possessed one, as though I were protecting my past from the exposure of publication. Al Jazeera was streaming in a separate window: "Given the gutted institutions," somebody said, "a true transition could take years." Sirens in the distance. I tapped and then banged on the actual window to try to dislodge the stout-bodied passerine—I always felt like I was interacting with the same bird no matter where I encountered it in the city—but it only preened and repositioned itself a little. (I just Googled *pigeon* and learned they aren't true passerines; along with doves, they constitute the distinct bird clade *Columbidae*.) "Now we turn to weather developments in the Caribbean." After a while I left for campus to meet a student.

An unusually large cyclonic system with a warm core was approaching New York; it was still a few days away off the coast of Nicaragua. Soon the mayor would divide the city into zones, mandate evacuations from the lower-lying ones, and shut down the entire subway system. For the second time in a year, we were facing once-in-a-generation weather. Outside it was still just unseasonably warm, but there was a sense of imminent, man-made excitation in the air. "Here we go again," a neighbor said to me, smiling, when he passed me on the street; he only seemed to acknowledge my presence when our world was threatening to end.

I was still on leave, but I kept in touch with graduate students whose manuscripts I was informally advising and two or three undergraduates who were working on honors theses of naïve ambition; otherwise I was making myself as scarce as possible. But I had to fill out some forms to fix my tax withholding in Human Resources anyway, so I decided to make a rare appearance on campus and meet one of the graduate poets, Calvin, in my office.

In the last few months, Calvin's messages to me had become both more frequent and harder to parse. Instead of sending me revisions of poems or comments about the readings I'd suggested, his rambling e-mails had begun to include long passages about "the poetics of civilizational collapse" and "the radical eschatological horizon of revolutionary praxis." Then they would switch suddenly back into a more mundane register as he complained quite sanely about tuition and fees and his sense that graduate school wasn't making him a better writer. He also expressed a great deal of concern about my health, despite my having already insisted it was fine, because he'd read the story in *The New Yorker*.

I took the 2 to Flatbush, accepting, as I left the station, some glossy apocalyptic literature from an elderly Jehovah's Witness. There was more security at the front gate than usual and when I walked onto the lawn I realized there was an Occupy-style protest, a large circle in front of the hall where my office was housed. When I joined the group, however, I realized it wasn't a protest, but rather an organizational meeting preparing for hurricane relief. I was impressed with how smoothly the leaderless meeting was run; by the time I broke off from the group to meet Calvin in my office, I'd volunteered to serve as a liaison between the campus and the co-op, helping them coordinate food drives; it was just a question of e-mail introductions. One of the most vocal students in the circle, Makada, had been in my undergraduate seminar the year before; I took a totally unjustified pride in her acumen and poise, which made me feel avuncular and old.

I felt that something was seriously wrong with Calvin as soon as I saw him sitting on the floor before my locked and dark office door, his back against it, a book open in his lap, but his eyes staring blankly at the opposite wall, his earbuds blasting something, but there was nothing unusual about encountering a student thus. When I greeted him and moved to unlock the door, there was a strange mixture of urgency and slowness of response, as if he had to keep reminding himself to react to external stimuli, but then reacted violently.

When I finally found the correct key and opened the door I was surprised by a sudden blast of wind, a few papers swirling in it. The large window facing the lawn was open some ten inches, had perhaps been that way for many months, although the computer and desk would prove to be dry, undamaged. As I took in my office from the doorway, I felt I was looking into the office of a dead man—a mildly musty smell, despite the open window; the disarranged papers, a leftover plastic Starbucks cup that had once held iced coffee, a small plastic bag of almonds, an open copy of the *Cantos* facedown on the desk: it felt like somebody had planned to be right back and never returned, dissected. I picked up the papers and hastily organized the desk, then turned on my computer, reassured by the Apple start-up chime, F-sharp major chord, a registered trademark.

My desk faced the wall; I swiveled around in my chair so I was facing Calvin in his; although we'd often sat in these positions before, he kept looking either at the screen or the window behind me with such fixed intensity that I couldn't help but turn around to see what he was seeing (nothing). I asked him how he was.

"I've been good, I've been good," he said.

I asked what he'd been doing, how his work was coming.

"It's been amazing, amazing." He was bouncing his right leg up and down rapidly, a habit I had, but which in him alarmed me. I suspected his energy had its origin in prescription amphetamines, which I had used, before my aortic diagnosis, semirecreationally.

"Did you read the O'Brien poems?"

"Man, I have been reading everything. Have been reading

and not sleeping." Adderall. Or, paradoxically, withdrawal from Adderall. He put a piece of gum in his mouth, and offered me some, which I accepted.

"What did you think of *Metropole*?" It was the O'Brien book we were due to discuss.

"You know how those poems just spider out, how those poems just spider out on the page?"

"Go on," I said, unfamiliar with the phrase, which made me uneasy.

"How they can move in any direction, how you can read one line a thousand different ways, the syntax shifts as you go." This was true, was often true of poems, but was particularly true of O'Brien's work. I was relieved by the comment's applicability, since I feared Calvin and I were in distinct universes. I said some things about the form of *Metropole* I thought he might find useful, and he took notes, head bent over a legal pad. But when I stopped talking, he kept writing.

"So has reading *Metropole* made you think any more about the prose poems at the center of your manuscript, how you might strategically disrupt your sentences, for instance?"

And writing.

"Calvin?" Finally he looked up from the paper and met my eyes. His were hazel, shining, although the shine I probably imagined. I felt a manic energy of my own, as if I'd had too much coffee.

"Do you see this?" he said, holding the pad up to me, which was now largely covered in a kind of microscript.

"You have bad handwriting," I said.

"How the materiality of the writing destroys its sense, like we talked about in class. You start by writing and then you're drawing. Or you start by reading and then you're looking. Poetics of modal instability. Pushed past the point of collapse."

I recommended a famous essay about the visual components of writing, in an attempt to reassimilate Calvin's frightening energy to the academic. I swiveled around to the computer and searched an academic database to get the full citation. When I turned back around he was looking out the window the way Joan of Arc looks out of the painting. Was he being called?

"What kind of gum is this?" I asked.

It took him a while to look at me. He smiled. "Nicotine gum." That's why I was a little nauseated. It was strong. I didn't spit it out: it was one of the few things connecting us.

"Are you quitting?"

"No, but my mom bought me a ton of this at Christmas."

"How is stuff going beyond poetry?" I felt I could ask, after the mention of family.

"Well, you said once that we shouldn't worry about our literary careers, should worry about being underwater." I must have been joking around in class—half joking. "And in any new civilization you need those who have a sense of usable history and can reconstruct at least the basic concepts from science. Also there is the literalization of all literature because the sky is falling, if you know what I mean—that's no longer just a phrase. A lot of people can't handle it, how everything becomes hieroglyphic. I lost my girlfriend over that. Body without organs, for instance. I can swallow but there is a cost to swallowing in the sense that I don't have the same kind of throat. That's a metaphor but it has real effects, which is what she couldn't understand. What's tricky is you want to test it, take poison or whatever to show how you can absorb it, but you don't know in that instance if it will be symbolic or spider out."

The college did not have good psychiatric services. He was twenty-six; no one could force him to get help or even legally contact his parents, whoever they were.

"Nobody thinks we've been told the truth about Fukushima. Think about the milk you're buying from a bodega, the hot particles there, I mean in addition to the hormones and what those do. There are rabbits being born there with three ears. The seas are poisoned. Look at this"—here he pulled his hair back, maybe to indicate his widow's peak; I wasn't sure—"that wasn't there when I lived in Colorado. And I know that some of the bone mass in my jaw has thinned, can feel that when it clicks, but I can't afford insurance. And now there is this storm, but who selects its name? You have a committee of like five guys in a situation room generating the names *before* they form. The World Meteorological Organization's Regional Association IV Hurricane Committee—I looked it up. And ever since I looked it up I can't get service on my phone. Every call is just dropped."

"I agree it's a crazy time," I said. "But I think in times like these we have to try to stay connected to people. And we have to try to make our own days, despite all the chaos. We have to focus on feeling comfortable in our own skin, and we need to be open to getting help with that." I was desperately trying to channel my parents.

"Exactly. And the skin is where a lot of the information is entering now. The pores. The pores are the poets of the skin. Who said that? And people try to seal them, silence them. I guess I did. My girlfriend would seal the pores on her face with egg whites and other shit and she'd have no idea where that was coming from, even if the companies say all natural or organic. Why do you think they sell so much makeup at airports? They don't need to test them on animals; they have supercomputers that can basically feel pain at this point. It's like molecular caulking but you're not going to keep particles out that way and you're just shutting yourself off from the social. From what's coming."

"Calvin"—I spoke slowly—"a lot of the things you're saying aren't really making sense to me." Was that true? "I get the feeling you've been really stressed. This is a stressful place, a stressful time. Sounds like you're going through a breakup. I often feel really worn out when I've been spending a lot of time trying to write." He looked at me with hurt surprise. "I'm wondering if you're seeing anyone or maybe could consider seeing somebody. Just to talk through things."

"Okay, wow. Wow. You want to pathologize me, too. I guess that's your job. You represent the institution. The institution speaks through you. But let me ask you something"—I sized Calvin up physically; he was taller than I was, nearly as tall as the protester, but thin, almost lanky; I involuntarily visualized punching him in the throat if he attacked me—"can you look at me and say you think this," and here he swept the air with his arm in a way that made "this" indicate something very large, "is going to continue? You deny there's poison coming at us from a million points? Do you want to tell me these storms aren't man-made, even if they're now out of the government's control? You don't think the FBI is fucking with our phones? The language is just becoming marks, drawings of words, not words—you should know that as well as anybody. Or are you on drugs? Are you letting them regulate you?" He stood up so suddenly I flinched, then felt bad for flinching. "Sorry for wasting your time," he said, maybe holding back tears, and stormed out of my office, forgetting his legal pad.

How would Whitman have tended such an illness, what gifts would he have distributed? No sides, no uniforms, no nation to be forged out of the suffering. I did the things one does, the institution speaking through me. I e-mailed my closest colleagues and the chair about my concerns and asked for advice. I e-mailed two students I thought were friends with Calvin and asked if they'd been in touch with him lately, without saying why. Then I e-mailed Calvin to say I was sorry if I'd upset him, but I was concerned about him and wanted to be of whatever help I could. I did not say that our society could not, in its present form, go on, or that I believed the storms were in part man-made, or that poison was coming at us from a million points, or that the FBI fucks with citizens' phones, although all of that was to my mind plainly true. And that my mood was regulated by drugs. And that sometimes the language was a jumble of marks.

I looked closely at the legal pad. At the top were some phrases I'd used about O'Brien's writing, placed in quotations, and then some of Calvin's phrases about those phrases, e.g., "Could apply to Waldrop's trilogy," which were starred. But the bulk of the writing resembled a private code of miniaturized and simplified letters and vertical strokes or, in places, seismographic readouts—a shorthand for what our language couldn't represent, a poem.

o

Around the time the storm struck Cuba, devastating Santiago, the box of books arrived at my apartment. I'd spared no expense on the self-publishing website, opting for a run of fifty hardcovers with full-color images—each book had cost around forty dollars. Anita wanted copies to mail to family in El Salvador; Aaron planned to put one in each of the classroom libraries; Roberto would want to share them with friends. I liked to think selling my unwritten novel had paid for these unsalable volumes, was proud of the excess I'd keep secret from Roberto. Eager to see what they looked like, I carried the surprisingly heavy box, no doubt increasing my intrathoracic pressure dramatically, upstairs to my apartment, where I opened it hurriedly, cutting away the brown packing tape with a key.

I realized I'd never been as happy to receive any of my own published volumes. Ripping the tape off, I suddenly had the strange sensation that I was opening a box filled with copies of the book for which I was being paid in advance; I hesitated, my eagerness evaporating, then opened the lid and saw the handsome copies of *To the Future*. The text itself was only four pages long, but those four pages were the result of months of Internet research, outlining, drafting by hand, typing, revising, formatting—each stage in the process of composition dilated into an academic lesson about grammar, computer literacy, etc. Professionally bound, it had a certain heft; it did not feel like a vanity project, but like a real children's book. I was excited to think how excited Roberto would be.

Even the fifteen copies I was carrying grew heavy as I walked up Fourth Avenue toward Sunset Park, sweating profusely in the unseasonable humidity. The line at the BP gas station on Douglass Street stretched around the corner, motorists hoarding fuel before the storm, some filling red plastic containers in addition to their cars, but otherwise there was no sign of an imminent disaster. Eventually I moved to Fifth Avenue to avoid all the fencing and construction walkways where the new condos were going up on Fourth, "the latest in urban living." By the time I reached Green-Wood Cemetery, my arms and shoulders ached from the weight of the little books, as if they had more than a material heaviness. As I passed I could hear the monk parakeets singing in the spires of the cemetery's gate; generations of the bright green birds had been nesting there since they first escaped from a damaged crate at JFK. Before I reached the school, it occurred to me, not for the first time, that the $2,000 could be used by Roberto's family in much more practical ways. But then, Anita—assuming she needed it—would never accept money from me. Maybe Aaron could help arrange some small anonymous scholarship for Roberto once we'd finished working together; my advance could secretly fund more than one kind of largesse simultaneously. Or maybe I should be bankrolling Calvin's therapy. Or maybe—I interrupted myself: You should celebrate, not second-guess, this kind of reckless expenditure; don't calculate opportunity costs or insert it into the network of abstract exchange.

Roberto, however, was not in a celebratory mood. He smiled politely at the books, flipped through one, but didn't seem proud or particularly impressed; I had to fight off the desire to tell him how much they'd cost to make. I kept congratulating him enthusiastically on becoming a published author, but to no avail. Instead, he wanted to talk about what he referred to as the "superstorm," how he was worried he'd have to go live with his cousins in Pittsburgh. I explained, as Aaron had no doubt already explained, that Sunset Park was high up, out of reach of the water, and that, while his building or the school might lose power for a while, he had nothing to fear; he could rest assured his parents were prepared. But what if we run out of water to drink? he asked me. What if there are "water wars"? He'd clearly seen another special on the Discovery Channel.

Almost half of humanity will face water scarcity by 2030, but I assured him he had no reason to worry, and tried to refocus his attention on the high production value of our own study of extinction.

"What are we going to do next?" he asked. "Our next project?"

"I'm not sure," I responded, frustrated. I wasn't even sure how much longer I could work with Roberto once my leave ended and I began to face a real deadline for my book or became a kind of father. I'd imagined that *To the Future* might help bring us closure.

"Will we do another book?" He sounded as though he hoped we wouldn't.

"You haven't even looked at this one," I said, trying to sound light, and not disappointed. "This is the product of all our hard work. We sweated over every sentence."

"Because I want to make a movie next," Roberto said, smiling a little apologetically. A mature incisor was coming in at a problematic angle, a new development since I'd left for Marfa. "Your iPhone has a movie camera. We can add lots of special effects and post it on YouTube."

"Anybody can make a movie on their iPhone," I said, "not everybody has published a book like this." I rapped my knuckles on the hardcover. I felt like a used-car salesman.

"We could make a movie of the tsunami," he said, meaning the hurricane. "It's also good to have a camera to film people so they don't try to rob you. Beat you up. To have surveying," he said, meaning surveillance.

"Roberto," I said, making myself smile, channeling Peggy Noonan, who was herself a channel, "what is this book about if not how science is always improving, correcting its past mistakes?" I thought of Judd's boxes in the desert, their terrible patience. "A young future scientist like you should have some faith in our ability to fix things," in our ability to colonize the moon. The future doesn't belong to the faint-hearted; it belongs to the brave—to brave people with *papeles*, I didn't go on to say. "People are going to work together to develop new solutions to all these problems you're worried about. For instance," I said, "they"—whoever they were—"are developing new seawalls to keep the water out, special floodgates." I resolved to continue our work together: "Maybe we should write a book about that next? If you really want, maybe we can make a book trailer for it, I mean a little movie about it on the iPhone." I opened one of the books and stood it on the desk. "But we should take a minute to feel good about this, okay?"

We sat there smiling anxiously at one another, our masterpiece between us. Roberto nodded, but didn't speak. The room had that particular quality of silence that obtains when many loud bodies have recently left. I could hear kids laughing and shrieking on the street below as they were handed off to relatives and guardians; I thought I could detect an added hint of desperation, as if the children had registered a precipitous change in atmospheric pressure. I could hear Chancho, the class's hamster, scurrying around in the cage against the wall behind me, imagined Daniel was refilling its water bottle, resisted the temptation to turn around. In the distance: a jackhammer, airplane noise, the bell of a pushcart vendor selling nieves. A car blasting cumbia stopped at the nearest corner; the music receded once the light turned green.

TO THE FUTURE

by Roberto Ortiz

TABLE OF CONTENTS

CHAPTER ONE: THE MISTAKE

Othniel Marsh was the paleontologist who in 1877 discovered a dinosaur called the apatosaurus. "apatosaurus" means "deceptive lizard." This is a funny name since Marsh himself would be deceived about the "apatosaurus."

In 1879 Marsh thought he had found another species of dinosaur. In fact, he had found more apatosaurus bones but no head. He found a head that he thought belonged to a new dinosaur, but really it was the skull of a camarasaurus. He named this fake dinosaur brontosaurus! "Brontosaurus" means "thunder lizard" in Greek.

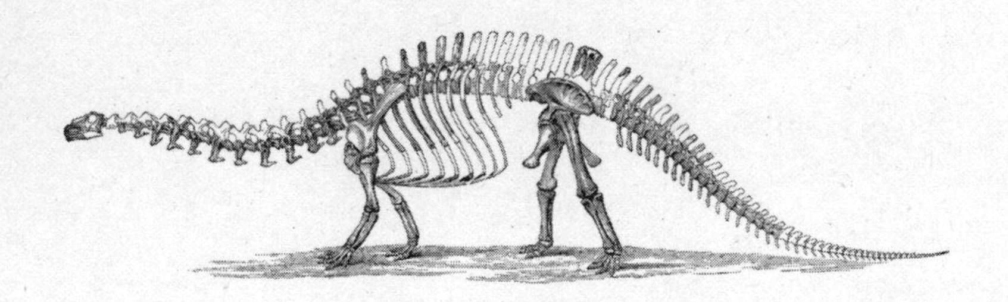

CHAPTER TWO: THE CORRECTION

In 1903 the scientists found out that the brontosaurus was a fake! They realized that the brontosaurus was really an apatosaurus with the wrong head. However, although the scientists realized their mistake, most people didn't know about their new discovery. Many people thought that the brontosaurus still existed because museums kept using the name on their labels—and because the brontosaurus was really, really popular! So even though the scientists discovered their error, most of us didn't know.

This stamp shows how popular the brontosaurus was. Even in 1989, when this stamp was made, which was 86 years after scientists discovered the brontosaurus didn't exist, people were still using the name "brontosaurus" and imagining that dinosaur.

CHAPTER THREE: THE TRUE DINOSAUR

The apatosaurus lived in the Jurassic period, around 150 million years ago. The apatosaurus was one of the biggest animals that ever lived. It weighed more than 30 tons, was up to 90 feet long, and could be 15 feet tall at the hips. Its head was less than two feet long, which is small for such a big body. It had a long skull and a tiny brain. Its teeth were thin, like pencils. Its tail was up to fifty feet long. The apatosaurus was an herbivore, which means it ate only plants. It ate stones that helped it grind up and digest the plants.

One strange fact about the apatosaurus is that its nostrils were located on top of its head. Scientists don't know why. At first they thought this maybe helped the apatosaurus breathe in water, but since apatosaurus fossils have been found far away from any bodies of water, scientists no longer think this is true. It remains a mystery.

CONCLUSION: SCIENCE ON THE MOVE

The story of the apatosaurus shows how science always changes. It shows this because first Othniel Marsh discovered a dinosaur called the apatosaurus. Later he thought he found a new species of dinosaur. But it was just an apatosaurus with a different head. Then this false dinosaur got famous. Scientists corrected their mistake, but many museum labels didn't. People still think there is a dinosaur called the brontosaurus.

Scientists are learning that every day there is something new to discover. Many new discoveries change our thoughts about the past. So science is infinite and goes on forever. Science is always on the move with its face to the future.

THE END

o

Again we did the things one does: filled every suitable container we could find with water, unplugged various appliances, located some batteries for the radio and flashlights, drew the bath. Then we got into bed and projected *Back to the Future* onto the wall; it could be our tradition for once-in-a-generation weather, I'd suggested to Alex, the way some families watch the same movie every Christmas, except we weren't a family. Branches scraped against the windows, casting their shadows in the 1980s, the 1950s; a couple of plastic trash cans were blown down the street, and rain hit the skylight hard enough that it sounded like hail. By the time the storm made landfall, Marty was teaching Chuck Berry how to play rock and roll in the past, which meant that, when he got back to the future, white people would have invented, not appropriated, that musical form; I spent a few minutes describing this ideological mechanism to Alex before I realized she was asleep. I drifted off too, and when I woke, I walked to the window; it was still raining hard, but the yellow of the streetlamps revealed a mundane scene; a few large branches had fallen, but no trees. We never lost power. Another historic storm had failed to arrive, as though we lived outside of history or were falling out of time.

Except it had arrived, just not for us. Subway and traffic tunnels in lower Manhattan had filled with water, drowning who knows how many rats; I couldn't help imagining their screams. Power and water were knocked out below Thirty-ninth Street and in Red Hook, Coney Island, the Rockaways, much of Staten Island. Hospitals were being evacuated after backup generators failed; newborn babies and patients recovering from heart surgery were carried gingerly down flights of stairs and placed in ambulances that rushed them uptown, where the storm had never happened. Houses up and down the coast had been obliterated, flooded, soon a neighborhood in Queens would burn. Emergency workers were fishing out the bodies of those who had drowned during the surge; who knew how many of the homeless had perished? Scores of Chelsea galleries had been inundated and soon the insurers would be welcoming the newly totaled art into their vast warehouses. Alena's work wasn't on a ground floor, I remembered; besides, she strategically damaged her paintings in advance; they were storm-proof.

The next day we went to the co-op and bought food to donate—there was a relay set up between the co-op and the Rockaways, in part facilitated by "my" students. We talked constantly about the urgency of the situation, but were still unable to feel it, as the festive atmosphere in the higher-elevation areas of Brooklyn recalled a snow day: parents and kids staying home from work and school, playing in the park; the only visible damage within six blocks of us was a large tree that had crushed an empty car. There were no shortages of food or water in the local stores; the restaurants were full. Everyone we knew was okay; our friends in lower Manhattan had evacuated or, like Alena, were camping out with sufficient supplies. Friends of Alex's had an apartment flooded with the infinitely filthy water of the Gowanus Canal, but, within our immediate community, that was the upper limit of destruction.

On the second day after the storm I called Sinai to confirm that Alex's appointment had not been changed; they said nothing at the hospital had been disrupted. It was a sunny, unseasonably warm day. There were some buses going into Manhattan from downtown Brooklyn, but the lines were so long, and the routes so confusing, I convinced Alex to let us take a cab. The traffic was slow, but not intolerable; it flowed easily enough once we crossed the Brooklyn Bridge into unelectrified lower Manhattan, although we had to treat every intersection as though it had a stop sign, since the traffic lights were out. Police were everywhere, but it seemed more like they were preparing for a parade than dealing with the aftermath of a disaster. Many businesses looked open, although I did see a few dumpsters overflowing with what I assumed were discarded perishables. The streets were relatively empty, as though it were an early Sunday morning. As we progressed north—past intermittent clusters of FEMA, Con Edison, and news trucks—Manhattan shaded rapidly back to normal. Our driver pointed out a crane in the distance above Midtown; it had come loose from a giant condo building during the hurricane and was now dangling precariously above an evacuated block. Other than that, with lower Manhattan behind us, it was a day like any other.

We arrived at the office nearly an hour early, having overestimated how long the journey from Brooklyn would take. We watched—there was no position in the waiting room from which you could avoid watching—the coverage of the storm we kept failing to experience. They spliced Doppler images of the swirling tentacular mass with footage of it reaching landfall, of houses being swept away, of emergency rescues of the elderly. Then the president was talking about the damage, projecting, as they say, leadership; the elections were rapidly approaching. For the first time, national politicians were speaking openly, if obliquely, about extreme weather's relation to climate change, about the need to stormproof our cities. Then the governor of New Jersey was surveying damage from a helicopter. I reminded Alex that in 2010 Stephen Hawking claimed the survival of the species depended on moon colonization. She reminded me the Mayan calendar indicated the world would end this coming December 22. She found a *New Yorker* on the table among the parenting magazines; "I can't get away from this thing," she said, moving her jaw around, probably unconsciously, as if it were sore. I thought of Calvin claiming his had thinned from radiation. At least one of the Indian Point reactors had been taken offline as a result of the storm.

Say that, from a small swivel chair beside the plastic reclining one, I watch as the doctor covers Alex's stomach and the sonographic wand with clear gel. The GE Vivid 7 Dimension Ultrasound System is the Rolls-Royce of ultrasound machinery, offering 4-D imaging capabilities along with blood-flow imaging, tissue tracking, and color flow. Normally the sonogram is conducted by a tech, not the doctor herself, but the tech, the doctor explains, lives in the Rockaways—or at least she did before the hurricane. On the flat-screen hung high up on the wall, we see the image of the coming storm, its limbs moving in real time, the brain visible in its translucent skull. The doctor dwells on the rapidly beating heart, then lets us hear it at high volume. It has only been a couple of months since I heard mine on a similar machine. The heartbeat is strong, she says, perfect, which is welcome news; Alex has had some unexplained bleeding, even some clotting, which we've been warned increases the already high rate of miscarriage. Confirming a heartbeat lowers the risk, although the chances the creature will never make landfall remain significant. It will be months before we can look closely at the aorta. As the doctor measures the diameter of the child's head, I can't avoid thinking of the baby octopuses. Neither Alex nor I speak, have any questions for the doctor, or take each other's hand, but there is that intimacy of parallel gazes I feel when we stand before a canvas or walk across a bridge.

Then we were walking. We moved slowly south along the

park in silence. Given the storm, the normality felt bizarre: a tourist asked me to take her and her friends' picture on the steps of the Met; I looked into the viewfinder and half expected to see inside their bodies. The pushcarts were out selling pretzels and hot dogs; there were joggers and dog walkers and nannies pushing multiples in thousand-dollar strollers. There was nothing in the speech or laughter or arguments I overheard to indicate crisis or emergency, no erratic behavior among the squirrels or *Columbidae.*

Around Fifty-ninth Street we decided we should determine how to get a bus back to Brooklyn, but it was harder to figure out on my phone than I expected, and my network connection was slow, intermittent. I realized I couldn't smell the sad horses that were normally hitched to carriages along Central Park South; where did they hide them in the storm? We decided to keep heading downtown and, as night fell, I told Alex we should take another taxi; although, according to the GYN, the recent bleeding was unrelated to physical exertion, I thought she should take it relatively easy until she'd made it out of the first trimester. It was impossible, however, to hail a cab, although there was a steady stream of them; I wasn't sure if this was because it was around five, when the cabs have their shift change, or because they didn't want to head south because of the storm; regardless, innumerable yellow cabs passed us, but they were all off-duty. Still, I was confident we'd get one eventually if we just kept trying as we walked; I raised my arm each time I saw one approaching and finally, in the upper Thirties, one stopped, albeit tentatively. At the very mention of the word *Brooklyn*, however, he sped away. This happened two more times and soon we arrived at the threshold of electrification, the streets below us dark.

Reader, we walked on. A couple of restaurants and bars

were open, selling drinks, at least, by candlelight. There was a diverse crowd on the corner of Eighteenth, and when we joined it, we saw that people were taking bottles of water from ten or twelve boxes that somebody had stacked there, probably the National Guard. No cab would stop, and Alex had to pee. When we got to Union Square, multiple food trucks were operating, and people were charging cell phones on their outlets. FEMA seemed to be using the park as a kind of hub. Somehow the giant Whole Foods had power, the illumination startling amid all the dark buildings. I hadn't been there since the night before the last hurricane. I waited outside while Alex went to the bathroom. A reporter was filming a segment nearby and I walked within range of the camera and tungsten lights and waved; maybe you saw me.

When Alex emerged from the store, a bus stopped on the corner, but it was so full only the first few people in line were allowed on; it was heading south, but we had no reason to think it would ferry us to Brooklyn. I asked a cop on the corner of Broadway and Fifteenth how we could get back to Brooklyn, and he just shrugged dismissively; to my surprise, I felt a surge of rage, fantasized about striking him, and only then realized how many contradictory emotions were colliding and recombining within me. My smile was probably strange and Alex asked if I was okay. Between Whole Foods and the various generators police and city trucks were using, Union Square had been relatively bright; as we walked farther south, the dark was enveloping, cut less and less frequently by headlights; driving in the unregulated night was dangerous. Trying to remember the bustling uptown neighborhoods we'd left an hour or two ago, let alone the Brooklyn we'd set out from early that afternoon, was like trying to recall a different epoch. The sense of stability, the Upper East Side architecture, French Renaissance and Federal, seemed to belong to a former age, innocent and gilded, while the ultrasound technology seemed to me in the dark like a premonition from the future; both were too alien to integrate into a narrative. I felt equidistant from all my memories as my sense of time collapsed: blue sparks in Monique's mouth when she bit down on wintergreen candy; hallucinating from a fever in Mexico City; watching the shuttle disaster on live TV. I looked up at the looming buildings whose presence I could now sense more than see and wondered how many people were still inside them. Here and there you could perceive a beam moving across a window, a flame, the glow of an LED, but the overall effect was of emptiness. I told Alex I felt fine. For some reason I imagined there were Sabbath elevators in each building, imagined that they were still running quietly, drawing their power from some other source, some other time.

We must have headed east as streets had dead-ended, because we were on Lafayette and Canal when two men approached us, at least one of them drunk, and asked for money. In the absence of streetlights and established order there was a long moment in which I couldn't tell if they were begging or threatening to rob us, making a demand; relations were newly indeterminate, the cues hard for me to read, as if, along with power, we'd lost a kind of social proprioception. I said I didn't have any, and the men persisted, but without any explicit threat; before I could decide what to do or say, Alex gave the men a couple of dollars, and they vanished.

It was getting cold. We saw a bright glow to the east among the dark towers of the Financial District, like the eyeshine of some animal. Later we would learn it was Goldman Sachs, see photographs in which one of the few illuminated buildings in the skyline was the investment banking firm, an image I'd use for the cover of my book—not the one I was contracted to write about fraudulence, but the one I've written in its place for you, to you, on the very edge of fiction. Its generators must have been immense; or did they have special access to a secret grid? Soon we were heading south and west and the dark felt briefly total; I thought of Marfa, the buildings around me like permanent installations in the desert night. I tried to describe this feeling to Alex, but my voice sounded weird in the lightless streets—loud, conspicuous, although there was plenty of other noise: somebody was hammering something nearby; I could hear, but not see, a helicopter; the slow, high-pitched braking of a large truck in the near distance sounded submarine, like whale song. A cab surprised us as we turned onto Park Place, the felt absence of the twin towers now difficult to distinguish from the invisible buildings. I had the sensation that if power were suddenly restored, the towers would be there, swaying a little. Although I could see that someone was in the back of the car, someone I imagined as on both sides of the poem—Bernard and Natali's daughter, Liza, Ari—I tried to hail the cab; I'd heard cabs could pick up multiple fares as a result of the storm, fares from multiple worlds, but it didn't stop for us.

I asked Alex how she was holding up; she said that she was fine, but I knew she was tired and cold. What if she were eight months pregnant and I'd accidentally led her into this state of nature? You haven't led me anywhere, she said, laughing, when I expressed the concern aloud. There was a small mammal developing within her—this was the week for taste buds, teeth buds. We would work out my involvement as we went along. A bodega was weakly illuminated by a generator and I went in to get a bottle of water and a couple of granola bars, as we hadn't eaten since our early lunch. There was a strong smell of vegetable rot; the refrigerated cases had all been emptied, but there was some old produce on a shelf, and the floors were still wet. I didn't see any water, but when I asked for it, the man behind the counter produced a large bottle. I asked him how much it was and he said ten dollars. I saw the other goods he had secured behind the counter like the treasures that they were: packages of batteries, flashlights, strike-anywhere matches, Clif bars, instant coffee. I asked the price of each in turn, and each time he said ten dollars, smiling. A few miles away they would cost no more than before the storm; prices rise in the dark. I bought the water and a Luna bar for Alex with the weakening currency and we resumed our walk.

As we passed City Hall and approached the Brooklyn Bridge there were plenty of people and headlights, police were directing traffic, and there were clusters of city trucks—fire, ambulances, sanitation, etc. There were two military jeeps parked on Centre Street. Brooklyn was illuminated across the river, sparkling in a different era. We had already walked some seven miles, having not planned to walk more than one; I asked Alex if she wanted me to inquire about a bus, but she said no, that she'd prefer to "do it all." A steady current of people attired in the usual costumes was entering the walkway onto the bridge and there was a strange energy crackling among us; part parade, part flight, part protest. Each woman I imagined as pregnant, then I imagined all of us were dead, flowing over London Bridge. What I mean is that our faceless presences were flickering, every one disintegrated, yet part of the scheme. I'm quoting now, like John Gillespie Magee. When we were over the water, under the cables, we stopped and looked back. Uptown the city was brighter than ever, although as you looked north you saw the darkened projects against the light. They looked two-dimensional, like cardboard cutouts in a stagecraft foreground. Lower Manhattan was black behind us, its densities intuitive. The fireworks celebrating the completion of the bridge exploded above us in 1883, spidering out across the page. The moon is high in the sky and you can see its light on the water. I want to say something to the schoolchildren of America:

In Brooklyn we will catch the B63 and take it up Atlantic. After a few stops, I will stand and offer my seat to an elderly woman with two large houseplants in black plastic bags. My feet will ache only then, my knees stiffen a little. A snake plant, a philodendron. Everything will be as it had been. Then, even though it would sound improbable in fiction, the woman with the plants will turn to Alex and say: Are you expecting? She will explain there is a certain glow. She'll guess it is a girl. The sonar pings will prove to be the ringtone of a teenager in the seat behind me who will answer her phone by yelling, "I'm basically there. Chill, I'm basically there." It and everything else I hear tonight will sound like Whitman, the similitudes of the past, and those of the future, corresponding. We'll get off where the bus turns right onto Fifth and walk east. It's all part of the process of exploration and discovery. We'll see the ghost bike—a memorial for a dead cyclist—chained to the street sign. We'll see the sidewalk littered with flowers from an early-blooming Callery pear. The plywood placard will say her name was Liz Padilla; Why not dedicate, Alex will ask, this book to her? The small flame in a gas lamp on Saint Mark's will flicker across genres. We'll give wide berth to a discarded box spring near the curb, as it might contain bedbugs, but tonight even parasitic insects will appear to me as a bad form of collectivity that can stand as a figure of its possibility, circulating blood from host to host. Like a joke cycle, like a prosody. Don't get carried away, Alex will say, when she offers me a penny—no—strong six figures for my thoughts. In 1986, I put a penny under my tongue in an attempt to increase my temperature and trick the school nurse into sending me home so I could watch a movie. Did it work?

We will stop to get something to eat at a sushi restaurant in Prospect Heights—just vegetable rolls, as Alex is pregnant and the seas are poisoned and the superstorm has shut down all the ports. A couple beside us will debate the relative merits of condos and co-ops, the woman insisting with increasing intensity that her partner "doesn't understand the process," that this isn't "the developing world." Sitting at a small table looking through our reflection in the window onto Flatbush Avenue, I will begin to remember our walk in the third person, as if I'd seen it from the Manhattan Bridge, but, at the time of writing, as I lean against the chain-link fence intended to stop jumpers, I am looking back at the totaled city in the second person plural. I know it's hard to understand / I am with you, and I know how it is.

"Never has there been a more exciting time to be alive, a time of rousing wonder and heroic achievement. As they said in the film Back to the Future, *'Where we're going, we don't need roads.'" —Ronald Reagan, State of the Union Address, February 4, 1986*

ACKNOWLEDGMENTS

Thank you, Ari. Thanks to my editor, Mitzi Angel, and to my agent, Anna Stein. I'm grateful for readings by: Michael Clune, Cyrus Console, Stephen Davis, Michael Helm, Sheila Heti, Aaron Kunin, Rachel Kushner, Stephen Lerner, Tao Lin, Eric McHenry, Anna Moschovakis, Maggie Nelson, Geoffrey G. O'Brien, Ellen Rosenbush, Peter Sacks, Ed Skoog, and Lorin Stein. This book was written in conversation with Harriet Lerner; what's best in it is for her.

I'm indebted to the Lannan Foundation for a residency in Marfa, Texas.

The story "The Golden Vanity" appeared in *The New Yorker*. Two excerpts of this book appeared in *The Paris Review*. The poem I wrote in Marfa, "The Dark Threw Patches Down Upon Me Also," was made into a chapbook by the Center for Book and Paper Arts at Columbia College under the Epicenter imprint and was published separately in *Lana Turner: A Journal of Poetry and Opinion*. I am grateful to the artists at Columbia College and to the editors of these publications.

The "Institute for Totaled Art" is modeled on Elka Krajewska's Salvage Art Institute; my description of the fictional version overlaps with my account of Krajewska's actual work in "Damage Control," an essay that appeared in *Harper's Magazine*. The narrator's collaboration with "Roberto" is based on a self-published book I cowrote with Elias Garcia, but "Roberto" is otherwise a work of fiction.

Time in this novel (when *The Clock* was viewable in New York, when a particular storm made landfall, etc.) does not always correspond to time in the world. I never had the chance to see *The Clock* reach midnight; I've borrowed details from Daniel Zalewski's essay on Christian Marclay, "The Hours," in *The New Yorker.*

I first encountered the text I use as an epigraph in Georgio Agamben's *The Coming Community*, translated from the Italian by Michael Hardt. It is typically attributed to Walter Benjamin.

10 Jules Bastien-Lepage (1848–1884), *Joan of Arc* (detail), 1879. Oil on canvas, 100×110". The Metropolitan Museum of Art, New York, gift of Erwin Davis, 1889 (89.21.1). Photograph copyright © The Metropolitan Museum of Art. Image source: Art Resource, NY.

10 Image from the film *Back to the Future* provided courtesy of Photofest.

16 Photograph of Christa McAuliffe by Keith Meyers of *The New York Times* provided courtesy of Great Images in NASA.

25 Paul Klee (1879–1940), *Angelus Novus*, 1920. Oil transfer and watercolor on paper, 12½×9½". The Israel Museum, Jerusalem, gift of Fania and Gershom Scholem, Jerusalem, and John Herring, Marlene and Paul Herring, and Jo Carole and Ronald Lauder, New York (B87.0994). Photograph by Elie Posner, copyright © The Israel Museum, Jerusalem.

69 Photograph of the Cydonia region of Mars taken by the *Viking 1* orbiter provided courtesy of Great Images in NASA.

135 Photograph of Claude Roy on the Brooklyn Bridge, New York, 1947, by Henri Cartier-Bresson (1908–2004) provided courtesy of Magnum Photos.

195 Photograph of graffito in Chinati (Marfa, Texas) provided by Tim Johnson. Copyright © 2013 by Tim Johnson.

226 Image of brontosaurus skeleton provided by Wikimedia Commons: http://en.wikipedia.org/wiki/File:Brontosaurus_skeleton_1880s.jpg.

227 Brontosaurus © 1989 United States Postal Service. All Rights Reserved. Used with Permission.

228 Illustration of apatosaurus provided by Scott Hartman. Copyright © 2013 by Scott Hartman.

229 Photograph provided courtesy of the author.

241 Vija Celmins (b. 1938), *Concentric Bearings B*, 1984. Aquatint, drypoint, and mezzotint on paper. Image left: 4 15/16×4 5/16", image right: 4 11/16×3 11/16". Tate, London, acquired jointly with the National Galleries of Scotland through the d'Offay Donation with assistance from the National Heritage Memorial Fund and the Art Fund 2008. Photograph copyright © 2014 by Tate, London.